CRANFORD

CRANFORD

ELIZABETH GASKELL

This edition published in 2023 by Arcturus Publishing Limited
26/27 Bickels Yard, 151–153 Bermondsey Street,
London SE1 3HA

Typesetting by Palimpsest Book Production Limited

Cover design: Peter Ridley
Cover illustration: Peter Gray
Design: Steve Flight

AD007633UK

Printed in the UK

Contents

Contents

Introduction

Elizabeth Gaskell was born on 29 September 1810 in Chelsea to William and Elizabeth Stevenson. Gaskell had a tumultuous childhood. She was one of only two of her parent's eight children to survive infancy. Her mother died when she was just 13 months old, and shortly after her father sent her to live with her aunt in Knutsford in Cheshire. She never developed a close relationship with her father, who had remarried when she was four years old, and she would see little of him during her childhood.

Elizabeth married the Reverend William Gaskell in 1832. He was the assistant minister at Cross Street Unitarian Chapel in Manchester. For the first few years of married life, she was content to play the model minister's wife, teaching at Sunday School, providing charity to needy parishoners and raising her children. Gaskell was delighted by motherhood. Her first daughter Marianne was born in 1834, a year after she had suffered through a traumatic stillbirth, and the couple had five children in total.

It was around this time that Gaskell began writing. Her first published work was a joint effort with her husband – the poem 'Sketches Among the Poor', which appeared in *Blackwood's Magazine* in 1837. Tragedy struck again in 1845 when her infant son William died of scarlet fever. Gaskell turned to writing for solace and began her first novel, *Mary Barton*, which was published in 1848. As with most of her work, it focused on the lives of ordinary people. The area where she and her husband lived in Manchester was one of the poorest in the city, and every day Gaskell encountered the challenges brought about by the industrial revolution. In the preface to the book, she wrote: 'I had always felt a deep sympathy with the care-worn men, who looked as if doomed to struggle through their lives in strange alternations between work and want; tossed to and fro by circumstances'.

Though published anonymously, *Mary Barton* was an immediate success, and it soon attracted the attention of Charles Dickens, who would refer to her as his 'dear Scheherazade'. He invited Gaskell to contribute to his magazine *Household Words*, and over the next few years he published many of Gaskell's stories, including her next major work, *Cranford*, which began life as a serialised novel in Dickens' magazine in 1851 before eventually being published as a book in June 1853. At first, Gaskell did not intend *Cranford* as a novel – she had hoped to create a series of sketches to help Americans understand English country life. The fictional town of Cranford of the title was inspired by Knutsford, the town she had grown up in, and it drew deeply on her own experiences.

By 1850, the Gaskell family had moved to a larger home, and her social life was thriving. Her circle of friends included such eminent personages as Charlotte Brontë, Florence Nightingale, Charles Kingsley and John Ruskin, and her friendship with the former led her to publish *The Life of Charlotte Brontë* in 1857, the first biography written of the esteemed writer. Through the 1850s she continued her career in fiction, too, as she published the novels *Ruth* in 1853, *North and South* in 1855 and *Sylvia's Lovers* in 1863.

Gaskell died suddenly on 12 November 1865 while working on her last novel, *Wives and Daughters*. The unfinished novel appeared posthumously in *Cornhill Magazine* in 1866. Today, she is considered one of the great British Victorian novelists, and her work continues to attract praise from literary critics and the general public alike.

CHAPTER I
OUR SOCIETY

In the first place, Cranford is in possession of the Amazons; all the holders of houses above a certain rent are women. If a married couple come to settle in the town, somehow the gentleman disappears; he is either fairly frightened to death by being the only man in the Cranford evening parties, or he is accounted for by being with his regiment, his ship, or closely engaged in business all the week in the great neighbouring commercial town of Drumble, distant only twenty miles on a railroad. In short, whatever does become of the gentlemen, they are not at Cranford. What could they do if they were there? The surgeon has his round of thirty miles, and sleeps at Cranford; but every man cannot be a surgeon. For keeping the trim gardens full of choice flowers without a weed to speck them; for frightening away little boys who look wistfully at the said flowers through the railings; for rushing out at the geese that occasionally venture in to the gardens if the gates are left open; for deciding all questions of literature and politics without troubling themselves with unnecessary reasons or arguments; for obtaining clear and correct knowledge of everybody's affairs in the parish; for keeping their neat maid-servants in admirable order; for kindness (somewhat dictatorial) to the poor, and real tender good offices to each other whenever they are in distress, the ladies of Cranford are quite sufficient. 'A man,' as one of them observed to me once, 'is *so* in the way in the house!' Although the ladies of Cranford know all each other's proceedings, they are exceedingly indifferent to each other's opinions. Indeed, as each has her own individuality, not to say eccentricity, pretty strongly developed, nothing is so easy as verbal retaliation; but, somehow, goodwill reigns among them to a considerable degree.

The Cranford ladies have only an occasional little quarrel, spirited out in a few peppery words and angry jerks of the head; just enough to prevent the even tenor of their lives from becoming too flat. Their dress is very independent of fashion; as they observe, 'What does it signify how we dress here at Cranford, where everybody knows us?' And if they go from home, their reason is equally cogent, 'What does it signify how we dress here, where nobody knows us?' The materials of their clothes are, in general, good and plain, and most of them are nearly as scrupulous as Miss Tyler, of cleanly memory; but I will answer for it, the last gigot, the last tight and scanty petticoat in wear in England, was seen in Cranford – and seen without a smile.

I can testify to a magnificent family red silk umbrella, under which a gentle little spinster, left alone of many brothers and sisters, used to patter to church on rainy days. Have you any red silk umbrellas in London? We had a tradition of the first that had ever been seen in Cranford; and the little boys mobbed it, and called it 'a stick in petti-coats'. It might have been the very red silk one I have described, held by a strong father over a troop of little ones; the poor little lady – the survivor of all – could scarcely carry it.

Then there were rules and regulations for visiting and calls; and they were announced to any young people who might be staying in the town, with all the solemnity with which the old Manx laws were read once a year on the Tinwald Mount.

'Our friends have sent to inquire how you are after your journey tonight, my dear' (fifteen miles in a gentleman's carriage); 'they will give you some rest tomorrow, but the next day, I have no doubt, they will call; so be at liberty after twelve – from twelve to three are our calling hours.'

Then, after they had called –

'It is the third day; I dare say your mamma has told you, my dear, never to let more than three days elapse between receiving a call and returning it; and also, that you are never to stay longer than a quarter of an hour.'

'But am I to look at my watch? How am I to find out when a quarter of an hour has passed?'

'You must keep thinking about the time, my dear, and not allow yourself to forget it in conversation.'

As everybody had this rule in their minds, whether they received or paid a call, of course no absorbing subject was ever spoken about. We kept ourselves to short sentences of small talk, and were punctual to our time.

I imagine that a few of the gentlefolks of Cranford were poor, and had some difficulty in making both ends meet; but they were like the Spartans, and concealed their smart under a smiling face. We none of us spoke of money, because that subject savoured of commerce and trade, and though some might be poor, we were all aristocratic. The Cranfordians had that kindly *esprit de corps* which made them overlook all deficiencies in success when some among them tried to conceal their poverty. When Mrs Forrester, for instance, gave a party in her baby-house of a dwelling, and the little maiden disturbed the ladies on the sofa by a request that she might get the tea-tray out from underneath, everyone took this novel proceeding as the most natural thing in the world, and talked on about household forms and ceremonies as if we all believed that our hostess had a regular servants' hall, second table, with housekeeper and steward, instead of the one little charity-school maiden, whose short ruddy arms could never have been strong enough to carry the tray upstairs, if she had not been assisted in private by her mistress, who now sat in state, pretending not to know what cakes were sent up, though she knew, and we knew, and she knew that we knew, and we knew that she knew that we knew, she had been busy all the morning making tea-bread and sponge-cakes.

There were one or two consequences arising from this general but unacknowledged poverty, and this very much acknowledged gentility, which were not amiss, and which might be introduced into many circles of society to their great improvement. For instance, the inhabitants of Cranford kept early hours, and clattered home in their pattens, under the guidance of a lantern-bearer, about nine o'clock at night; and the whole town was abed and asleep by half-past ten. Moreover, it was considered 'vulgar' (a tremendous word in Cranford) to give anything expensive, in the way of eatable or drinkable, at the evening entertainments. Wafer bread-and-butter and sponge-biscuits were all that the Honourable Mrs Jamieson gave; and she was sister-in-law to the late Earl of Glenmire, although she did practise such 'elegant economy'.

'Elegant economy!' How naturally one falls back into the phraseology of Cranford! There, economy was always 'elegant,' and money-spending always 'vulgar and ostentatious'; a sort of sour-grapeism which made us very peaceful and satisfied. I never shall forget the dismay felt when a certain Captain Brown came to live at Cranford, and openly spoke about his being poor – not in a whisper to an intimate friend, the doors and windows being previously closed, but in the public street! in a loud military voice! alleging his poverty as a reason for not taking a particular house. The ladies of Cranford were already rather moaning over the invasion of their territories by a man and a gentleman. He was a half-pay captain, and had obtained some situation on a neighbouring railroad, which had been vehemently petitioned against by the little town; and if, in addition to his masculine gender, and his connection with the obnoxious railroad, he was so brazen as to talk of being poor – why, then, indeed, he must be sent to Coventry. Death was as true and as common as poverty; yet people never spoke about that, loud out in the streets. It was a word not to be mentioned to ears polite. We had tacitly agreed to ignore that any with whom we associated on terms of visiting equality could ever be prevented by poverty from doing anything that they wished. If we walked to or from a party, it was because the night was *so* fine, or the air *so* refreshing, not because sedan-chairs were expensive. If we wore prints, instead of summer silks, it was because we preferred a washing material; and so on, till we blinded ourselves to the vulgar fact that we were, all of us, people of very moderate means. Of course, then, we did not know what to make of a man who could speak of poverty as if it was not a disgrace. Yet, somehow, Captain Brown made himself respected in Cranford, and was called upon, in spite of all resolutions to the contrary. I was surprised to hear his opinions quoted as authority at a visit which I paid to Cranford about a year after he had settled in the town. My own friends had been among the bitterest opponents of any proposal to visit the Captain and his daughters, only twelve months before; and now he was even admitted in the tabooed hours before twelve. True, it was to discover the cause of a smoking chimney, before the fire was lighted; but still Captain Brown walked upstairs, nothing daunted, spoke in a voice too large for the room, and joked quite in the way of a tame man about the house. He had been blind to all the small slights, and omissions of trivial ceremonies, with which he had been received. He had been friendly, though the Cranford ladies had been cool; he had answered small sarcastic compliments in good faith; and with his manly frankness had overpowered all the shrinking which met him as a man who was not ashamed to be poor. And, at last, his excellent masculine common sense, and his facility in devising expedients to overcome domestic dilemmas, had gained him an extraordinary place as authority among the Cranford ladies. He himself went on in his course, as unaware of his popularity as he had been of the reverse; and I am sure he was startled one day when he found his advice so highly esteemed as to make some counsel which he had given in jest to be taken in sober, serious earnest.

It was on this subject: An old lady had an Alderney cow, which she looked upon as a daughter. You could not pay the short quarter of an hour call without being told of the wonderful milk or wonderful intelligence of this animal. The whole town knew and kindly regarded Miss Betsy Barker's Alderney; therefore great was the sympathy and regret when, in an unguarded moment, the poor cow tumbled into a lime-pit. She moaned so loudly that she was soon heard and rescued; but meanwhile the poor beast had lost most of her hair, and came out looking naked, cold, and miserable, in a bare skin. Everybody pitied the animal, though a few could not restrain their smiles at her droll appearance. Miss Betsy Barker absolutely cried with sorrow and dismay; and it was said she thought of trying a bath of oil. This remedy, perhaps, was recommended by someone of the number whose advice she asked; but the proposal, if ever it was made, was knocked on the head by Captain Brown's decided 'Get her a flannel waistcoat and flannel drawers, ma'am, if you wish to keep her alive. But my advice is, kill the poor creature at once.'

Miss Betsy Barker dried her eyes, and thanked the Captain heartily; she set to work, and by-and-by all the town turned out to see the Alderney meekly going to her pasture, clad in dark grey flannel. I have watched her myself many a time. Do you ever see cows dressed in grey flannel in London?

Captain Brown had taken a small house on the outskirts of the town, where he lived with his two daughters. He must have been upwards of sixty at the time of the first visit I paid to Cranford after I had left it as a residence. But he had a wiry, well-trained, elastic figure, a stiff military throw-back of his head, and a springing step, which made him appear much younger than he was. His eldest daughter looked almost as old as himself, and betrayed the fact that his real was more than his apparent age. Miss Brown must have been forty; she had a sickly, pained, careworn expression on her face, and looked as if the gaiety of youth had long faded out of sight. Even when young she must have been plain and hard-featured. Miss Jessie Brown was ten years younger than her sister, and twenty shades prettier. Her face was round and dimpled. Miss Jenkyns once said, in a passion against Captain Brown (the cause of which I will tell you presently), 'that she thought it was time for Miss Jessie to leave off her dimples, and not always to be trying to look like a child.' It was true there was something childlike in her face; and there will be, I think, till she dies, though she should live to a hundred. Her eyes were large blue wondering eyes, looking straight at you; her nose was unformed and snub, and her lips were red and dewy; she wore her hair, too, in little rows of curls, which heightened this appearance. I do not know whether she was pretty or not; but I liked her face, and so did everybody, and I do not think she could help her dimples. She had something of her father's jauntiness of gait and manner; and any female observer might detect a slight difference in the attire of the two sisters – that of Miss Jessie being about two pounds per annum more expensive than Miss Brown's. Two pounds was a large sum in Captain Brown's annual disbursements.

Such was the impression made upon me by the Brown family when I first saw them all together in Cranford Church. The Captain I had met before – on the occasion of the smoky chimney, which he had cured by some simple alteration in the flue. In church, he held his double eye-glass to his eyes during the Morning Hymn, and then lifted up his head erect and sang out loud and joyfully. He made the responses louder than the clerk – an old man with a piping feeble voice, who, I think, felt aggrieved at the Captain's sonorous bass, and quivered higher and higher in consequence.

On coming out of church, the brisk Captain paid the most gallant attention to his two daughters. He nodded and smiled to his acquaintances; but he shook hands with none until he had helped Miss Brown to unfurl her umbrella, had relieved her of her prayer-book, and had waited patiently till she, with trembling nervous hands, had taken up her gown to walk through the wet roads.

I wonder what the Cranford ladies did with Captain Brown at their parties. We had often rejoiced, in former days, that there was no gentleman to be attended to, and to find conversation for, at the card-parties. We had congratulated ourselves upon the snugness of the evenings; and, in our love for gentility, and distaste of mankind, we had almost persuaded ourselves that to be a man was to be 'vulgar'; so that when I found my friend and hostess, Miss Jenkyns, was going to have a party in my honour, and that Captain and the Miss Browns were invited, I wondered much what would be the course of the evening. Card-tables, with green baize tops, were set out by daylight, just as usual; it was the third week in November, so the evenings closed in about four. Candles, and clean packs of cards, were arranged on each table. The fire was made up; the neat maid-servant had received her last directions; and there we stood, dressed in our best, each with a candle-lighter in our hands, ready to dart at the candles as soon as the first knock came. Parties in Cranford were solemn festivities, making the ladies feel gravely elated as they sat together in their best dresses. As soon as three had arrived, we sat down to 'Preference', I being the unlucky fourth. The next four comers were put down immediately to another table; and presently the tea-trays, which I had seen set out in the storeroom as I passed in the morning, were placed each on the middle of a card-table. The china was delicate egg-shell; the old-fashioned silver glittered with polishing; but the eatables were of the slightest description. While the trays were yet on the tables, Captain and the Miss Browns came in; and I could see that, somehow or other, the Captain was a favourite with all the ladies present. Ruffled brows were smoothed, sharp voices lowered at his approach. Miss Brown looked ill, and depressed almost to gloom. Miss Jessie smiled as usual, and seemed nearly as popular as her father. He immediately and quietly assumed the man's place in the room; attended to everyone's wants, lessened the pretty maid-servant's labour by waiting on empty cups and bread-and-butterless ladies; and yet did it all in so easy and digni-fied a manner, and so much as if it were a matter of course for the strong to attend to the weak, that he was a true man throughout. He played for threepenny points with as grave an interest as if they had been pounds; and yet, in all his attention to strangers, he had an eye on his suffering daughter – for suffering I was sure she was, though to many eyes she might only appear to be irritable. Miss Jessie could not play cards: but she talked to the sitters-out, who, before her coming, had been rather inclined to be cross. She sang, too, to an old cracked piano, which I think had been a spinet in its youth. Miss Jessie sang, 'Jock of Hazeldean' a little out of tune; but we were none of us musical, though Miss Jenkyns beat time, out of time, by way of appearing to be so.

It was very good of Miss Jenkyns to do this; for I had seen that, a little before, she had been a good deal annoyed by Miss Jessie Brown's unguarded admission (à propos of Shetland wool) that she had an uncle, her mother's brother, who was a shopkeeper in Edinburgh. Miss

Jenkyns tried to drown this confession by a terrible cough – for the
Honourable Mrs Jamieson was sitting at a card-table nearest Miss
Jessie, and what would she say or think if she found out she was in
the same room with a shopkeeper's niece! But Miss Jessie Brown (who
had no tact, as we all agreed the next morning) *would* repeat the
information, and assure Miss Pole she could easily get her the identical
Shetland wool required, 'through my uncle, who has the best assortment
of Shetland goods of anyone in Edinbro'.' It was to take the taste of
this out of our mouths, and the sound of this out of our ears, that Miss
Jenkyns proposed music; so I say again, it was very good of her to
beat time to the song.

When the trays re-appeared with biscuits and wine, punctually at a
quarter to nine, there was conversation, comparing of cards, and talking
over tricks; but by-and-by Captain Brown sported a bit of literature.

'Have you seen any numbers of *The Pickwick Papers*?' said he.
(They were then publishing in parts.) 'Capital thing!'

Now Miss Jenkyns was daughter of a deceased rector of Cranford;
and, on the strength of a number of manuscript sermons, and a pretty
good library of divinity, considered herself literary, and looked upon any
conversation about books as a challenge to her. So she answered and
said, 'Yes, she had seen them; indeed, she might say she had read them.'

'And what do you think of them?' exclaimed Captain Brown. 'Aren't
they famously good?'

So urged Miss Jenkyns could not but speak.

'I must say, I don't think they are by any means equal to Dr Johnson.
Still, perhaps, the author is young. Let him persevere, and who knows
what he may become if he will take the great Doctor for his model?'
This was evidently too much for Captain Brown to take placidly; and
I saw the words on the tip of his tongue before Miss Jenkyns had
finished her sentence.

'It is quite a different sort of thing, my dear madam,' he began.

'I am quite aware of that,' returned she. 'And I make allowances,
Captain Brown.'

'Just allow me to read you a scene out of this month's number,'
pleaded he. 'I had it only this morning, and I don't think the company
can have read it yet.'

'As you please,' said she, settling herself with an air of resignation.
He read the account of the 'swarry' which Sam Weller gave at Bath.

Some of us laughed heartily. *I* did not dare, because I was staying in the house. Miss Jenkyns sat in patient gravity. When it was ended, she turned to me, and said with mild dignity –

'Fetch me *Rasselas*, my dear, out of the book-room.'

When I had brought it to her, she turned to Captain Brown –

'Now allow *me* to read you a scene, and then the present company can judge between your favourite, Mr Boz, and Dr Johnson.'

She read one of the conversations between Rasselas and Imlac, in a high-pitched, majestic voice: and when she had ended, she said, 'I imagine I am now justified in my preference of Dr Johnson as a writer of fiction.' The Captain screwed his lips up, and drummed on the table, but he did not speak. She thought she would give him a finishing blow or two.

'I consider it vulgar, and below the dignity of literature, to publish in numbers.'

'How was the *Rambler* published, ma'am?' asked Captain Brown in a low voice, which I think Miss Jenkyns could not have heard.

'Dr Johnson's style is a model for young beginners. My father recommended it to me when I began to write letters – I have formed my own style upon it; I recommended it to your favourite.'

'I should be very sorry for him to exchange his style for any such pompous writing,' said Captain Brown.

Miss Jenkyns felt this as a personal affront, in a way of which the Captain had not dreamed. Epistolary writing she and her friends considered as her *forte*. Many a copy of many a letter have I seen written and corrected on the slate, before she 'seized the half-hour just previous to post-time to assure' her friends of this or of that; and Dr Johnson was, as she said, her model in these compositions. She drew herself up with dignity, and only replied to Captain Brown's last remark by saying, with marked emphasis on every syllable, 'I prefer Dr Johnson to Mr Boz.'

It is said – I won't vouch for the fact – that Captain Brown was heard to say, *sotto voce*, 'Damn Dr Johnson!' If he did, he was penitent afterwards, as he showed by going to stand near Miss Jenkyns' arm-chair, and endeavouring to beguile her into conversation on some more pleasing subject. But she was inexorable. The next day she made the remark I have mentioned about Miss Jessie's dimples.

CHAPTER II
THE CAPTAIN

It was impossible to live a month at Cranford and not know the daily habits of each resident; and long before my visit was ended I knew much concerning the whole Brown trio. There was nothing new to be discovered respecting their poverty; for they had spoken simply and openly about that from the very first. They made no mystery of the necessity for their being economical. All that remained to be discovered was the Captain's infinite kindness of heart, and the various modes in which, unconsciously to himself, he manifested it. Some little anecdotes were talked about for some time after they occurred. As we did not read much, and as all the ladies were pretty well suited with servants, there was a dearth of subjects for conversation. We therefore discussed the circumstance of the Captain taking a poor old woman's dinner out of her hands one very slippery Sunday. He had met her returning from the bakehouse as he came from church, and noticed her precarious footing; and, with the grave dignity with which he did everything, he relieved her of her burden, and steered along the street by her side, carrying her baked mutton and potatoes safely home. This was thought very eccentric; and it was rather expected that he would pay a round of calls, on the Monday morning, to explain and apologise to the Cranford sense of propriety: but he did no such thing: and then it was decided that he was ashamed, and was keeping out of sight. In a kindly pity for him, we began to say, 'After all, the Sunday morning's occurrence showed great goodness of heart,' and it was resolved that he should be comforted on his next appearance amongst us; but, lo! he came down upon us, untouched by any sense of shame, speaking loud and bass as ever, his head thrown back, his wig as jaunty and well-curled as usual, and we were obliged to conclude he had forgotten all about Sunday.

Miss Pole and Miss Jessie Brown had set up a kind of intimacy on the strength of the Shetland wool and the new knitting stitches; so it happened that when I went to visit Miss Pole I saw more of the Browns than I had done while staying with Miss Jenkyns, who had never got over what she called Captain Brown's disparaging remarks upon Dr

Johnson as a writer of light and agreeable fiction. I found that Miss
Brown was seriously ill of some lingering, incurable complaint, the
pain occasioned by which gave the uneasy expression to her face that
I had taken for unmitigated crossness. Cross, too, she was at times,
when the nervous irritability occasioned by her disease became past
endurance. Miss Jessie bore with her at these times, even more patiently
than she did with the bitter self-upbraidings by which they were invariably succeeded. Miss Brown used to accuse herself, not merely of
hasty and irritable temper, but also of being the cause why her father
and sister were obliged to pinch, in order to allow her the small luxuries
which were necessaries in her condition. She would so fain have made
sacrifices for them, and have lightened their cares, that the original
generosity of her disposition added acerbity to her temper. All this was
borne by Miss Jessie and her father with more than placidity – with
absolute tenderness. I forgave Miss Jessie her singing out of tune, and
her juvenility of dress, when I saw her at home. I came to perceive
that Captain Brown's dark Brutus wig and padded coat (alas! too often
threadbare) were remnants of the military smartness of his youth, which
he now wore unconsciously. He was a man of infinite resources, gained
in his barrack experience. As he confessed, no one could black his
boots to please him except himself; but, indeed, he was not above
saving the little maid-servant's labours in every way – knowing, most
likely, that his daughter's illness made the place a hard one.

He endeavoured to make peace with Miss Jenkyns soon after the
memorable dispute I have named, by a present of a wooden fire-shovel
(his own making), having heard her say how much the grating of an
iron one annoyed her. She received the present with cool gratitude,
and thanked him formally. When he was gone, she bade me put it
away in the lumber-room; feeling, probably, that no present from a
man who preferred Mr Boz to Dr Johnson could be less jarring than
an iron fire-shovel.

Such was the state of things when I left Cranford and went to
Drumble. I had, however, several correspondents, who kept me *au fait*
as to the proceedings of the dear little town. There was Miss Pole,
who was becoming as much absorbed in crochet as she had been once
in knitting, and the burden of whose letter was something like, 'But
don't you forget the white worsted at Flint's' of the old song; for at
the end of every sentence of news came a fresh direction as to some

crochet commission which I was to execute for her. Miss Matilda Jenkyns (who did not mind being called Miss Matty, when Miss Jenkyns was not by) wrote nice, kind, rambling letters, now and then venturing into an opinion of her own; but suddenly pulling herself up, and either begging me not to name what she had said, as Deborah thought differently, and *she* knew, or else putting in a postscript to the effect that, since writing the above, she had been talking over the subject with Deborah, and was quite convinced that, etc. – (here probably followed a recantation of every opinion she had given in the letter). Then came Miss Jenkyns – *Debörah*, as she liked Miss Matty to call her, her father having once said that the Hebrew name ought to be so pronounced. I secretly think she took the Hebrew prophetess for a model in character; and, indeed, she was not unlike the stern prophetess in some ways, making allowance, of course, for modern customs and difference in dress. Miss Jenkyns wore a cravat, and a little bonnet like a jockey-cap, and altogether had the appearance of a strong-minded woman; although she would have despised the modern idea of women being equal to men. Equal, indeed! she knew they were superior. But to return to her letters. Everything in them was stately and grand like herself. I have been looking them over (dear Miss Jenkyns, how I honoured her!) and I will give an extract, more especially because it relates to our friend Captain Brown: –

'The Honourable Mrs Jamieson has only just quitted me; and, in the course of conversation, she communicated to me the intelligence that she had yesterday received a call from her revered husband's quondam friend, Lord Mauleverer. You will not easily conjecture what brought his lordship within the precincts of our little town. It was to see Captain Brown, with whom, it appears, his lordship was acquainted in the "plumed wars", and who had the privilege of averting destruction from his lordship's head when some great peril was impending over it, off the misnomered Cape of Good Hope. You know our friend the Honourable Mrs Jamieson's deficiency in the spirit of innocent curiosity, and you will therefore not be so much surprised when I tell you she was quite unable to disclose to me the exact nature of the peril in question. I was anxious, I confess, to ascertain in what manner Captain Brown, with his limited establishment, could receive so distinguished a guest; and I discovered that his lordship retired to rest, and, let us hope, to refreshing slumbers, at the Angel Hotel; but shared the

Brunonian meals during the two days that he honoured Cranford with his august presence. Mrs Johnson, our civil butcher's wife, informs me that Miss Jessie purchased a leg of lamb; but, besides this, I can hear of no preparation whatever to give a suitable reception to so distinguished a visitor. Perhaps they entertained him with "the feast of reason and the flow of soul"; and to us, who are acquainted with Captain Brown's sad want of relish for "the pure wells of English undefiled", it may be matter for congratulation that he has had the opportunity of improving his taste by holding converse with an elegant and refined member of the British aristocracy. But from some mundane failings who is altogether free?'

Miss Pole and Miss Matty wrote to me by the same post. Such a piece of news as Lord Mauleverer's visit was not to be lost on the Cranford letter-writers: they made the most of it. Miss Matty humbly apologised for writing at the same time as her sister, who was so much more capable than she to describe the honour done to Cranford; but in spite of a little bad spelling, Miss Matty's account gave me the best idea of the commotion occasioned by his lordship's visit, after it had occurred; for, except the people at the Angel, the Browns, Mrs Jamieson, and a little lad his lordship had sworn at for driving a dirty hoop against the aristocratic legs, I could not hear of anyone with whom his lordship had held conversation.

My next visit to Cranford was in the summer. There had been neither births, deaths, nor marriages since I was there last. Everybody lived in the same house, and wore pretty nearly the same well-preserved, old-fashioned clothes. The greatest event was, that Miss Jenkyns had purchased a new carpet for the drawing-room. Oh, the busy work Miss Matty and I had in chasing the sunbeams, as they fell in an afternoon right down on this carpet through the blindless window! We spread newspapers over the places and sat down to our book or our work; and, lo! in a quarter of an hour the sun had moved, and was blazing away on a fresh spot; and down again we went on our knees to alter the position of the newspapers. We were very busy, too, one whole morning, before Miss Jenkyns gave her party, in following her directions, and in cutting out and stitching together pieces of newspaper so as to form little paths to every chair set for the expected visitors, lest their shoes might dirty or defile the purity of the carpet. Do you make paper paths for every guest to walk upon in London?

Captain Brown and Miss Jenkyns were not very cordial to each other. The literary dispute, of which I had seen the beginning, was a 'raw', the slightest touch on which made them wince. It was the only difference of opinion they had ever had; but that difference was enough. Miss Jenkyns could not refrain from talking *at* Captain Brown; and, though he did not reply, he drummed with his fingers, which action she felt and resented as very disparaging to Dr Johnson. He was rather ostentatious in his preference of the writings of Mr Boz; would walk through the streets so absorbed in them that he all but ran against Miss Jenkyns; and though his apologies were earnest and sincere, and though he did not, in fact, do more than startle her and himself, she owned to me she had rather he had knocked her down, if he had only been reading a higher style of literature. The poor, brave Captain! he looked older, and more worn, and his clothes were very threadbare. But he seemed as bright and cheerful as ever, unless he was asked about his daughter's health.

'She suffers a great deal, and she must suffer more: we do what we can to alleviate her pain; – God's will be done!' He took off his hat at these last words. I found, from Miss Matty, that everything had been done, in fact. A medical man, of high repute in that country neighbour-hood, had been sent for, and every injunction he had given was attended to, regardless of expense. Miss Matty was sure they denied themselves many things in order to make the invalid comfortable; but they never spoke about it; and as for Miss Jessie! – 'I really think she's an angel,' said poor Miss Matty, quite overcome. 'To see her way of bearing with Miss Brown's crossness, and the bright face she puts on after she's been sitting up a whole night and scolded above half of it, is quite beautiful. Yet she looks as neat and as ready to welcome the Captain at breakfast-time as if she had been asleep in the Queen's bed all night. My dear! you could never laugh at her prim little curls or her pink bows again if you saw her as I have done.' I could only feel very penitent, and greet Miss Jessie with double respect when I met her next. She looked faded and pinched; and her lips began to quiver, as if she was very weak, when she spoke of her sister. But she brightened, and sent back the tears that were glittering in her pretty eyes, as she said –

'But, to be sure, what a town Cranford is for kindness! I don't suppose anyone has a better dinner than usual cooked but the best part of all comes in a little covered basin for my sister. The poor people will leave their earliest vegetables at our door for her. They speak short and gruff, as if they were ashamed of it: but I am sure it often goes to my heart to see their thoughtfulness.' The tears now came back and overflowed; but after a minute or two she began to scold herself, and ended by going away the same cheerful Miss Jessie as ever.

'But why does not this Lord Mauleverer do something for the man who saved his life?' said I.

'Why, you see, unless Captain Brown has some reason for it, he never speaks about being poor; and he walked along by his lordship looking as happy and cheerful as a prince; and as they never called attention to their dinner by apologies, and as Miss Brown was better that day, and all seemed bright, I dare say his lordship never knew how much care there was in the background. He did send game in the winter pretty often, but now he is gone abroad.'

I had often occasion to notice the use that was made of fragments and small opportunities in Cranford; the rose-leaves that were gathered ere they fell to make into a potpourri for someone who had no garden; the little bundles of lavender flowers sent to strew the drawers of some town-dweller, or to burn in the chamber of some invalid. Things that many would despise, and actions which it seemed scarcely worthwhile to perform, were all attended to in Cranford. Miss Jenkyns stuck an apple full of cloves, to be heated and smell pleasantly in Miss Brown's room; and as she put in each clove she uttered a Johnsonian sentence. Indeed, she never could think of the Browns without talking Johnson; and, as they were seldom absent from her thoughts just then, I heard many a rolling, three-piled sentence.

Captain Brown called one day to thank Miss Jenkyns for many little kindnesses, which I did not know until then that she had rendered. He had suddenly become like an old man; his deep bass voice had a quavering in it, his eyes looked dim, and the lines on his face were deep. He did not – could not – speak cheerfully of his daughter's state, but he talked with manly, pious resignation, and not much. Twice over he said, 'What Jessie has been to us, God only knows!' and after the second time, he got up hastily, shook hands all round without speaking, and left the room.

That afternoon we perceived little groups in the street, all listening with faces aghast to some tale or other. Miss Jenkyns wondered what could be the matter for some time before she took the undignified step of sending Jenny out to inquire.

Jenny came back with a white face of terror. 'Oh, ma'am! Oh, Miss Jenkyns, ma'am! Captain Brown is killed by them nasty cruel railroads!' and she burst into tears. She, along with many others, had experienced the poor Captain's kindness.

'How? – where – where? Good God! Jenny, don't waste time in crying, but tell us something.' Miss Matty rushed out into the street at once, and collared the man who was telling the tale.

'Come in – come to my sister at once, Miss Jenkyns, the rector's daughter. Oh, man, man! say it is not true,' she cried, as she brought the affrighted carter, sleeking down his hair, into the drawing-room, where he stood with his wet boots on the new carpet, and no one regarded it.

'Please, mum, it is true. I seed it myself,' and he shuddered at the recollection. 'The Captain was a-reading some new book as he was deep in, a-waiting for the down train; and there was a little lass as wanted to come to its mammy, and gave its sister the slip, and came toddling across the line. And he looked up sudden, at the sound of the train coming, and seed the child, and he darted on the line and cotched it up, and his foot slipped, and the train came over him in no time. O Lord, Lord! Mum, it's quite true, and they've come over to tell his daughters. The child's safe, though, with only a bang on its shoulder as he threw it to its mammy. Poor Captain would be glad of that, mum, wouldn't he? God bless him!' The great rough carter puckered up his manly face, and turned away to hide his tears. I turned to Miss Jenkyns. She looked very ill, as if she were going to faint, and signed to me to open the window.

'Matilda, bring me my bonnet. I must go to those girls. God pardon me, if ever I have spoken contemptuously to the Captain!'

Miss Jenkyns arrayed herself to go out, telling Miss Matilda to give the man a glass of wine. While she was away, Miss Matty and I huddled over the fire, talking in a low and awe-struck voice. I know we cried quietly all the time.

Miss Jenkyns came home in a silent mood, and we durst not ask her many questions. She told us that Miss Jessie had fainted, and that she and Miss Pole had had some difficulty in bringing her round; but that, as soon as she recovered, she begged one of them to go and sit with her sister.

'Mr Hoggins says she cannot live many days, and she shall be spared this shock,' said Miss Jessie, shivering with feelings to which she dared not give way.

'But how can you manage, my dear?' asked Miss Jenkyns; 'you cannot bear up, she must see your tears.'

'God will help me – I will not give way – she was asleep when the news came; she may be asleep yet. She would be so utterly miserable, not merely at my father's death, but to think of what would become of me; she is so good to me.' She looked up earnestly in their faces with her soft true eyes, and Miss Pole told Miss Jenkyns afterwards she could hardly bear it, knowing, as she did, how Miss Brown treated her sister.

However, it was settled according to Miss Jessie's wish. Miss Brown was to be told her father had been summoned to take a short journey on railway business. They had managed it in some way – Miss Jenkyns could not exactly say how. Miss Pole was to stop with Miss Jessie. Mrs Jamieson had sent to inquire. And this was all we heard that night; and a sorrowful night it was. The next day a full account of the fatal accident was in the county paper which Miss Jenkyns took in. Her eyes were very weak, she said, and she asked me to read it. When I came to the 'gallant gentleman was deeply engaged in the perusal of a number of *Pickwick*, which he had just received,' Miss Jenkyns shook her head long and solemnly, and then sighed out, 'Poor, dear, infatuated man!'

The corpse was to be taken from the station to the parish church, there to be interred. Miss Jessie had set her heart on following it to the grave; and no dissuasives could alter her resolve. Her restraint upon herself made her almost obstinate; she resisted all Miss Pole's entreaties and Miss Jenkyns' advice. At last Miss Jenkyns gave up the point; and after a silence, which I feared portended some deep displeasure against Miss Jessie, Miss Jenkyns said she should accompany the latter to the funeral.

'It is not fit for you to go alone. It would be against both propriety and humanity were I to allow it.'

Miss Jessie seemed as if she did not half like this arrangement; but her obstinacy, if she had any, had been exhausted in her determination to go to the interment. She longed, poor thing, I have no doubt, to cry alone over the grave of the dear father to whom she had been all in all, and to give way, for one little half-hour, uninterrupted by sympathy and unobserved by friendship. But it was not to be. That afternoon Miss Jenkyns sent out for a yard of black crape, and employed herself busily in trimming the little black silk bonnet I have spoken about. When it was finished she put it on, and looked at us for approbation – admiration she despised. I was full of sorrow, but, by one of those whimsical thoughts which come unbidden into our heads, in times of deepest grief, I no sooner saw the bonnet than I was reminded of a helmet; and in that hybrid bonnet, half helmet, half jockey-cap, did Miss Jenkyns attend Captain Brown's funeral, and, I believe, supported Miss Jessie with a tender, indulgent firmness which was invaluable, allowing her to weep her passionate fill before they left.

Miss Pole, Miss Matty, and I, meanwhile attended to Miss Brown: and hard work we found it to relieve her querulous and never-ending complaints. But if we were so weary and dispirited, what must Miss Jessie have been! Yet she came back almost calm as if she had gained a new strength. She put off her mourning dress, and came in, looking pale and gentle, thanking us each with a soft long pressure of the hand. She could even smile – a faint, sweet, wintry smile – as if to reassure us of her power to endure; but her look made our eyes fill suddenly with tears, more than if she had cried outright.

It was settled that Miss Pole was to remain with her all the watching livelong night; and that Miss Matty and I were to return in the morning to relieve them, and give Miss Jessie the opportunity for a few hours of sleep. But when the morning came, Miss Jenkyns appeared at the breakfast-table, equipped in her helmet-bonnet, and ordered Miss Matty to stay at home, as she meant to go and help to nurse. She was evidently in a state of great friendly excitement, which she showed by eating her breakfast standing, and scolding the household all round.

No nursing – no energetic strong-minded woman could help Miss Brown now. There was that in the room as we entered which was stronger than us all, and made us shrink into solemn awestruck helplessness. Miss Brown was dying. We hardly knew her voice, it was so devoid of the complaining tone we had always associated with it. Miss Jessie told me afterwards that it, and her face too, were just what they had been formerly, when her mother's death left her the young anxious head of the family, of whom only Miss Jessie survived.

She was conscious of her sister's presence, though not, I think, of ours. We stood a little behind the curtain: Miss Jessie knelt with her face near her sister's, in order to catch the last soft awful whispers.

'Oh, Jessie! Jessie! How selfish I have been! God forgive me for letting you sacrifice yourself for me as you did! I have so loved you – and yet I have thought only of myself. God forgive me!'

'Hush, love! hush!' said Miss Jessie, sobbing.

'And my father, my dear, dear father! I will not complain now, if God will give me strength to be patient. But, oh, Jessie! tell my father how I longed and yearned to see him at last, and to ask his forgiveness. He can never know now how I loved him – oh! if I might but tell him, before I die! What a life of sorrow his has been, and I have done so little to cheer him!'

A light came into Miss Jessie's face. 'Would it comfort you, dearest, to think that he does know? – would it comfort you, love, to know that his cares, his sorrows' – Her voice quivered, but she steadied it into calmness – 'Mary! he has gone before you to the place where the weary are at rest. He knows now how you loved him.'

A strange look, which was not distress, came over Miss Brown's face. She did not speak for some time, but then we saw her lips form the words, rather than heard the sound – 'Father, mother, Harry, Archy;' – then, as if it were a new idea throwing a filmy shadow over her darkened mind – 'But you will be alone, Jessie!'

Miss Jessie had been feeling this all during the silence, I think; for the tears rolled down her cheeks like rain, at these words, and she could not answer at first. Then she put her hands together tight, and lifted them up, and said – but not to us – 'Though He slay me, yet will I trust in Him.'

In a few moments more Miss Brown lay calm and still – never to sorrow or murmur more.

After this second funeral, Miss Jenkyns insisted that Miss Jessie should come to stay with her rather than go back to the desolate house, which, in fact, we learned from Miss Jessie, must now be given up, as she had not wherewithal to maintain it. She had something above twenty pounds a year, besides the interest of the money for which the furniture would sell; but she could not live upon that: and so we talked over her qualifications for earning money.

'I can sew neatly,' said she, 'and I like nursing. I think, too, I could manage a house, if anyone would try me as housekeeper; or I would go into a shop as a saleswoman, if they would have patience with me at first.'

Miss Jenkyns declared, in an angry voice, that she should do no such thing; and talked to herself about 'some people having no idea of their rank as a captain's daughter', nearly an hour afterwards, when she brought Miss Jessie up a basin of delicately-made arrowroot, and stood over her like a dragoon until the last spoonful was finished: then she disappeared. Miss Jessie began to tell me some more of the plans which had suggested themselves to her, and insensibly fell into talking of the days that were past and gone, and interested me so much I neither knew nor heeded how time passed. We were both startled when Miss Jenkyns reappeared, and caught us crying. I was afraid lest she would be displeased, as she often said that crying hindered digestion, and I knew she wanted Miss Jessie to get strong; but, instead, she looked queer and excited, and fidgeted round us without saying anything. At last she spoke.

'I have been so much startled – no, I've not been at all startled – don't mind me, my dear Miss Jessie – I've been very much surprised – in fact, I've had a caller, whom you knew once, my dear Miss Jessie' –

Miss Jessie went very white, then flushed scarlet, and looked eagerly at Miss Jenkyns.

'A gentleman, my dear, who wants to know if you would see him.'

'Is it? – it is not' – stammered out Miss Jessie – and got no farther.

'This is his card,' said Miss Jenkyns, giving it to Miss Jessie; and while her head was bent over it, Miss Jenkyns went through a series of winks and odd faces to me, and formed her lips into a long sentence, of which, of course, I could not understand a word.

'May he come up?' asked Miss Jenkyns at last.

'Oh, yes! certainly!' said Miss Jessie, as much as to say, this is your house, you may show any visitor where you like. She took up some knitting of Miss Matty's and began to be very busy, though I could see how she trembled all over.

Miss Jenkyns rang the bell, and told the servant who answered it to show Major Gordon upstairs; and, presently, in walked a tall, fine, frank-looking man of forty or upwards. He shook hands with Miss Jessie; but he could not see her eyes, she kept them so fixed on the ground. Miss Jenkyns asked me if I would come and help her to tie up the preserves in the storeroom; and though Miss Jessie plucked at my gown, and even looked up at me with begging eye, I durst not refuse to go where Miss Jenkyns asked. Instead of tying up preserves in the storeroom, however, we went to talk in the dining-room; and there Miss Jenkyns told me what Major Gordon had told her; how he had served in the same regiment with Captain Brown, and had become acquainted with Miss Jessie, then a sweet-looking, blooming girl of eighteen; how the acquaintance had grown into love on his part, though it had been some years before he had spoken; how, on becoming possessed, through the will of an uncle, of a good estate in Scotland, he had offered and been refused, though with so much agitation and evident distress that he was sure she was not indifferent to him; and how he had discovered that the obstacle was the fell disease which was, even then, too surely threatening her sister. She had mentioned that the surgeons foretold intense suffering; and there was no one but herself to nurse her poor Mary, or cheer and comfort her father during the time of illness. They had had long discussions; and on her refusal to pledge herself to him as his wife when all should be over, he had grown angry, and broken off entirely, and gone abroad, believing that she was a cold-hearted person whom he would do well to forget. He had been travelling in the East, and was on his return home when, at Rome, he saw the account of Captain Brown's death in *Galignani*.

Just then Miss Matty, who had been out all the morning, and had only lately returned to the house, burst in with a face of dismay and outraged propriety.

'Oh, goodness me!' she said. 'Deborah, there's a gentleman sitting in the drawing-room with his arm round Miss Jessie's waist!' Miss Matty's eyes looked large with terror.

Miss Jenkyns snubbed her down in an instant.

'The most proper place in the world for his arm to be in. Go away, Matilda, and mind your own business.' This from her sister, who had hitherto been a model of feminine decorum, was a blow for poor Miss Matty, and with a double shock she left the room.

The last time I ever saw poor Miss Jenkyns was many years after this. Mrs Gordon had kept up a warm and affectionate intercourse with all at Cranford. Miss Jenkyns, Miss Matty, and Miss Pole had all been to visit her, and returned with wonderful accounts of her house, her husband, her dress, and her looks. For, with happiness, something of her early bloom returned; she had been a year or two younger than we had taken her for. Her eyes were always lovely, and, as Mrs Gordon, her dimples were not out of place. At the time to which I have referred, when I last saw Miss Jenkyns, that lady was old and feeble, and had lost something of her strong mind. Little Flora Gordon was staying with the Misses Jenkyns, and when I came in she was reading aloud to Miss Jenkyns, who lay feeble and changed on the sofa. Flora put down the *Rambler* when I came in.

'Ah!' said Miss Jenkyns, 'you find me changed, my dear. I can't see as I used to do. If Flora were not here to read to me, I hardly know how I should get through the day. Did you ever read the *Rambler*? It's a wonderful book – wonderful! and the most improving reading for Flora' (which I dare say it would have been, if she could have read half the words without spelling, and could have understood the meaning of a third), 'better than that strange old book, with the queer name, poor Captain Brown was killed for reading – that book by Mr Boz, you know – "Old Poz"; when I was a girl – but that's a long time ago – I acted Lucy in "Old Poz".' She babbled on long enough for Flora to get a good long spell at the *Christmas Carol*, which Miss Matty had left on the table.

CHAPTER III

A LOVE AFFAIR OF LONG AGO

I thought that probably my connection with Cranford would cease after Miss Jenkyns's death; at least, that it would have to be kept up by correspondence, which bears much the same relation to personal intercourse that the books of dried plants I sometimes see (*Hortus Siccus*, I think they call the thing) do to the living and fresh flowers in the lanes and meadows. I was pleasantly surprised, therefore, by receiving a letter from Miss Pole (who had always come in for a supplementary week after my annual visit to Miss Jenkyns) proposing that I should go and stay with her; and then, in a couple of days after my acceptance, came a note from Miss Matty, in which, in a rather circuitous and very humble manner, she told me how much pleasure I should confer if I could spend a week or two with her, either before or after I had been at Miss Pole's; 'for,' she said, 'since my dear sister's death I am well aware I have no attractions to offer; it is only to the kindness of my friends that I can owe their company.'

Of course I promised to come to dear Miss Matty as soon as I had ended my visit to Miss Pole; and the day after my arrival at Cranford I went to see her, much wondering what the house would be like without Miss Jenkyns, and rather dreading the changed aspect of things. Miss Matty began to cry as soon as she saw me. She was evidently nervous from having anticipated my call. I comforted her as well as I could; and I found the best consolation I could give was the honest praise that came from my heart as I spoke of the deceased. Miss Matty slowly shook her head over each virtue as it was named and attributed to her sister; and at last she could not restrain the tears which had long been silently flowing, but hid her face behind her handkerchief and sobbed aloud.

'Dear Miss Matty,' said I, taking her hand – for indeed I did not know in what way to tell her how sorry I was for her, left deserted in the world. She put down her handkerchief and said –

'My dear, I'd rather you did not call me Matty. *She* did not like it; but I did many a thing she did not like, I'm afraid – and now she's gone! If you please, my love, will you call me Matilda?'

I promised faithfully, and began to practise the new name with Miss Pole that very day; and, by degrees, Miss Matilda's feeling on the subject was known through Cranford, and we all tried to drop the more familiar name, but with so little success that by-and-by we gave up the attempt.

My visit to Miss Pole was very quiet. Miss Jenkyns had so long taken the lead in Cranford that now she was gone, they hardly knew how to give a party. The Honourable Mrs Jamieson, to whom Miss Jenkyns herself had always yielded the post of honour, was fat and inert, and very much at the mercy of her old servants. If they chose that she should give a party, they reminded her of the necessity for so doing: if not, she let it alone. There was all the more time for me to hear old-world stories from Miss Pole, while she sat knitting, and I making my father's shirts. I always took a quantity of plain sewing to Cranford; for, as we did not read much, or walk much, I found it a capital time to get through my work. One of Miss Pole's stories related to a shadow of a love affair that was dimly perceived or suspected long years before.

Presently, the time arrived when I was to remove to Miss Matilda's house. I found her timid and anxious about the arrangements for my comfort. Many a time, while I was unpacking, did she come backwards and forwards to stir the fire which burned all the worse for being so frequently poked.

'Have you drawers enough, dear?' asked she. 'I don't know exactly how my sister used to arrange them. She had capital methods. I am sure she would have trained a servant in a week to make a better fire than this, and Fanny has been with me four months.'

This subject of servants was a standing grievance, and I could not wonder much at it; for if gentlemen were scarce, and almost unheard of in the 'genteel society' of Cranford, they or their counterparts – handsome young men – abounded in the lower classes. The pretty neat servant-maids had their choice of desirable 'followers'; and their mistresses, without having the sort of mysterious dread of men and matrimony that Miss Matilda had, might well feel a little anxious lest the heads of their comely maids should be turned by the joiner, or the butcher, or the gardener, who were obliged, by their callings, to come to the house, and who, as ill-luck would have it, were generally handsome and unmarried. Fanny's lovers, if she had any – and Miss Matilda

suspected her of so many flirtations that, if she had not been very
pretty, I should have doubted her having one – were a constant anxiety
to her mistress. She was forbidden, by the articles of her engagement,
to have 'followers'; and though she had answered, innocently enough,
doubling up the hem of her apron as she spoke, 'Please, ma'am, I
never had more than one at a time,' Miss Matty prohibited that one.
But a vision of a man seemed to haunt the kitchen. Fanny assured me
that it was all fancy, or else I should have said myself that I had seen
a man's coat-tails whisk into the scullery once, when I went on an
errand into the storeroom at night; and another evening, when, our
watches having stopped, I went to look at the clock, there was a very
odd appearance, singularly like a young man squeezed up between the
clock and the back of the open kitchen-door: and I thought Fanny
snatched up the candle very hastily, so as to throw the shadow on the
clock face, while she very positively told me the time half an hour too
early, as we found out afterwards by the church clock. But I did not
add to Miss Matty's anxieties by naming my suspicions, especially as
Fanny said to me, the next day, that it was such a queer kitchen for
having odd shadows about it, she really was almost afraid to stay; 'for
you know, miss,' she added, 'I don't see a creature from six o'clock
tea, till Missus rings the bell for prayers at ten.'

However, it so fell out that Fanny had to leave and Miss Matilda
begged me to stay and 'settle her' with the new maid; to which I
consented, after I had heard from my father that he did not want me
at home. The new servant was a rough, honest-looking, country girl,
who had only lived in a farm place before; but I liked her looks when
she came to be hired; and I promised Miss Matilda to put her in the
ways of the house. The said ways were religiously such as Miss Matilda
thought her sister would approve. Many a domestic rule and regulation
had been a subject of plaintive whispered murmur to me during Miss
Jenkyns's life; but now that she was gone, I do not think that even I,
who was a favourite, durst have suggested an alteration. To give an
instance: we constantly adhered to the forms which were observed, at
meal-times, in 'my father, the rector's house'. Accordingly, we had
always wine and dessert; but the decanters were only filled when there
was a party, and what remained was seldom touched, though we had
two wine glasses apiece every day after dinner, until the next festive
occasion arrived, when the state of the remainder wine was examined

into in a family council. The dregs were often given to the poor: but occasionally, when a good deal had been left at the last party (five months ago, it might be), it was added to some of a fresh bottle, brought up from the cellar. I fancy poor Captain Brown did not much like wine, for I noticed he never finished his first glass, and most military men take several. Then, as to our dessert, Miss Jenkyns used to gather currants and gooseberries for it herself, which I sometimes thought would have tasted better fresh from the trees; but then, as Miss Jenkyns observed, there would have been nothing for dessert in summer-time. As it was, we felt very genteel with our two glasses apiece, and a dish of gooseberries at the top, of currants and biscuits at the sides, and two decanters at the bottom. When oranges came in, a curious proceeding was gone through. Miss Jenkyns did not like to cut the fruit; for, as she observed, the juice all ran out nobody knew where; sucking (only I think she used some more recondite word) was in fact the only way of enjoying oranges; but then there was the unpleasant association with a ceremony frequently gone through by little babies; and so, after dessert, in orange season, Miss Jenkyns and Miss Matty used to rise up, possess themselves each of an orange in silence, and withdraw to the privacy of their own rooms to indulge in sucking oranges.

I had once or twice tried, on such occasions, to prevail on Miss Matty to stay, and had succeeded in her sister's lifetime. I held up a screen, and did not look, and, as she said, she tried not to make the noise very offensive; but now that she was left alone, she seemed quite horrified when I begged her to remain with me in the warm dining-parlour, and enjoy her orange as she liked best. And so it was in everything. Miss Jenkyns's rules were made more stringent than ever, because the trainer of them was gone where there could be no appeal. In all things else Miss Matilda was meek and undecided to a fault. I have heard Fanny turn her round twenty times in a morning about dinner, just as the little hussy chose; and I sometimes fancied she worked on Miss Matilda's weakness in order to bewilder her, and to make her feel more in the power of her clever servant. I determined that I would not leave her till I had seen what sort of a person Martha was; and, if I found her trustworthy, I would tell her not to trouble her mistress with every little decision.

Martha was blunt and plain-spoken to a fault; otherwise she was a brisk, well-meaning, but very ignorant girl. She had not been with us a week before Miss Matilda and I were astounded one morning by the receipt of a letter from a cousin of hers, who had been twenty or thirty years in India, and who had lately, as we had seen by the *Army List*, returned to England, bringing with him an invalid wife who had never been introduced to her English relations. Major Jenkyns wrote to propose that he and his wife should spend a night at Cranford, on his way to Scotland – at the inn, if it did not suit Miss Matilda to receive them into her house; in which case they should hope to be with her as much as possible during the day. Of course it *must* suit her, as she said; for all Cranford knew that she had her sister's bedroom at liberty; but I am sure she wished the Major had stopped in India and forgotten his cousins out and out.

'Oh! how must I manage?' asked she helplessly. 'If Deborah had been alive she would have known what to do with a gentleman-visitor. Must I put razors in his dressing-room? Dear! dear! and I've got none. Deborah would have had them. And slippers, and coat-brushes?' I suggested that probably he would bring all these things with him. 'And after dinner, how am I to know when to get up and leave him to his wine? Deborah would have done it so well; she would have been quite in her element. Will he want coffee, do you think?' I undertook the management of the coffee, and told her I would instruct Martha in the art of waiting – in which it must be owned she was terribly deficient – and that I had no doubt Major and Mrs Jenkyns would understand the quiet mode in which a lady lived by herself in a country town. But she was sadly fluttered. I made her empty her decanters and bring up two fresh bottles of wine. I wished I could have prevented her from being present at my instructions to Martha, for she frequently cut in with some fresh direction, muddling the poor girl's mind as she stood open-mouthed, listening to us both.

'Hand the vegetables round,' said I (foolishly, I see now – for it was aiming at more than we could accomplish with quietness and simplicity); and then, seeing her look bewildered, I added, 'take the vegetables round to people, and let them help themselves.'

'And mind you go first to the ladies,' put in Miss Matilda. 'Always go to the ladies before gentlemen when you are waiting.'

'I'll do it as you tell me, ma'am,' said Martha; 'but I like lads best.'

We felt very uncomfortable and shocked at this speech of Martha's, yet I don't think she meant any harm; and, on the whole, she attended very well to our directions, except that she 'nudged' the Major when he did not help himself as soon as she expected to the potatoes, while she was handing them round.

The major and his wife were quiet unpretending people enough when they did come; languid, as all East Indians are, I suppose. We were rather dismayed at their bringing two servants with them, a Hindoo body-servant for the Major, and a steady elderly maid for his wife; but they slept at the inn, and took off a good deal of the responsibility by attending carefully to their master's and mistress's comfort. Martha, to be sure, had never ended her staring at the East Indian's white turban and brown complexion, and I saw that Miss Matilda shrunk away from him a little as he waited at dinner. Indeed, she asked me, when they were gone, if he did not remind me of Blue Beard? On the whole, the visit was most satisfactory, and is a subject of conversation even now with Miss Matilda; at the time it greatly excited Cranford, and even stirred up the apathetic and Honourable Mrs Jamieson to some expression of interest, when I went to call and thank her for the kind answers she had vouchsafed to Miss Matilda's inquiries as to the arrangement of a gentleman's dressing-room – answers which I must confess she had given in the wearied manner of the Scandinavian prophetess –

'Leave me, leave me to repose.'

And *now* I come to the love affair.

It seems that Miss Pole had a cousin, once or twice removed, who had offered to Miss Matty long ago. Now this cousin lived four or five miles from Cranford on his own estate; but his property was not large enough to entitle him to rank higher than a yeoman; or rather, with something of the 'pride which apes humility', he had refused to push himself on, as so many of his class had done, into the ranks of the squires. He would not allow himself to be called Thomas Holbrook, *Esq.*; he even sent back letters with this address, telling the post-mistress at Cranford that his name was *Mr* Thomas Holbrook, yeoman. He rejected all domestic innovations; he would have the house door stand open in summer and shut in winter, without knocker or bell to summon a servant. The closed fist or the knob of a stick did this office for him if he found the door locked. He despised every refinement which had not its root deep down in humanity. If people were not ill, he saw no necessity for moderating his voice. He spoke the dialect of the country in perfection, and constantly used it in conversation; although Miss

Pole (who gave me these particulars) added, that he read aloud more beautifully and with more feeling than anyone she had ever heard, except the late rector.

'And how came Miss Matilda not to marry him?' asked I.

'Oh, I don't know. She was willing enough, I think; but you know Cousin Thomas would not have been enough of a gentleman for the rector and Miss Jenkyns.'

'Well! but they were not to marry him,' said I, impatiently.

'No; but they did not like Miss Matty to marry below her rank. You know she was the rector's daughter, and somehow they are related to Sir Peter Arley: Miss Jenkyns thought a deal of that.'

'Poor Miss Matty!' said I.

'Nay, now, I don't know anything more than that he offered and was refused. Miss Matty might not like him – and Miss Jenkyns might never have said a word – it is only a guess of mine.'

'Has she never seen him since?' I inquired.

'No, I think not. You see Woodley, Cousin Thomas's house, lies halfway between Cranford and Misselton; and I know he made Misselton his market-town very soon after he had offered to Miss Matty; and I don't think he has been into Cranford above once or twice since – once, when I was walking with Miss Matty, in High Street, and suddenly she darted from me, and went up Shire Lane. A few minutes after I was startled by meeting Cousin Thomas.'

'How old is he?' I asked, after a pause of castle-building.

'He must be about seventy, I think, my dear,' said Miss Pole, blowing up my castle, as if by gunpowder, into small fragments.

Very soon after – at least during my long visit to Miss Matilda – I had the opportunity of seeing Mr Holbrook; seeing, too, his first encounter with his former love, after thirty or forty years' separation. I was helping to decide whether any of the new assortment of coloured silks which they had just received at the shop would do to match a grey and black *mousseline-de-laine* that wanted a new breadth, when a tall, thin, Don Quixote-looking old man came into the shop for some woollen gloves. I had never seen the person (who was rather striking) before, and I watched him rather attentively while Miss Matty listened to the shopman. The stranger wore a blue coat with brass buttons, drab breeches, and gaiters, and drummed with his fingers on the counter until he was attended to. When he answered the shop boy's question,

'What can I have the pleasure of showing you today, sir?' I saw Miss Matilda start, and then suddenly sit down; and instantly I guessed who it was. She had made some inquiry which had to be carried round to the other shopman.

'Miss Jenkyns wants the black sarsenet two-and-twopence the yard'; and Mr Holbrook had caught the name, and was across the shop in two strides.

'Matty – Miss Matilda – Miss Jenkyns! God bless my soul! I should not have known you. How are you? how are you?' He kept shaking her hand in a way which proved the warmth of his friendship; but he repeated so often, as if to himself, 'I should not have known you!' that any sentimental romance which I might be inclined to build was quite done away with by his manner.

However, he kept talking to us all the time we were in the shop; and then waving the shopman with the unpurchased gloves on one side, with 'Another time, sir! another time!' he walked home with us. I am happy to say my client, Miss Matilda, also left the shop in an equally bewildered state, not having purchased either green or red silk. Mr Holbrook was evidently full with honest loud-spoken joy at meeting his old love again; he touched on the changes that had taken place; he even spoke of Miss Jenkyns as 'Your poor sister! Well, well! we have all our faults'; and bade us goodbye with many a hope that he should soon see Miss Matty again. She went straight to her room, and never came back till our early tea-time, when I thought she looked as if she had been crying.

CHAPTER IV

A VISIT TO AN OLD BACHELOR

A few days after, a note came from Mr Holbrook, asking us – impartially asking both of us – in a formal, old-fashioned style, to spend a day at his house – a long June day – for it was June now. He named that he had also invited his cousin, Miss Pole; so that we might join in a fly, which could be put up at his house.

I expected Miss Matty to jump at this invitation; but, no! Miss Pole and I had the greatest difficulty in persuading her to go. She thought it was improper; and was even half annoyed when we utterly ignored the idea of any impropriety in her going with two other ladies to see her old lover. Then came a more serious difficulty. She did not think Deborah would have liked her to go. This took us half a day's good hard talking to get over; but, at the first sentence of relenting, I seized the opportunity, and wrote and despatched an acceptance in her name – fixing day and hour, that all might be decided and done with.

The next morning she asked me if I would go down to the shop with her; and there, after much hesitation, we chose out three caps to be sent home and tried on, that the most becoming might be selected to take with us on Thursday.

She was in a state of silent agitation all the way to Woodley. She had evidently never been there before; and, although she little dreamt I knew anything of her early story, I could perceive she was in a tremor at the thought of seeing the place which might have been her home, and round which it is probable that many of her innocent girlish imaginations had clustered. It was a long drive there, through paved jolting lanes. Miss Matilda sat bolt upright, and looked wistfully out of the windows as we drew near the end of our journey. The aspect of the country was quiet and pastoral. Woodley stood among fields; and there was an old-fashioned garden where roses and currant-bushes touched each other, and where the feathery asparagus formed a pretty background to the pinks and gilly-flowers; there was no drive up to the door. We got out at a little gate, and walked up a straight box-edged path.

'My cousin might make a drive, I think,' said Miss Pole, who was afraid of earache, and had only her cap on.

'I think it is very pretty,' said Miss Matty, with a soft plaintiveness in her voice, and almost in a whisper, for just then Mr Holbrook appeared at the door, rubbing his hands in very effervescence of hospitality. He looked more like my idea of Don Quixote than ever, and yet the likeness was only external. His respectable housekeeper stood modestly at the door to bid us welcome; and, while she led the elder ladies upstairs to a bedroom, I begged to look about the garden. My request evidently pleased the old gentleman, who took me all round the place and showed me his six-and-twenty cows, named after the different letters of the alphabet. As we went along, he surprised me occasionally by repeating apt and beautiful quotations from the poets, ranging easily from Shakespeare and George Herbert to those of our own day. He did this as naturally as if he were thinking aloud, and their true and beautiful words were the best expression he could find for what he was thinking or feeling. To be sure he called Byron 'my Lord Byrron', and pronounced the name of Goethe strictly in accordance with the English sound of the letters – 'As Goethe says, "Ye ever-verdant palaces",' &c. Altogether, I never met with a man, before or since, who had spent so long a life in a secluded and not impressive country, with ever-increasing delight in the daily and yearly change of season and beauty.

When he and I went in, we found that dinner was nearly ready in the kitchen – for so I suppose the room ought to be called, as there were oak dressers and cupboards all round, all over by the side of the fireplace, and only a small Turkey carpet in the middle of the flag-floor. The room might have been easily made into a handsome dark oak dining-parlour by removing the oven and a few other appurtenances of a kitchen, which were evidently never used, the real cooking-place being at some distance. The room in which we were expected to sit was a stiffly-furnished, ugly apartment; but that in which we did sit was what Mr Holbrook called the counting-house, where he paid his labourers their weekly wages at a great desk near the door. The rest of the pretty sitting-room – looking into the orchard, and all covered over with dancing tree-shadows – was filled with books. They lay on the ground, they covered the walls, they strewed the table. He was evidently half ashamed and half proud of his extravagance in this respect. They were of all kinds – poetry and wild weird tales prevailing. He evidently chose his books in accordance with his own tastes, not because such and such were classical or established favourites.

'Ah!' he said, 'we farmers ought not to have much time for reading; yet somehow one can't help it.'

'What a pretty room!' said Miss Matty, *sotto voce*.

'What a pleasant place!' said I, aloud, almost simultaneously.

'Nay! if you like it,' replied he; 'but can you sit on these great, black leather, three-cornered chairs? I like it better than the best parlour; but I thought ladies would take that for the smarter place.'

It was the smarter place, but, like most smart things, not at all pretty, or pleasant, or home-like; so, while we were at dinner, the servant-girl dusted and scrubbed the counting-house chairs, and we sat there all the rest of the day.

We had pudding before meat; and I thought Mr Holbrook was going to make some apology for his old-fashioned ways, for he began –

'I don't know whether you like newfangled ways.'

'Oh, not at all!' said Miss Matty.

'No more do I,' said he. 'My housekeeper *will* have these in her new fashion; or else I tell her that, when I was a young man, we used to keep strictly to my father's rule, "No broth, no ball; no ball, no beef"; and always began dinner with broth. Then we had suet puddings, boiled in the broth with the beef: and then the meat itself. If we did not sup our broth, we had no ball, which we liked a deal better; and the beef came last of all, and only those had it who had done justice to the broth and the ball. Now folks begin with sweet things, and turn their dinners topsy-turvy.'

When the ducks and green peas came, we looked at each other in dismay; we had only two-pronged, black-handled forks. It is true the steel was as bright as silver; but what were we to do? Miss Matty picked up her peas, one by one, on the point of the prongs, much as Aminé ate her grains of rice after her previous feast with the Ghoul. Miss Pole sighed over her delicate young peas as she left them on one side of her plate untasted, for they *would* drop between the prongs. I looked at my host: the peas were going wholesale into his capacious mouth, shovelled up by his large round-ended knife. I saw, I imitated, I survived! My friends, in spite of my precedent, could not muster up courage enough to do an ungenteel thing; and, if Mr Holbrook had not been so heartily hungry, he would probably have seen that the good peas went away almost untouched.

After dinner, a clay pipe was brought in, and a spittoon; and, asking us to retire to another room, where he would soon join us, if we disliked tobacco smoke, he presented his pipe to Miss Matty, and requested her to fill the bowl. This was a compliment to a lady in his youth; but it was rather inappropriate to propose it as an honour to Miss Matty, who had been trained by her sister to hold smoking of every kind in utter abhorrence. But if it was a shock to her refinement, it was also a gratification to her feelings to be thus selected; so she daintily stuffed the strong tobacco into the pipe, and then we withdrew.

'It is very pleasant dining with a bachelor,' said Miss Matty softly, as we settled ourselves in the counting-house. 'I only hope it is not improper; so many pleasant things are!'

'What a number of books he has!' said Miss Pole, looking round the room. 'And how dusty they are!'

'I think it must be like one of the great Dr Johnson's rooms,' said Miss Matty. 'What a superior man your cousin must be!'

'Yes!' said Miss Pole, 'he's a great reader; but I am afraid he has got into very uncouth habits with living alone.'

'Oh! uncouth is too hard a word. I should call him eccentric; very clever people always are!' replied Miss Matty.

When Mr Holbrook returned, he proposed a walk in the fields; but the two elder ladies were afraid of damp, and dirt, and had only very unbecoming calashes to put on over their caps; so they declined, and I was again his companion in a turn which he said he was obliged to take to see after his men. He strode along, either wholly forgetting my existence, or soothed into silence by his pipe – and yet it was not silence exactly. He walked before me with a stooping gait, his hands clasped behind him; and, as some tree or cloud, or glimpse of distant upland pastures, struck him, he quoted poetry to himself, saying it out loud in a grand sonorous voice, with just the emphasis that true feeling and appreciation give. We came upon an old cedar tree, which stood at one end of the house –

'The cedar spreads his dark-green layers of shade.'

'Capital term – "layers"! Wonderful man!' I did not know whether he was speaking to me or not; but I put in an assenting 'wonderful', although I knew nothing about it, just because I was tired of being forgotten, and of being consequently silent.

He turned sharp round. 'Ay! you may say "wonderful". Why, when I saw the review of his poems in *Blackwood*, I set off within an hour, and walked seven miles to Misselton (for the horses were not in the way) and ordered them. Now, what colour are ash-buds in March?'

Is the man going mad? thought I. He is very like Don Quixote.

'What colour are they, I say?' repeated he vehemently.

'I am sure I don't know, sir,' said I, with the meekness of ignorance.

'I knew you didn't. No more did I – an old fool that I am! – till this young man comes and tells me. "Black as ash-buds in March." And I've lived all my life in the country; more shame for me not to know. Black: they are jet-black, madam.' And he went off again, swinging along to the music of some rhyme he had got hold of.

When we came back, nothing would serve him but he must read us the poems he had been speaking of; and Miss Pole encouraged him in his proposal, I thought, because she wished me to hear his beautiful reading, of which she had boasted; but she afterwards said it was because she had got to a difficult part of her crochet, and wanted to count her stitches without having to talk. Whatever he had proposed would have been right to Miss Matty; although she did fall sound asleep within five minutes after he had begun a long poem, called *Locksley Hall*, and had a comfortable nap, unobserved, till he ended; when the cessation of his voice wakened her up, and she said, feeling that something was expected, and that Miss Pole was counting –

'What a pretty book!'

'Pretty, madam! it's beautiful! Pretty, indeed!'

'Oh yes! I meant beautiful!' said she, fluttered at his disapproval of her word. 'It is so like that beautiful poem of Dr Johnson's my sister used to read – I forget the name of it; what was it, my dear?' turning to me.

'Which do you mean, ma'am? What was it about?'

'I don't remember what it was about, and I've quite forgotten what the name of it was; but it was written by Dr Johnson, and was very beautiful, and very like what Mr Holbrook has just been reading.'

'I don't remember it,' said he reflectively. 'But I don't know Dr Johnson's poems well. I must read them.'

As we were getting into the fly to return, I heard Mr Holbrook say he should call on the ladies soon, and inquire how they got home; and this evidently pleased and fluttered Miss Matty at the time he said it; but after we had lost sight of the old house among the trees her sentiments towards the master of it were gradually absorbed into a distressing wonder as to whether Martha had broken her word, and seized on the opportunity of her mistress's absence to have a 'follower'. Martha looked good, and steady, and composed enough, as she came to help us out; she was always careful of Miss Matty, and tonight she made use of this unlucky speech –

'Eh! dear ma'am, to think of your going out in an evening in such a thin shawl! It's no better than muslin. At your age, ma'am, you should be careful.'

'My age!' said Miss Matty, almost speaking crossly, for her, for she was usually gentle – 'My age! Why, how old do you think I am, that you talk about my age?'

'Well, ma'am, I should say you were not far short of sixty: but folks' looks is often against them – and I'm sure I meant no harm.'

'Martha, I'm not yet fifty-two!' said Miss Matty, with grave emphasis; for probably the remembrance of her youth had come very vividly before her this day, and she was annoyed at finding that golden time so far away in the past.

But she never spoke of any former and more intimate acquaintance with Mr Holbrook. She had probably met with so little sympathy in her early love, that she had shut it up close in her heart; and it was only by a sort of watching, which I could hardly avoid since Miss Pole's confidence, that I saw how faithful her poor heart had been in its sorrow and its silence.

She gave me some good reason for wearing her best cap every day, and sat near the window, in spite of her rheumatism, in order to see, without being seen, down into the street.

He came. He put his open palms upon his knees, which were far apart, as he sat with his head bent down, whistling, after we had replied to his inquiries about our safe return. Suddenly he jumped up –

'Well, madam! have you any commands for Paris? I am going there in a week or two.'

'To Paris!' we both exclaimed.

'Yes, madam! I've never been there, and always had a wish to go; and I think if I don't go soon, I mayn't go at all; so as soon as the hay is got in I shall go, before harvest time.'

We were so much astonished that we had no commissions.

Just as he was going out of the room, he turned back, with his favourite exclamation –

'God bless my soul, madam! but I nearly forgot half my errand. Here are the poems for you you admired so much the other evening at my house.' He tugged away at a parcel in his coat-pocket. 'Goodbye, miss,' said he; 'goodbye, Matty! take care of yourself.' And he was gone. But he had given her a book, and he had called her Matty, just as he used to do thirty years ago.

'I wish he would not go to Paris,' said Miss Matilda anxiously. 'I don't believe frogs will agree with him; he used to have to be very careful what he ate, which was curious in so strong-looking a young man.'

Soon after this I took my leave, giving many an injunction to Martha to look after her mistress, and to let me know if she thought that Miss Matilda was not so well; in which case I would volunteer a visit to my old friend, without noticing Martha's intelligence to her.

Accordingly I received a line or two from Martha every now and then; and, about November I had a note to say her mistress was 'very low and sadly off her food'; and the account made me so uneasy that, although Martha did not decidedly summon me, I packed up my things and went.

I received a warm welcome, in spite of the little flurry produced by my impromptu visit, for I had only been able to give a day's notice. Miss Matilda looked miserably ill; and I prepared to comfort and cosset her.

I went down to have a private talk with Martha.

'How long has your mistress been so poorly?' I asked, as I stood by the kitchen fire.

'Well! I think it's better than a fortnight; it is, I know; it was one Tuesday, after Miss Pole had been, that she went into this moping way. I thought she was tired, and it would go off with a night's rest; but no! she has gone on and on ever since, till I thought it my duty to write to you, ma'am.'

'You did quite right, Martha. It is a comfort to think she has so faithful a servant about her. And I hope you find your place comfortable?'

'Well, ma'am, missus is very kind, and there's plenty to eat and drink, and no more work but what I can do easily – but – ' Martha hesitated.

'But what, Martha?'

'Why, it seems so hard of missus not to let me have any followers; there's such lots of young fellows in the town; and many a one has as much as offered to keep company with me; and I may never be in such a likely place again, and it's like wasting an opportunity. Many a girl as I know would have 'em unbeknownst to missus; but I've given my word, and I'll stick to it; or else this is just the house for missus never to be the wiser if they did come: and it's such a capable kitchen – there's such dark corners in it – I'd be bound to hide anyone. I counted up last Sunday night – for I'll not deny I was crying because I had to shut the door in Jem Hearn's face, and he's a steady young man, fit for any girl; only I had given missus my word.' Martha was all but crying again; and I had little comfort to give her, for I knew, from old experience, of the horror with which both the Miss Jenkynses looked upon 'followers'; and in Miss Matty's present nervous state this dread was not likely to be lessened.

I went to see Miss Pole the next day, and took her completely by surprise, for she had not been to see Miss Matilda for two days.

'And now I must go back with you, my dear, for I promised to let her know how Thomas Holbrook went on; and, I'm sorry to say, his housekeeper has sent me word today that he hasn't long to live. Poor Thomas! that journey to Paris was quite too much for him. His housekeeper says he has hardly ever been round his fields since, but just sits with his hands on his knees in the counting-house, not reading or anything, but only saying what a wonderful city Paris was! Paris has much to answer for if it's killed my cousin Thomas, for a better man never lived.'

'Does Miss Matilda know of his illness?' asked I – a new light as to the cause of her indisposition dawning upon me.

'Dear! to be sure, yes! Has not she told you? I let her know a fortnight ago, or more, when first I heard of it. How odd she shouldn't have told you!'

Not at all, I thought; but I did not say anything. I felt almost guilty of having spied too curiously into that tender heart, and I was not going to speak of its secrets – hidden, Miss Matty believed, from all the world. I ushered Miss Pole into Miss Matilda's little drawing-room, and then left them alone. But I was not surprised when Martha came to my bedroom door, to ask me to go down to dinner alone, for that missus had one of her bad headaches. She came into the drawing-room at tea-time, but it was evidently an effort to her; and, as if to make up for some reproachful feeling against her late sister, Miss Jenkyns, which had been troubling her all the afternoon, and for which she now felt penitent, she kept telling me how good and how clever Deborah was in her youth; how she used to settle what gowns they were to wear at all the parties (faint, ghostly ideas of grim parties, far away in the distance, when Miss Matty and Miss Pole were young!); and how Deborah and her mother had started the benefit society for the poor, and taught girls cooking and plain sewing; and how Deborah had once danced with a lord; and how she used to visit at Sir Peter Arley's, and tried to remodel the quiet rectory establishment on the plans of Arley Hall, where they kept thirty servants; and how she had nursed Miss Matty through a long, long illness, of which I had never heard before, but which I now dated in my own mind as following the dismissal of the suit of Mr Holbrook. So we talked softly and quietly of old times through the long November evening.

The next day Miss Pole brought us word that Mr Holbrook was dead. Miss Matty heard the news in silence; in fact, from the account of the previous day, it was only what we had to expect. Miss Pole kept calling upon us for some expression of regret, by asking if it was not sad that he was gone, and saying –

'To think of that pleasant day last June, when he seemed so well! And he might have lived this dozen years if he had not gone to that wicked Paris, where they are always having revolutions.'

She paused for some demonstration on our part. I saw Miss Matty could not speak, she was trembling so nervously; so I said what I really felt; and after a call of some duration – all the time of which I have no doubt Miss Pole thought Miss Matty received the news very calmly – our visitor took her leave.

Miss Matty made a strong effort to conceal her feelings – a conceal-ment she practised even with me, for she has never alluded to Mr Holbrook again, although the book he gave her lies with her Bible on the little table by her bedside. She did not think I heard her when she asked the little milliner of Cranford to make her caps something like the Honourable Mrs Jamieson's, or that I noticed the reply –

'But she wears widows' caps, ma'am?'

'Oh! I only meant something in that style; not widows', of course, but rather like Mrs Jamieson's.'

This effort at concealment was the beginning of the tremulous motion of head and hands which I have seen ever since in Miss Matty.

The evening of the day on which we heard of Mr Holbrook's death, Miss Matilda was very silent and thoughtful; after prayers she called Martha back and then she stood uncertain what to say.

'Martha!' she said, at last, 'you are young' – and then she made so long a pause that Martha, to remind her of her half-finished sentence, dropped a curtsey, and said –

'Yes, please, ma'am; two-and-twenty last third of October, please, ma'am.'

'And, perhaps, Martha, you may some time meet with a young man you like, and who likes you. I did say you were not to have followers; but if you meet with such a young man, and tell me, and I find he is respectable, I have no objection to his coming to see you once a week. God forbid!' said she in a low voice, 'that I should grieve any young hearts.' She spoke as if she were providing for some distant contingency, and was rather startled when Martha made her ready eager answer –

'Please, ma'am, there's Jem Hearn, and he's a joiner making three-and-sixpence a day, and six foot one in his stocking-feet, please, ma'am; and if you'll ask about him tomorrow morning, everyone will give him a character for steadiness; and he'll be glad enough to come tomorrow night, I'll be bound.'

Though Miss Matty was startled, she submitted to Fate and Love.

CHAPTER V

OLD LETTERS

I have often noticed that almost everyone has his own individual small economies – careful habits of saving fractions of pennies in some one peculiar direction – any disturbance of which annoys him more than spending shillings or pounds on some real extravagance. An old gentleman of my acquaintance, who took the intelligence of the failure of a Joint-Stock Bank, in which some of his money was invested, with stoical mildness, worried his family all through a long summer's day because one of them had torn (instead of cutting) out the written leaves of his now useless bank-book; of course, the corresponding pages at the other end came out as well, and this little unnecessary waste of paper (his private economy) chafed him more than all the loss of his money. Envelopes fretted his soul terribly when they first came in; the only way in which he could reconcile himself to such waste of his cherished article was by patiently turning inside out all that were sent to him, and so making them serve again. Even now, though tamed by age, I see him casting wistful glances at his daughters when they send a whole inside of a half-sheet of note paper, with the three lines of acceptance to an invitation, written on only one of the sides. I am not above owning that I have this human weakness myself. String is my foible. My pockets get full of little hanks of it, picked up and twisted together, ready for uses that never come. I am seriously annoyed if anyone cuts the string of a parcel instead of patiently and faithfully undoing it fold by fold. How people can bring themselves to use india-rubber rings, which are a sort of deification of string, as lightly as they do, I cannot imagine. To me an india-rubber ring is a precious treasure. I have one which is not new – one that I picked up off the floor nearly six years ago. I have really tried to use it, but my heart failed me, and I could not commit the extravagance.

Small pieces of butter grieve others. They cannot attend to conversation because of the annoyance occasioned by the habit which some people have of invariably taking more butter than they want. Have you not seen the anxious look (almost mesmeric) which such persons fix on the article? They would feel it a relief if they might bury it out of their sight by popping it into their own mouths and swallowing it down; and they are really made happy if the person on whose plate it lies unused suddenly breaks off a piece of toast (which he does not want at all) and eats up his butter. They think that this is not waste.

Now Miss Matty Jenkyns was chary of candles. We had many devices to use as few as possible. In the winter afternoons she would sit knitting for two or three hours – she could do this in the dark, or by firelight – and when I asked if I might not ring for candles to finish stitching my wristbands, she told me to 'keep blind man's holiday'. They were usually brought in with tea; but we only burnt one at a time. As we lived in constant preparation for a friend who might come in any evening (but who never did), it required some contrivance to keep our two candles of the same length, ready to be lighted, and to look as if we burnt two always. The candles took it in turns; and, whatever we might be talking about or doing, Miss Matty's eyes were habitually fixed upon the candle, ready to jump up and extinguish it and to light the other before they had become too uneven in length to be restored to equality in the course of the evening.

One night, I remember this candle economy particularly annoyed me. I had been very much tired of my compulsory 'blind man's holiday', especially as Miss Matty had fallen asleep, and I did not like to stir the fire and run the risk of awakening her; so I could not even sit on the rug, and scorch myself with sewing by firelight, according to my usual custom. I fancied Miss Matty must be dreaming of her early life; for she spoke one or two words in her uneasy sleep bearing reference to persons who were dead long before. When Martha brought in the lighted candle and tea, Miss Matty started into wakefulness, with a strange, bewildered look around, as if we were not the people she expected to see about her. There was a little sad expression that shad-owed her face as she recognised me; but immediately afterwards she tried to give me her usual smile. All through tea-time her talk ran upon the days of her childhood and youth. Perhaps this reminded her of the desirableness of looking over all the old family letters, and destroying such as ought not to be allowed to fall into the hands of strangers; for she had often spoken of the necessity of this task, but had always shrunk from it, with a timid dread of something painful. Tonight, however, she rose up after tea and went for them – in the dark; for she piqued herself on the precise neatness of all her chamber arrangements, and used to look uneasily at me when I lighted a bed-candle to go to another room for anything. When she returned there was a faint, pleasant smell of Tonquin beans in the room. I had always noticed this scent about any of the things which had belonged to her mother; and many of the letters were addressed to her – yellow bundles of love-letters, sixty or seventy years old.

Miss Matty undid the packet with a sigh; but she stifled it directly, as if it were hardly right to regret the flight of time, or of life either. We agreed to look them over separately, each taking a different letter out of the same bundle and describing its contents to the other before destroying it. I never knew what sad work the reading of old letters was before that evening, though I could hardly tell why. The letters were as happy as letters could be – at least those early letters were. There was in them a vivid and intense sense of the present time, which seemed so strong and full, as if it could never pass away, and as if the warm, living hearts that so expressed themselves could never die, and be as nothing to the sunny earth. I should have felt less melancholy, I believe, if the letters had been more so. I saw the tears stealing down the well-worn furrows of Miss Matty's cheeks, and her spectacles often wanted wiping. I trusted at last that she would light the other candle, for my own eyes were rather dim, and I wanted more light to see the pale, faded ink; but no, even through her tears, she saw and remembered her little economical ways.

The earliest set of letters were two bundles tied together, and ticketed (in Miss Jenkyns's handwriting) 'Letters interchanged between my ever-honoured father and my dearly-beloved mother, prior to their marriage, in July 1774.' I should guess that the rector of Cranford was about twenty-seven years of age when he wrote those letters; and Miss Matty told me that her mother was just eighteen at the time of her wedding. With my idea of the rector derived from a picture in the dining-parlour, stiff and stately, in a huge full-bottomed wig, with gown, cassock, and bands, and his hand upon a copy of the only sermon he ever published – it was strange to read these letters. They were full of eager, passionate ardour; short homely sentences, right fresh from the heart (very different from the grand Latinised, Johnsonian style of the printed sermon preached before some judge at assize time). His letters were a curious contrast to those of his girl-bride. She was evidently rather annoyed at his demands upon her for expressions of love, and could not quite understand what he meant by repeating the same thing over in so many different ways; but what she was quite clear about was a longing for a white 'Paduasoy' – whatever that might be; and six or seven letters were principally occupied in asking her lover to use his influence with her parents (who evidently kept her in good order) to obtain this or that article of dress, more especially the white 'Paduasoy'. He cared nothing how she was dressed; she was always lovely enough for him, as he took pains to assure her, when she begged him to express in his answers a predilection for particular pieces of finery, in order that she might show what he said to her parents. But at length he seemed to find out that she would not be married till she had a 'trousseau' to her mind; and then he sent her a letter, which had evidently accompanied a whole box full of finery, and in which he requested that she might be dressed in everything her heart desired. This was the first letter, ticketed in a frail, delicate hand, 'From my dearest John.' Shortly afterwards they were married, I suppose, from the intermission in their correspondence.

'We must burn them, I think,' said Miss Matty, looking doubtfully at me. 'No one will care for them when I am gone.' And one by one she dropped them into the middle of the fire, watching each blaze up, die out, and rise away, in faint, white, ghostly semblance, up the chimney, before she gave another to the same fate. The room was light enough now; but I, like her, was fascinated into watching the destruction of those letters, into which the honest warmth of a manly heart had been poured forth.

The next letter, likewise docketed by Miss Jenkyns, was endorsed, 'Letter of pious congratulation and exhortation from my venerable grandfather to my beloved mother, on occasion of my own birth. Also some practical remarks on the desirability of keeping warm the extremities of infants, from my excellent grandmother.'

The first part was, indeed, a severe and forcible picture of the responsibilities of mothers, and a warning against the evils that were in the world, and lying in ghastly wait for the little baby of two days old. His wife did not write, said the old gentleman, because he had forbidden it, she being indisposed with a sprained ankle, which (he said) quite incapacitated her from holding a pen. However, at the foot of the page was a small 't.o.', and on turning it over, sure enough, there was a letter to 'my dear, dearest Molly', begging her, when she left her room, whatever she did, to go *up* stairs before going *down*: and telling her to wrap her baby's feet up in flannel, and keep it warm by the fire, although it was summer, for babies were so tender.

It was pretty to see from the letters, which were evidently exchanged with some frequency between the young mother and the grandmother, how the girlish vanity was being weeded out of her heart by love for her baby. The white 'Paduasoy' figured again in the letters, with almost as much vigour as before. In one, it was being made into a christening cloak for the baby. It decked it when it went with its parents to spend a day or two at Arley Hall. It added to its charms, when it was 'the prettiest little baby that ever was seen. Dear mother, I wish you could see her! Without any parshality, I do think she will grow up a regular bewty!' I thought of Miss Jenkyns, grey, withered, and wrinkled, and I wondered if her mother had known her in the courts of heaven: and then I knew that she had, and that they stood there in angelic guise.

There was a great gap before any of the rector's letters appeared. And then his wife had changed her mode of her endorsement. It was no longer from, 'My dearest John'; it was from 'My Honoured Husband'. The letters were written on occasion of the publication of the same sermon which was represented in the picture. The preaching before 'My Lord Judge', and the 'publishing by request', was evidently the culminating point – the event of his life. It had been necessary for him to go up to London to superintend it through the press. Many friends had to be called upon and consulted before he could decide on any printer fit for so onerous a task; and at length it was arranged that J. and J. Rivingtons were to have the honourable responsibility. The worthy rector seemed to be strung up by the occasion to a high literary pitch, for he could hardly write a letter to his wife without cropping out into Latin. I remember the end of one of his letters ran thus: 'I shall ever hold the virtuous qualities of my Molly in remembrance, *dum memor ipse mei, dum spiritus regit artus*', which, considering that the English of his correspondent was sometimes at fault in grammar, and often in spelling, might be taken as a proof of how much he 'idealised his Molly'; and, as Miss Jenkyns used to say, 'People talk a great deal about idealising nowadays, whatever that may mean.' But this was nothing to a fit of writing classical poetry which soon seized him, in which his Molly figured away as 'Maria'. The letter containing the *carmen* was endorsed by her, 'Hebrew verses sent me by my honoured husband. I thowt to have had a letter about killing the pig, but must wait. Mem., to send the poetry to Sir Peter Arley, as my husband desires.' And in a post-scriptum note in his handwriting it was stated that the Ode had appeared in the *Gentleman's Magazine*, December 1782.

Her letters back to her husband (treasured as fondly by him as if they had been *M. T. Ciceronis Epistolæ*) were more satisfactory to an absent husband and father than his could ever have been to her. She told him how Deborah sewed her seam very neatly every day, and read to her in the books he had sent her; how she was a very 'forrard', good child, but would ask questions her mother could not answer, but how she did not let herself down by saying she did not know, but took to stirring the fire, or sending the 'forrard' child on an errand. Matty was now the mother's darling, and promised (like her sister at her age), to be a great beauty. I was reading this aloud to Miss Matty, who smiled and sighed a little at the hope, so fondly expressed, that 'little Matty might not be vain, even if she were a bewty.'

'I had very pretty hair, my dear,' said Miss Matilda; 'and not a bad mouth.' And I saw her soon afterwards adjust her cap and draw herself up.

But to return to Mrs Jenkyns's letters. She told her husband about the poor in the parish; what homely domestic medicines she had administered; what kitchen physic she had sent. She had evidently held his displeasure as a rod in pickle over the heads of all the ne'er-do-wells. She asked for his directions about the cows and pigs; and did not always obtain them, as I have shown before.

The kind old grandmother was dead when a little boy was born, soon after the publication of the sermon; but there was another letter of exhortation from the grandfather, more stringent and admonitory than ever, now that there was a boy to be guarded from the snares of the world. He described all the various sins into which men might fall, until I wondered how any man ever came to a natural death. The gallows seemed as if it must have been the termination of the lives of most of the grandfather's friends and acquaintance; and I was not surprised at the way in which he spoke of this life being 'a vale of tears'.

It seemed curious that I should never have heard of this brother before; but I concluded that he had died young, or else surely his name would have been alluded to by his sisters.

By-and-by we came to packets of Miss Jenkyns's letters. These Miss Matty did regret to burn. She said all the others had been only interesting to those who loved the writers, and that it seemed as if it would have hurt her to allow them to fall into the hands of strangers, who had not known her dear mother, and how good she was, although she did not always spell, quite in the modern fashion; but Deborah's letters were so very superior! Anyone might profit by reading them. It was a long time since she had read Mrs Chapone, but she knew she used to think that Deborah could have said the same things quite as well; and as for Mrs Carter! people thought a deal of her letters, just because she had written *Epictetus*, but she was quite sure Deborah would never have made use of such a common expression as 'I canna be fashed!'

Miss Matty did grudge burning these letters, it was evident. She would not let them be carelessly passed over with any quiet reading, and skipping, to myself. She took them from me, and even lighted the second candle in order to read them aloud with a proper emphasis, and without stumbling over the big words. Oh dear! how I wanted facts instead of reflections, before those letters were concluded! They lasted us two nights; and I won't deny that I made use of the time to think of many other things, and yet I was always at my post at the end of each sentence.

The rector's letters, and those of his wife and mother-in-law, had all been tolerably short and pithy, written in a straight hand, with the lines very close together. Sometimes the whole letter was contained on a mere scrap of paper. The paper was very yellow, and the ink very brown; some of the sheets were (as Miss Matty made me observe) the old original post, with the stamp in the corner representing a post-boy riding for life and twanging his horn. The letters of Mrs Jenkyns and her mother were fastened with a great round red wafer; for it was before Miss Edgeworth's *Patronage* had banished wafers from polite society. It was evident, from the tenor of what was said, that franks were in great request, and were even used as a means of paying debts by needy members of Parliament. The rector sealed his epistles with an immense coat of arms, and showed by the care with which he had performed this ceremony that he expected they should be cut open, not broken by any thoughtless or impatient hand. Now, Miss Jenkyns's letters were of a later date in form and writing. She wrote on the square sheet which we have learned to call old-fashioned. Her hand was admirably calculated, together with her use of many-syllabled words, to fill up a sheet, and then came the pride and delight of crossing. Poor Miss Matty got sadly puzzled with this, for the words gathered size like snowballs, and towards the end of her letter Miss Jenkyns used to become quite sesquipedalian. In one to her father, slightly theological and controversial in its tone, she had spoken of Herod, Tetrarch of Idumea. Miss Matty read it 'Herod Petrarch of Etruria,' and was just as well pleased as if she had been right.

I can't quite remember the date, but I think it was in 1805 that Miss Jenkyns wrote the longest series of letters – on occasion of her absence on a visit to some friends near Newcastle-upon-Tyne. These friends were intimate with the commandant of the garrison there, and heard from him of all the preparations that were being made to repel the invasion of Buonaparte, which some people imagined might take place at the mouth of the Tyne. Miss Jenkyns was evidently very much alarmed; and the first part of her letters was often written in pretty intelligible English, conveying particulars of the preparations which were made in the family with whom she was residing against the dreaded event; the bundles of clothes that were packed up ready for a flight to Alston Moor (a wild hilly piece of ground between Northumberland and Cumberland); the signal that was to be given for this flight, and for the simultaneous turning out of the volunteers under arms – which said signal was to consist (if I remember rightly) in ringing the church bells in a particular and ominous manner. One day, when Miss Jenkyns and her hosts were at a dinner party in Newcastle, this warning summons was actually given (not a very wise proceeding, if there be any truth in the moral attached to the fable of the Boy and the Wolf; but so it was), and Miss Jenkyns, hardly recovered from her fright, wrote the next day to describe the sound, the breathless shock, the hurry and alarm; and then, taking breath, she added, 'How trivial, my dear father, do all our apprehensions of the last evening appear, at the present moment, to calm and enquiring minds!' And here Miss Matty broke in with –

'But, indeed, my dear, they were not at all trivial or trifling at the time. I know I used to wake up in the night many a time and think I heard the tramp of the French entering Cranford. Many people talked of hiding themselves in the salt mines – and meat would have kept capitally down there, only perhaps we should have been thirsty. And

my father preached a whole set of sermons on the occasion; one set
in the mornings, all about David and Goliath, to spirit up the people
to fighting with spades or bricks, if need were; and the other set in
the afternoons, proving that Napoleon (that was another name for Bony,
as we used to call him) was all the same as an Apollyon and Abaddon.
I remember my father rather thought he should be asked to print this
last set; but the parish had, perhaps, had enough of them with hearing.'

Peter Marmaduke Arley Jenkyns ('poor Peter!' as Miss Matty began
to call him) was at school at Shrewsbury by this time. The rector took
up his pen, and rubbed up his Latin once more, to correspond with
his boy. It was very clear that the lad's were what are called show
letters. They were of a highly mental description, giving an account
of his studies, and his intellectual hopes of various kinds, with an
occasional quotation from the classics; but, now and then, the animal
nature broke out in such a little sentence as this, evidently written in
a trembling hurry, after the letter had been inspected: 'Mother dear,
do send me a cake, and put plenty of citron in.' The 'mother dear'
probably answered her boy in the form of cakes and 'goody', for there
were none of her letters among this set; but a whole collection of the
rector's, to whom the Latin in his boy's letters was like a trumpet to
the old war-horse. I do not know much about Latin, certainly, and it
is, perhaps, an ornamental language, but not very useful, I think – at
least to judge from the bits I remember out of the rector's letters. One
was, 'You have not got that town in your map of Ireland; but *Bonus
Bernardus non videt omnia*, as the Proverbia say.' Presently it became
very evident that 'poor Peter' got himself into many scrapes. There
were letters of stilted penitence to his father, for some wrong-doing;
and among them all was a badly-written, badly-sealed, badly-directed,
blotted note: – 'My dear, dear, dear, dearest mother, I will be a better
boy; I will, indeed; but don't, please, be ill for me; I am not worth it;
but I will be good, darling mother.'

Miss Matty could not speak for crying, after she had read this note.
She gave it to me in silence, and then got up and took it to her sacred
recesses in her own room, for fear, by any chance, it might get burnt.
'Poor Peter!' she said; 'he was always in scrapes; he was too easy.
They led him wrong, and then left him in the lurch. But he was too
fond of mischief. He could never resist a joke. Poor Peter!'

CHAPTER VI
POOR PETER

Poor Peter's career lay before him rather pleasantly mapped out by kind friends, but *Bonus Bernardus non videt omnia*, in this map too. He was to win honours at the Shrewsbury School, and carry them thick to Cambridge, and after that, a living awaited him, the gift of his godfather, Sir Peter Arley. Poor Peter! his lot in life was very different to what his friends had hoped and planned. Miss Matty told me all about it, and I think it was a relief when she had done so.

He was the darling of his mother, who seemed to dote on all her children, though she was, perhaps, a little afraid of Deborah's superior acquirements. Deborah was the favourite of her father, and when Peter disappointed him, she became his pride. The sole honour Peter brought away from Shrewsbury was the reputation of being the best good fellow that ever was, and of being the captain of the school in the art of practical joking. His father was disappointed, but set about remedying the matter in a manly way. He could not afford to send Peter to read with any tutor, but he could read with him himself; and Miss Matty told me much of the awful preparations in the way of dictionaries and lexicons that were made in her father's study the morning Peter began.

'My poor mother!' said she. 'I remember how she used to stand in the hall, just near enough the study door, to catch the tone of my father's voice. I could tell in a moment if all was going right, by her face. And it did go right for a long time.'

'What went wrong at last?' said I. 'That tiresome Latin, I dare say.'

'No! it was not the Latin. Peter was in high favour with my father, for he worked up well for him. But he seemed to think that the Cranford people might be joked about, and made fun of, and they did not like it; nobody does. He was always hoaxing them; "hoaxing" is not a pretty word, my dear, and I hope you won't tell your father I used it, for I should not like him to think that I was not choice in my language, after living with such a woman as Deborah. And be sure you never use it yourself. I don't know how it slipped out of my mouth, except it was that I was thinking of poor Peter and it was always his expression. But he was a very gentlemanly boy in many things. He was like dear Captain Brown in always being ready to help any old person or a child. Still, he did like joking and making fun; and he seemed to think the old ladies in Cranford would believe anything. There were many old ladies living here then; we are principally ladies now, I know, but we are not so old as the ladies used to be when I was a girl. I could laugh to think of some of Peter's jokes. No, my dear, I won't tell you of them, because they might not shock you as they ought to do, and they were very shocking. He even took in my father once, by dressing himself up as a lady that was passing through the town and wished to see the Rector of Cranford, "who had published that admirable Assize Sermon". Peter said he was awfully frightened himself when he saw how my father took it all in, and even offered to copy out all his Napoleon Buonaparte sermons for her – him, I mean – no, her, for Peter was a lady then. He told me he was more terrified than he ever was before, all the time my father was speaking. He did not think my father would have believed him; and yet if he had not, it would have been a sad thing for Peter. As it was, he was none so glad of it, for my father kept him hard at work copying out all those twelve Buonaparte sermons for the lady – that was for Peter himself, you know. He was the lady. And once when he wanted to go fishing, Peter said, "Confound the woman!" – very bad language, my dear, but Peter was not always so guarded as he should have been; my father was so angry with him, it nearly frightened me out of my wits: and yet I could hardly keep from laughing at the little curtseys Peter kept making, quite slyly, whenever my father spoke of the lady's excellent taste and sound discrimination.'

'Did Miss Jenkyns know of these tricks?' said I.

'Oh, no! Deborah would have been too much shocked. No, no one knew but me. I wish I had always known of Peter's plans; but sometimes he did not tell me. He used to say the old ladies in the town wanted something to talk about; but I don't think they did. They had the *St James's Chronicle* three times a week, just as we have now, and we have plenty to say; and I remember the clacking noise there always was when some of the ladies got together. But, probably, schoolboys talk more than ladies. At last there was a terrible, sad thing happened.' Miss Matty got up, went to the door, and opened it; no one was there. She rang the bell for Martha, and when Martha came, her mistress told her to go for eggs to a farm at the other end of the town.

'I will lock the door after you, Martha. You are not afraid to go, are you?'

'No, ma'am, not at all; Jem Hearn will be only too proud to go with me.'

Miss Matty drew herself up, and as soon as we were alone, she wished that Martha had more maidenly reserve.

'We'll put out the candle, my dear. We can talk just as well by firelight, you know. There! Well, you see, Deborah had gone from home for a fortnight or so; it was a very still, quiet day, I remember, overhead; and the lilacs were all in flower, so I suppose it was spring. My father had gone out to see some sick people in the parish; I recollect seeing him leave the house with his wig and shovel-hat and cane. What possessed our poor Peter I don't know; he had the sweetest temper, and yet he always seemed to like to plague Deborah. She never laughed at his jokes, and thought him ungenteel, and not careful enough about improving his mind; and that vexed him.

'Well! he went to her room, it seems, and dressed himself in her old gown, and shawl, and bonnet; just the things she used to wear in Cranford, and was known by everywhere; and he made the pillow into a little – you are sure you locked the door, my dear, for I should not like anyone to hear – into – into a little baby, with white long clothes. It was only, as he told me afterwards, to make something to talk about in the town; he never thought of it as affecting Deborah. And he went and walked up and down in the Filbert walk – just half-hidden by the rails, and half-seen; and he cuddled his pillow, just like a baby, and talked to it all the nonsense people do. Oh dear! and my father came stepping stately up the street, as he always did; and what should he see but a little black crowd of people – I dare say as many as twenty – all peeping through his garden rails. So he thought, at first, they were only looking at a new rhododendron that was in full bloom, and that he was very proud of; and he walked slower, that they might have more time to admire. And he wondered if he could make out a sermon from the occasion, and thought, perhaps, there was some relation between the rhododendrons and the lilies of the field. My poor father! When he came nearer, he began to wonder that they did not see him; but their heads were all so close together, peeping and peeping! My father was amongst them, meaning, he said, to ask them to walk into the garden with him, and admire the beautiful vegetable production, when – oh, my dear, I tremble to think of it – he looked through the rails himself, and saw – I don't know what he thought he saw, but old Clare told me his face went quite grey-white with anger, and his eyes blazed out under his frowning black brows; and he spoke out – oh, so terribly! – and bade them all stop where they were – not one of them to go, not one of them to stir a step; and, swift as light, he was in at the garden door, and down the Filbert walk, and seized hold of poor Peter, and tore his clothes off his back – bonnet, shawl, gown, and all – and threw the pillow among the people over the railings: and then he was very, very angry indeed, and before all the people he lifted up his cane and flogged Peter!

'My dear, that boy's trick, on that sunny day, when all seemed going straight and well, broke my mother's heart, and changed my father for life. It did, indeed. Old Clare said, Peter looked as white as my father; and stood as still as a statue to be flogged; and my father struck hard! When my father stopped to take breath, Peter said, "Have you done enough, sir?" quite hoarsely, and still standing quite quiet. I don't know what my father said – or if he said anything. But old Clare said, Peter turned to where the people outside the railing were, and made them a low bow, as grand and as grave as any gentleman; and then walked slowly into the house. I was in the storeroom helping my mother to make cowslip wine. I cannot abide the wine now, nor the scent of the flowers; they turn me sick and faint, as they did that day, when Peter came in, looking as haughty as any man – indeed, looking like a man, not like a boy. "Mother!" he said, "I am come to say, God bless you for ever." I saw his lips quiver as he spoke; and I think he durst not say anything more loving, for the purpose that was in his heart. She looked at him rather frightened, and wondering, and asked him what was to do. He did not smile or speak, but put his arms round her and kissed her as if he did not know how to leave off; and before she could speak again, he was gone. We talked it over, and could not understand it, and she bade me go and seek my father, and ask what it was all about. I found him walking up and down, looking very highly displeased.

'"Tell your mother I have flogged Peter, and that he richly deserved it."

'I durst not ask any more questions. When I told my mother, she sat down, quite faint, for a minute. I remember, a few days after, I saw the poor, withered cowslip flowers thrown out to the leaf heap, to decay and die there. There was no making of cowslip wine that year at the rectory – nor, indeed, ever after.

'Presently my mother went to my father. I know I thought of Queen Esther and King Ahasuerus; for my mother was very pretty and delicate-looking, and my father looked as terrible as King Ahasuerus. Some time after they came out together; and then my mother told me what had happened, and that she was going up to Peter's room at my father's desire – though she was not to tell Peter this – to talk the matter over with him. But no Peter was there. We looked over the house; no Peter was there! Even my father, who had not liked to join in the search at first, helped us before long. The rectory was a very old house – steps up into a room, steps down into a room, all through. At first, my mother went calling low and soft, as if to reassure the poor boy, "Peter! Peter, dear! it's only me"; but, by-and-by, as the servants came back from the errands my father had sent them, in different directions, to find where Peter was – as we found he was not in the garden, nor the hayloft, nor anywhere about – my mother's cry grew louder and wilder, "Peter! Peter, my darling! where are you?" for then she felt and under-stood that that long kiss meant some sad kind of "goodbye". The afternoon went on – my mother never resting, but seeking again and again in every possible place that had been looked into twenty times before, nay, that she had looked into over and over again herself. My father sat with his head in his hands, not speaking except when his messengers came in, bringing no tidings; then he lifted up his face, so strong and sad, and told them to go again in some new direction. My mother kept passing from room to room, in and out of the house, moving noiselessly, but never ceasing. Neither she nor my father durst leave the house, which was the meeting-place for all the messengers. At last (and it was nearly dark), my father rose up. He took hold of my mother's arm as she came with wild, sad pace through one door, and quickly towards another. She started at the touch of his hand, for she had forgotten all in the world but Peter.

'"Molly!" said he, "I did not think all this would happen." He looked into her face for comfort – her poor face all wild and white; for neither she nor my father had dared to acknowledge – much less act upon – the terror that was in their hearts, lest Peter should have made away with himself. My father saw no conscious look in his wife's hot, dreary eyes, and he missed the sympathy that she had always been ready to give him – strong man as he was, and at the dumb despair in her face his tears began to flow. But when she saw this, a gentle sorrow came over her countenance, and she said, "Dearest John! don't cry; come with me, and we'll find him," almost as cheerfully as if she knew where he was. And she took my father's great hand in her little soft one, and led him along, the tears dropping as he walked on that same unceasing, weary walk, from room to room, through house and garden.

'Oh, how I wished for Deborah! I had no time for crying, for now all seemed to depend on me. I wrote for Deborah to come home. I sent a message privately to that same Mr Holbrook's house – poor Mr Holbrook; – you know who I mean. I don't mean I sent a message to him, but I sent one that I could trust to know if Peter was at his house. For at one time Mr Holbrook was an occasional visitor at the rectory – you know he was Miss Pole's cousin – and he had been very kind to Peter, and taught him how to fish – he was very kind to everybody, and I thought Peter might have gone off there. But Mr Holbrook was from home, and Peter had never been seen. It was night now; but the doors were all wide open, and my father and mother walked on and on; it was more than an hour since he had joined her, and I don't believe they had ever spoken all that time. I was getting the parlour fire lighted, and one of the servants was preparing tea, for I wanted them to have something to eat and drink and warm them, when old Clare asked to speak to me.

"'I have borrowed the nets from the weir, Miss Matty. Shall we drag the ponds tonight, or wait for the morning?"

'I remember staring in his face to gather his meaning; and when I did, I laughed out loud. The horror of that new thought – our bright, darling Peter, cold, and stark, and dead! I remember the ring of my own laugh now.

'The next day Deborah was at home before I was myself again. She would not have been so weak as to give way as I had done; but my screams (my horrible laughter had ended in crying) had roused my sweet dear mother, whose poor wandering wits were called back and collected as soon as a child needed her care. She and Deborah sat by my bedside; I knew by the looks of each that there had been no news of Peter – no awful, ghastly news, which was what I most had dreaded in my dull state between sleeping and waking.

'The same result of all the searching had brought something of the same relief to my mother, to whom, I am sure, the thought that Peter might even then be hanging dead in some of the familiar home places had caused that never-ending walk of yesterday. Her soft eyes never were the same again after that; they had always a restless, craving look, as if seeking for what they could not find. Oh! it was an awful time; coming down like a thunderbolt on the still sunny day when the lilacs were all in bloom.'

'Where was Mr Peter?' said I.

'He had made his way to Liverpool; and there was war then; and some of the king's ships lay off the mouth of the Mersey; and they were only too glad to have a fine likely boy such as him (five foot nine he was), come to offer himself. The captain wrote to my father, and Peter wrote to my mother. Stay! those letters will be somewhere here.'

We lighted the candle, and found the captain's letter and Peter's too. And we also found a little simple begging letter from Mrs Jenkyns to Peter, addressed to him at the house of an old schoolfellow whither she fancied he might have gone. They had returned it unopened; and unopened it had remained ever since, having been inadvertently put by among the other letters of that time. This is it: –

'MY DEAREST PETER, – You did not think we should be so sorry as we are, I know, or you would never have gone away. You are too good. Your father sits and sighs till my heart aches to hear him. He cannot hold up his head for grief; and yet he only did what he thought was right. Perhaps he has been too severe, and perhaps I have not been kind enough; but God knows how we love you, my dear only boy. Don looks so sorry you are gone. Come back, and make us happy, who love you so much. I know you will come back.'

But Peter did not come back. That spring day was the last time he ever saw his mother's face. The writer of the letter – the last – the only person who had ever seen what was written in it, was dead long ago; and I, a stranger, not born at the time when this occurrence took place, was the one to open it.

The captain's letter summoned the father and mother to Liverpool instantly, if they wished to see their boy; and, by some of the wild chances of life, the captain's letter had been detained somewhere, somehow.

Miss Matty went on, 'And it was racetime, and all the post-horses at Cranford were gone to the races; but my father and mother set off in our own gig – and oh! my dear, they were too late – the ship was gone! And now read Peter's letter to my mother!'

It was full of love, and sorrow, and pride in his new profession, and a sore sense of his disgrace in the eyes of the people at Cranford; but ending with a passionate entreaty that she would come and see him before he left the Mersey: 'Mother; we may go into battle. I hope we shall, and lick those French: but I must see you again before that time.'

'And she was too late,' said Miss Matty; 'too late!'

We sat in silence, pondering on the full meaning of those sad, sad words. At length I asked Miss Matty to tell me how her mother bore it.

'Oh!' she said, 'she was patience itself. She had never been strong, and this weakened her terribly. My father used to sit looking at her: far more sad than she was. He seemed as if he could look at nothing else when she was by; and he was so humble – so very gentle now. He would, perhaps, speak in his old way – laying down the law, as it were – and then, in a minute or two, he would come round and put his hand on our shoulders, and ask us in a low voice, if he had said anything to hurt us. I did not wonder at his speaking so to Deborah, for she was so clever; but I could not bear to hear him talking so to me.

'But, you see, he saw what we did not – that it was killing my mother. Yes! killing her (put out the candle, my dear; I can talk better in the dark), for she was but a frail woman, and ill-fitted to stand the fright and shock she had gone through; and she would smile at him and comfort him, not in words, but in her looks and tones, which were always cheerful when he was there. And she would speak of how she thought Peter stood a good chance of being admiral very soon – he was so brave and clever; and how she thought of seeing him in his navy uniform, and what sort of hats admirals wore; and how much more fit he was to be a sailor than a clergyman; and all in that way, just to make my father think she was quite glad of what came of that unlucky morning's work, and the flogging which was always in his mind, as we all knew. But oh, my dear! the bitter, bitter crying she had when she was alone; and at last, as she grew weaker, she could not keep her tears in when Deborah or me was by, and would give us message after message for Peter (his ship had gone to the Mediterranean, or somewhere down there, and then he was ordered off to India, and there was no overland route then); but she still said that no one knew where their death lay in wait, and that we were not to think hers was near. We did not think it, but we knew it, as we saw her fading away.

'Well, my dear, it's very foolish of me, I know, when in all likelihood I am so near seeing her again.

'And only think, love! the very day after her death – for she did not live quite a twelvemonth after Peter went away – the very day after – came a parcel for her from India – from her poor boy. It was a large, soft, white Indian shawl, with just a little narrow border all round; just what my mother would have liked.

'We thought it might rouse my father, for he had sat with her hand in his all night long; so Deborah took it in to him, and Peter's letter to her, and all. At first, he took no notice; and we tried to make a kind of light careless talk about the shawl, opening it out and admiring it. Then, suddenly, he got up, and spoke: "She shall be buried in it," he said; "Peter shall have that comfort; and she would have liked it."

'Well, perhaps it was not reasonable, but what could we do or say? One gives people in grief their own way. He took it up and felt it: "It is just such a shawl as she wished for when she was married, and her mother did not give it her. I did not know of it till after, or she should have had it – she should; but she shall have it now."

'My mother looked so lovely in her death! She was always pretty, and now she looked fair, and waxen, and young – younger than Deborah, as she stood trembling and shivering by her. We decked her in the long soft folds; she lay smiling, as if pleased; and people came – all Cranford came – to beg to see her, for they had loved her dearly, as well they might; and the countrywomen brought posies; old Clare's wife brought some white violets and begged they might lie on her breast.

'Deborah said to me, the day of my mother's funeral, that if she had a hundred offers she never would marry and leave my father. It was not very likely she would have so many – I don't know that she had one; but it was not less to her credit to say so. She was such a daughter to my father as I think there never was before or since. His eyes failed him, and she read book after book, and wrote, and copied, and was always at his service in any parish business. She could do many more things than my poor mother could; she even once wrote a letter to the bishop for my father. But he missed my mother sorely; the whole parish noticed it. Not that he was less active; I think he was more so, and more patient in helping everyone. I did all I could to set

Deborah at liberty to be with him; for I knew I was good for little, and that my best work in the world was to do odd jobs quietly, and set others at liberty. But my father was a changed man.'

'Did Mr Peter ever come home?'

'Yes, once. He came home a lieutenant; he did not get to be admiral. And he and my father were such friends! My father took him into every house in the parish, he was so proud of him. He never walked out without Peter's arm to lean upon. Deborah used to smile (I don't think we ever laughed again after my mother's death), and say she was quite put in a corner. Not but what my father always wanted her when there was letter-writing or reading to be done, or anything to be settled.'

'And then?' said I, after a pause.

'Then Peter went to sea again; and, by-and-by, my father died, blessing us both, and thanking Deborah for all she had been to him; and, of course, our circumstances were changed; and, instead of living at the rectory, and keeping three maids and a man, we had to come to this small house, and be content with a servant-of-all-work; but, as Deborah used to say, we have always lived genteelly, even if circumstances have compelled us to simplicity. Poor Deborah!'

'And Mr Peter?' asked I.

'Oh, there was some great war in India – I forget what they call it – and we have never heard of Peter since then. I believe he is dead myself; and it sometimes fidgets me that we have never put on mourning for him. And then again, when I sit by myself, and all the house is still, I think I hear his step coming up the street, and my heart begins to flutter and beat; but the sound always goes past – and Peter never comes.

'That's Martha back? No! *I'll* go, my dear; I can always find my way in the dark, you know. And a blow of fresh air at the door will do my head good, and it's rather got a trick of aching.'

So she pattered off. I had lighted the candle, to give the room a cheerful appearance against her return.

'Was it Martha?' asked I.

'Yes. And I am rather uncomfortable, for I heard such a strange noise, just as I was opening the door.'

'Where?' I asked, for her eyes were round with affright.

'In the street – just outside – it sounded like' –

'Talking?' I put in, as she hesitated a little.

'No! kissing' –

CHAPTER VII
VISITING

One morning, as Miss Matty and I sat at our work – it was before twelve o'clock, and Miss Matty had not changed the cap with yellow ribbons that had been Miss Jenkyns's best, and which Miss Matty was now wearing out in private, putting on the one made in imitation of Mrs Jamieson's at all times when she expected to be seen – Martha came up, and asked if Miss Betty Barker might speak to her mistress. Miss Matty assented, and quickly disappeared to change the yellow ribbons, while Miss Barker came upstairs; but, as she had forgotten her spectacles, and was rather flurried by the unusual time of the visit, I was not surprised to see her return with one cap on the top of the other. She was quite unconscious of it herself, and looked at us, with bland satisfaction. Nor do I think Miss Barker perceived it; for, putting aside the little circumstance that she was not so young as she had been, she was very much absorbed in her errand, which she delivered herself of with an oppressive modesty that found vent in endless apologies.

Miss Betty Barker was the daughter of the old clerk at Cranford who had officiated in Mr Jenkyns's time. She and her sister had had pretty good situations as ladies' maids, and had saved money enough to set up a milliner's shop, which had been patronised by the ladies in the neighbourhood. Lady Arley, for instance, would occasionally give Miss Barkers the pattern of an old cap of hers, which they immediately copied and circulated among the *élite* of Cranford. I say the *élite*, for Miss Barkers had caught the trick of the place, and piqued themselves upon their 'aristocratic connection'. They would not sell their caps and ribbons to anyone without a pedigree. Many a farmer's wife or daughter turned away huffed from Miss Barkers' select millinery, and went rather to the universal shop, where the profits of brown soap and moist sugar enabled the proprietor to go straight to (Paris, he said, until he found his customers too patriotic and John Bullish to wear what the Mounseers wore) London, where, as he often told his customers, Queen Adelaide had appeared, only the very week before, in a cap exactly like the one he showed them, trimmed with yellow and blue ribbons, and had been complimented by King William on the becoming nature of her headdress.

Miss Barkers, who confined themselves to truth, and did not approve of miscellaneous customers, throve notwithstanding. They were self-denying, good people. Many a time have I seen the eldest of them (she that had been maid to Mrs Jamieson) carrying out some delicate mess to a poor person. They only aped their betters in having 'nothing to do' with the class immediately below theirs. And when Miss Barker died, their profits and income were found to be such that Miss Betty was justified in shutting up shop and retiring from business. She also (as I think I have before said) set up her cow; a mark of respectability in Cranford almost as decided as setting up a gig is among some people. She dressed finer than any lady in Cranford; and we did not wonder at it; for it was understood that she was wearing out all the bonnets and caps and outrageous ribbons which had once formed her stock-in-trade. It was five or six years since she had given up shop, so in any other place than Cranford her dress might have been considered *passée*.

And now Miss Betty Barker had called to invite Miss Matty to tea at her house on the following Tuesday. She gave me also an impromptu invitation, as I happened to be a visitor – though I could see she had a little fear lest, since my father had gone to live in Drumble, he might have engaged in that 'horrid cotton trade', and so dragged his family down out of 'aristocratic society'. She prefaced this invitation with so many apologies that she quite excited my curiosity. 'Her presumption' was to be excused. What had she been doing? She seemed so overpowered by it I could only think that she had been writing to Queen Adelaide to ask for a receipt for washing lace; but the act which she so characterised was only an invitation she had carried to her sister's former mistress, Mrs Jamieson. 'Her former occupation considered, could Miss Matty excuse the liberty?' Ah! thought I, she has found out that double cap, and is going to rectify Miss Matty's headdress. No! it was simply to extend her invitation to Miss Matty and to me. Miss Matty bowed acceptance; and I wondered that, in the graceful action, she did not feel the unusual weight and extraordinary height of her headdress. But I do not think she did, for she recovered her balance, and went on talking to Miss Betty in a kind, condescending manner, very different from the fidgety way she would have had if she had suspected how singular her appearance was. 'Mrs Jamieson is coming, I think you said?' asked Miss Matty.

'Yes. Mrs Jamieson most kindly and condescendingly said she would be happy to come. One little stipulation she made, that she should bring Carlo. I told her that if I had a weakness, it was for dogs.'

'And Miss Pole?' questioned Miss Matty, who was thinking of her pool at Preference, in which Carlo would not be available as a partner.

'I am going to ask Miss Pole. Of course, I could not think of asking her until I had asked you, madam – the rector's daughter, madam. Believe me, I do not forget the situation my father held under yours.'

'And Mrs Forrester, of course?'

'And Mrs Forrester. I thought, in fact, of going to her before I went to Miss Pole. Although her circumstances are changed, madam, she was born at Tyrrell, and we can never forget her alliance to the Bigges, of Bigelow Hall.'

Miss Matty cared much more for the little circumstance of her being a very good card-player.

'Mrs Fitz-Adam – I suppose' –

'No, madam. I must draw a line somewhere. Mrs Jamieson would not, I think, like to meet Mrs Fitz-Adam. I have the greatest respect for Mrs Fitz-Adam – but I cannot think her fit society for such ladies as Mrs Jamieson and Miss Matilda Jenkyns.'

Miss Betty Barker bowed low to Miss Matty, and pursed up her mouth. She looked at me with sidelong dignity, as much as to say, although a retired milliner, she was no democrat, and understood the difference of ranks.

'May I beg you to come as near half-past six to my little dwelling, as possible, Miss Matilda? Mrs Jamieson dines at five, but has kindly promised not to delay her visit beyond that time – half-past six.' And with a swimming curtsey Miss Betty Barker took her leave.

My prophetic soul foretold a visit that afternoon from Miss Pole, who usually came to call on Miss Matilda after any event – or indeed in sight of any event – to talk it over with her.

'Miss Betty told me it was to be a choice and select few,' said Miss Pole, as she and Miss Matty compared notes.

'Yes, so she said. Not even Mrs Fitz-Adam.'

Now Mrs Fitz-Adam was the widowed sister of the Cranford surgeon, whom I have named before. Their parents were respectable farmers, content with their station. The name of these good people was Hoggins. Mr Hoggins was the Cranford doctor now; we disliked the name and considered it coarse; but, as Miss Jenkyns said, if he changed it to Piggins it would not be much better. We had hoped to discover a relationship between him and that Marchioness of Exeter whose name was Molly Hoggins; but the man, careless of his own interests, utterly ignored and denied any such relationship, although, as dear Miss Jenkyns had said, he had a sister called Mary, and the same Christian names were very apt to run in families.

Soon after Miss Mary Hoggins married Mr Fitz-Adam, she disappeared from the neighbourhood for many years. She did not move in a sphere in Cranford society sufficiently high to make any of us care to know what Mr Fitz-Adam was. He died and was gathered to his fathers without our ever having thought about him at all. And then Mrs Fitz-Adam reappeared in Cranford ('as bold as a lion', Miss Pole said), a well-to-do widow, dressed in rustling black silk, so soon after her husband's death that poor Miss Jenkyns was justified in the remark she made, that 'bombazine would have shown a deeper sense of her loss'.

I remember the convocation of ladies who assembled to decide whether or not Mrs Fitz-Adam should be called upon by the old blue-blooded inhabitants of Cranford. She had taken a large rambling house, which had been usually considered to confer a patent of gentility upon its tenant, because, once upon a time, seventy or eighty years before, the spinster daughter of an earl had resided in it. I am not sure if the inhabiting of this house was not also believed to convey some unusual power of intellect; for the earl's daughter, Lady Jane, had a sister, Lady Anne, who had married a general officer in the time of the American war, and this general officer had written one or two comedies, which were still acted on the London boards, and which, when we saw them advertised, made us all draw up, and feel that Drury Lane was paying a very pretty compliment to Cranford. Still, it was not at all a settled thing that Mrs Fitz-Adam was to be visited, when dear Miss Jenkyns died; and, with her, something of the clear knowledge of the strict code of gentility went out too. As Miss Pole observed, 'As most of the ladies of good family in Cranford were elderly spinsters, or widows without children, if we did not relax a little, and become less exclusive, by-and-by we should have no society at all.'

Mrs Forrester continued on the same side.

'She had always understood that Fitz meant something aristocratic; there was Fitz-Roy – she thought that some of the King's children had been called Fitz-Roy; and there was Fitz-Clarence, now – they were the children of dear good King William the Fourth. Fitz-Adam! – it was a pretty name, and she thought it very probably meant "Child of Adam". No one, who had not some good blood in their veins, would dare to be called Fitz; there was a deal in a name – she had had a cousin who spelt his name with two little ffs – ffoulkes – and he always looked down upon capital letters and said they belonged to lately-invented families. She had been afraid he would die a bachelor, he was so very choice. When he met with a Mrs ffarringdon, at a watering-place, he took to her immediately; and a very pretty genteel woman she was – a widow, with a very good fortune; and "my cousin", Mr ffoulkes, married her; and it was all owing to her two little ffs.'

Mrs Fitz-Adam did not stand a chance of meeting with a Mr Fitz-anything in Cranford, so that could not have been her motive for settling there. Miss Matty thought it might have been the hope of being admitted into the society of the place, which would certainly be a very agreeable rise for *ci-devant* Miss Hoggins; and if this had been her hope it would be cruel to disappoint her.

So everybody called upon Mrs Fitz-Adam – everybody but Mrs Jamieson, who used to show how honourable she was by never seeing Mrs Fitz-Adam when they met at the Cranford parties. There would be only eight or ten ladies in the room, and Mrs Fitz-Adam was the largest of all, and she invariably used to stand up when Mrs Jamieson came in, and curtsey very low to her whenever she turned in her direction – so low, in fact, that I think Mrs Jamieson must have looked at the wall above her, for she never moved a muscle of her face, no more than if she had not seen her. Still Mrs Fitz-Adam persevered.

The spring evenings were getting bright and long when three or four ladies in calashes met at Miss Barker's door. Do you know what a calash is? It is a covering worn over caps, not unlike the heads fastened on old-fashioned gigs; but sometimes it is not quite so large. This kind of headgear always made an awful impression on the children in Cranford; and now two or three left off their play in the quiet sunny little street, and gathered in wondering silence round Miss Pole, Miss Matty, and myself. We were silent too, so that we could hear loud, suppressed whispers inside Miss Barker's house: 'Wait, Peggy! wait till I've run upstairs and washed my hands. When I cough, open the door; I'll not be a minute.'

And, true enough it was not a minute before we heard a noise, between a sneeze and a crow; on which the door flew open. Behind it stood a round-eyed maiden, all aghast at the honourable company of calashes, who marched in without a word. She recovered presence of mind enough to usher us into a small room, which had been the shop, but was now converted into a temporary dressing-room. There we unpinned and shook ourselves, and arranged our features before the glass into a sweet and gracious company-face; and then, bowing backwards with 'After you, ma'am,' we allowed Mrs Forrester to take precedence up the narrow staircase that led to Miss Barker's drawing-room. There she sat, as stately and composed as though we had never heard that odd-sounding cough, from which her throat must have been even then sore and rough. Kind, gentle, shabbily-dressed Mrs Forrester was immediately conducted to the second place of honour – a seat arranged something like Prince Albert's near the Queen's – good, but not so good. The place of pre-eminence was, of course, reserved for the Honourable Mrs Jamieson, who presently came panting up the stairs – Carlo rushing round her on her progress, as if he meant to trip her up.

And now Miss Betty Barker was a proud and happy woman! She stirred the fire, and shut the door, and sat as near to it as she could, quite on the edge of her chair. When Peggy came in, tottering under the weight of the tea-tray, I noticed that Miss Barker was sadly afraid lest Peggy should not keep her distance sufficiently. She and her mistress were on very familiar terms in their everyday intercourse, and Peggy wanted now to make several little confidences to her, which Miss Barker was on thorns to hear, but which she thought it her duty, as a lady, to repress. So she turned away from all Peggy's asides and signs; but she made one or two very malapropos answers to what was said; and at last, seized with a bright idea, she exclaimed, 'Poor, sweet Carlo! I'm forgetting him. Come downstairs with me, poor little doggie, and it shall have its tea, it shall!'

In a few minutes she returned, bland and benignant as before; but I thought she had forgotten to give the 'poor little doggie' anything to eat, judging by the avidity with which he swallowed down chance pieces of cake. The tea-tray was abundantly loaded – I was pleased to see it, I was so hungry; but I was afraid the ladies present might think it vulgarly heaped up. I know they would have done at their own houses; but somehow the heaps disappeared here. I saw Mrs Jamieson eating seed-cake, slowly and considerately, as she did everything; and I was rather surprised, for I knew she had told us, on the occasion of her last party, that she never had it in her house, it reminded her so much of scented soap. She always gave us Savoy biscuits. However, Mrs Jamieson was kindly indulgent to Miss Barker's want of knowledge of the customs of high life; and, to spare her feelings, ate three large pieces of seed-cake, with a placid, ruminating expression of countenance, not unlike a cow's.

After tea there was some little demur and difficulty. We were six in number; four could play at Preference, and for the other two there was Cribbage. But all, except myself (I was rather afraid of the Cranford ladies at cards, for it was the most earnest and serious business they ever engaged in), were anxious to be of the 'pool'. Even Miss Barker, while declaring she did not know Spadille from Manille, was evidently hankering to take a hand. The dilemma was soon put an end to by a singular kind of noise. If a baron's daughter-in-law could ever be supposed to snore, I should have said Mrs Jamieson did so then; for, overcome by the heat of the room, and inclined to doze by nature, the temptation of that very comfortable armchair had been too much for her, and Mrs Jamieson was nodding. Once or twice she opened her eyes with an effort, and calmly but unconsciously smiled upon us; but by-and-by, even her benevolence was not equal to this exertion, and she was sound asleep.

'It is very gratifying to me,' whispered Miss Barker at the card-table to her three opponents, whom, notwithstanding her ignorance of the game, she was 'basting' most unmercifully – 'very gratifying indeed, to see how completely Mrs Jamieson feels at home in my poor little dwelling; she could not have paid me a greater compliment.'

Miss Barker provided me with some literature in the shape of three or four handsomely-bound fashion-books ten or twelve years old, observing, as she put a little table and a candle for my especial benefit, that she knew young people liked to look at pictures. Carlo lay and snorted, and started at his mistress's feet. He, too, was quite at home.

The card-table was an animated scene to watch; four ladies' heads, with niddle-noddling caps, all nearly meeting over the middle of the table in their eagerness to whisper quick enough and loud enough: and every now and then came Miss Barker's 'Hush, ladies! if you please, hush! Mrs Jamieson is asleep.'

It was very difficult to steer clear between Mrs Forrester's deafness and Mrs Jamieson's sleepiness. But Miss Barker managed her arduous task well. She repeated the whisper to Mrs Forrester, distorting her face considerably, in order to show, by the motions of her lips, what was said; and then she smiled kindly all round at us, and murmured to herself, 'Very gratifying, indeed; I wish my poor sister had been alive to see this day.'

Presently the door was thrown wide open; Carlo started to his feet, with a loud snapping bark, and Mrs Jamieson awoke: or, perhaps, she had not been asleep – as she said almost directly, the room had been so light she had been glad to keep her eyes shut, but had been listening with great interest to all our amusing and agreeable conversation. Peggy came in once more, red with importance. Another tray! 'Oh, gentility!' thought I, 'can yon endure this last shock?' For Miss Barker had ordered (nay, I doubt not, prepared, although she did say, 'Why, Peggy, what have you brought us?' and looked pleasantly surprised at the unexpected pleasure) all sorts of good things for supper – scalloped oysters, potted lobsters, jelly, a dish called 'little Cupids' (which was in great favour with the Cranford ladies, although too expensive to be given, except on solemn and state occasions – macaroons sopped in brandy, I should have called it, if I had not known its more refined and classical name). In short, we were evidently to be feasted with all that was sweetest and best; and we thought it better to submit graciously, even at the cost of our gentility – which never ate suppers in general, but which, like most non-supper-eaters, was particularly hungry on all special occasions.

Miss Barker, in her former sphere, had, I dare say, been made acquainted with the beverage they call cherry-brandy. We none of us had ever seen such a thing, and rather shrank back when she proffered it us – 'just a little, leetle glass, ladies; after the oysters and lobsters, you know. Shellfish are sometimes thought not very wholesome.' We all shook our heads like female mandarins; but, at last, Mrs Jamieson suffered herself to be persuaded, and we followed her lead. It was not exactly unpalatable, though so hot and so strong that we thought ourselves bound to give evidence that we were not accustomed to such things by coughing terribly – almost as strangely as Miss Barker had done, before we were admitted by Peggy.

'It's very strong,' said Miss Pole, as she put down her empty glass; 'I do believe there's spirit in it.'

'Only a little drop – just necessary to make it keep,' said Miss Barker. 'You know we put brandy-pepper over our preserves to make them keep. I often feel tipsy myself from eating damson tart.'

I question whether damson tart would have opened Mrs Jamieson's heart as the cherry-brandy did; but she told us of a coming event, respecting which she had been quite silent till that moment.

'My sister-in-law, Lady Glenmire, is coming to stay with me.'

There was a chorus of 'Indeed!' and then a pause. Each one rapidly reviewed her wardrobe, as to its fitness to appear in the presence of a baron's widow; for, of course, a series of small festivals were always held in Cranford on the arrival of a visitor at any of our friends' houses. We felt very pleasantly excited on the present occasion.

Not long after this the maids and the lanterns were announced. Mrs Jamieson had the sedan-chair, which had squeezed itself into Miss Barker's narrow lobby with some difficulty, and most literally 'stopped the way'. It required some skilful manoeuvring on the part of the old chairmen (shoemakers by day, but when summoned to carry the sedan dressed up in a strange old livery – long greatcoats, with small capes, coeval with the sedan, and similar to the dress of the class in Hogarth's pictures) to edge, and back, and try at it again, and finally to succeed in carrying their burden out of Miss Barker's front door. Then we heard their quick pit-a-pat along the quiet little street as we put on our calashes and pinned up our gowns; Miss Barker hovering about us with offers of help, which, if she had not remembered her former occupation, and wished us to forget it, would have been much more pressing.

CHAPTER VIII

'YOUR LADYSHIP'

Early the next morning – directly after twelve – Miss Pole made her appearance at Miss Matty's. Some very trifling piece of business was alleged as a reason for the call; but there was evidently something behind. At last out it came.

'By the way, you'll think I'm strangely ignorant; but, do you really know, I am puzzled how we ought to address Lady Glenmire. Do you say, "Your Ladyship", where you would say "you" to a common person? I have been puzzling all morning; and are we to say "My Lady", instead of "Ma'am"? Now you knew Lady Arley – will you kindly tell me the most correct way of speaking to the peerage?'

Poor Miss Matty! she took off her spectacles and she put them on again – but how Lady Arley was addressed, she could not remember.

'It is so long ago,' she said. 'Dear! dear! how stupid I am! I don't think I ever saw her more than twice. I know we used to call Sir Peter, "Sir Peter" – but he came much oftener to see us than Lady Arley did. Deborah would have known in a minute. "My lady" – "your ladyship". It sounds very strange, and as if it was not natural. I never thought of it before; but, now you have named it, I am all in a puzzle.'

It was very certain Miss Pole would obtain no wise decision from Miss Matty, who got more bewildered every moment, and more perplexed as to etiquettes of address.

'Well, I really think,' said Miss Pole, 'I had better just go and tell Mrs Forrester about our little difficulty. One sometimes grows nervous; and yet one would not have Lady Glenmire think we were quite ignorant of the etiquettes of high life in Cranford.'

'And will you just step in here, dear Miss Pole, as you come back, please, and tell me what you decide upon? Whatever you and Mrs Forrester fix upon, will be quite right, I'm sure. "Lady Arley", "Sir Peter",' said Miss Matty to herself, trying to recall the old forms of words.

'Who is Lady Glenmire?' asked I.

'Oh, she's the widow of Mr Jamieson – that's Mrs Jamieson's late husband, you know – widow of his eldest brother. Mrs Jamieson was a Miss Walker, daughter of Governor Walker. "Your ladyship". My dear, if they fix on that way of speaking, you must just let me practise a little on you first, for I shall feel so foolish and hot saying it the first time to Lady Glenmire.'

It was really a relief to Miss Matty when Mrs Jamieson came on a very unpolite errand. I notice that apathetic people have more quiet impertinence than others; and Mrs Jamieson came now to insinuate pretty plainly that she did not particularly wish that the Cranford ladies should call upon her sister-in-law. I can hardly say how she made this clear; for I grew very indignant and warm, while with slow deliberation she was explaining her wishes to Miss Matty, who, a true lady herself, could hardly understand the feeling which made Mrs Jamieson wish to appear to her noble sister-in-law as if she only visited 'county' families. Miss Matty remained puzzled and perplexed long after I had found out the object of Mrs Jamieson's visit.

When she did understand the drift of the honourable lady's call, it was pretty to see with what quiet dignity she received the intimation thus uncourteously given. She was not in the least hurt – she was of too gentle a spirit for that; nor was she exactly conscious of disapproving of Mrs Jamieson's conduct; but there was something of this feeling in her mind, I am sure, which made her pass from the subject to others in a less flurried and more composed manner than usual. Mrs Jamieson was, indeed, the more flurried of the two, and I could see she was glad to take her leave.

A little while afterwards Miss Pole returned, red and indignant. 'Well! to be sure! You've had Mrs Jamieson here, I find from Martha; and we are not to call on Lady Glenmire. Yes! I met Mrs Jamieson, halfway between here and Mrs Forrester's, and she told me; she took me so by surprise, I had nothing to say. I wish I had thought of something very sharp and sarcastic; I dare say I shall tonight. And Lady Glenmire is but the widow of a Scotch baron after all! I went on to look at Mrs Forrester's Peerage, to see who this lady was, that is to be kept under a glass case: widow of a Scotch peer – never sat in the House of Lords – and as poor as Job, I dare say; and she – fifth daughter of some Mr Campbell or other. You are the daughter of a rector, at any rate, and related to the Arleys; and Sir Peter might have been Viscount Arley, everyone says.'

Miss Matty tried to soothe Miss Pole, but in vain. That lady, usually so kind and good-humoured, was now in a full flow of anger.

'And I went and ordered a cap this morning, to be quite ready,' said
she at last, letting out the secret which gave sting to Mrs Jamieson's
intimation. 'Mrs Jamieson shall see if it is so easy to get me to make
fourth at a pool when she has none of her fine Scotch relations with
her!'

In coming out of church, the first Sunday on which Lady Glenmire
appeared in Cranford, we sedulously talked together, and turned our
backs on Mrs Jamieson and her guest. If we might not call on her, we
would not even look at her, though we were dying with curiosity to
know what she was like. We had the comfort of questioning Martha
in the afternoon. Martha did not belong to a sphere of society whose
observation could be an implied compliment to Lady Glenmire, and
Martha had made good use of her eyes.

'Well, ma'am! is it the little lady with Mrs Jamieson, you mean? I
thought you would like more to know how young Mrs Smith was
dressed; her being a bride.' (Mrs Smith was the butcher's wife).

Miss Pole said, 'Good gracious me! as if we cared about a Mrs
Smith;' but was silent as Martha resumed her speech.

'The little lady in Mrs Jamieson's pew had on, ma'am, rather an
old black silk, and a shepherd's plaid cloak, ma'am, and very bright
black eyes she had, ma'am, and a pleasant, sharp face; not over young,
ma'am, but yet, I should guess, younger than Mrs Jamieson herself.
She looked up and down the church, like a bird, and nipped up her
petticoats, when she came out, as quick and sharp as ever I see. I'll
tell you what, ma'am, she's more like Mrs Deacon, at the "Coach and
Horses", nor anyone.'

'Hush, Martha!' said Miss Matty, 'that's not respectful.'

'Isn't it, ma'am? I beg pardon, I'm sure; but Jem Hearn said so as
well. He said, she was just such a sharp, stirring sort of a body' –

'Lady,' said Miss Pole.

'Lady – as Mrs Deacon.'

Another Sunday passed away, and we still averted our eyes from
Mrs Jamieson and her guest, and made remarks to ourselves that we
thought were very severe – almost too much so. Miss Matty was
evidently uneasy at our sarcastic manner of speaking.

Perhaps by this time Lady Glenmire had found out that Mrs
Jamieson's was not the gayest, liveliest house in the world; perhaps
Mrs Jamieson had found out that most of the county families were in

London, and that those who remained in the country were not so alive as they might have been to the circumstance of Lady Glenmire being in their neighbourhood. Great events spring out of small causes; so I will not pretend to say what induced Mrs Jamieson to alter her determination of excluding the Cranford ladies, and send notes of invitation all round for a small party on the following Tuesday. Mr Mulliner himself brought them round. He *would* always ignore the fact of there being a back door to any house, and gave a louder rat-tat than his mistress, Mrs Jamieson. He had three little notes, which he carried in a large basket, in order to impress his mistress with an idea of their great weight, though they might easily have gone into his waistcoat pocket.

Miss Matty and I quietly decided that we would have a previous engagement at home: it was the evening on which Miss Matty usually made candle-lighters of all the notes and letters of the week; for on Mondays her accounts were always made straight – not a penny owing from the week before; so, by a natural arrangement, making candle-lighters fell upon a Tuesday evening, and gave us a legitimate excuse for declining Mrs Jamieson's invitation. But before our answer was written, in came Miss Pole, with an open note in her hand.

'So!' she said. 'Ah! I see you have got your note, too. Better late than never. I could have told my Lady Glenmire she would be glad enough of our society before a fortnight was over.'

'Yes,' said Miss Matty, 'we're asked for Tuesday evening. And perhaps you would just kindly bring your work across and drink tea with us that night. It is my usual regular time for looking over the last week's bills, and notes, and letters, and making candle-lighters of them; but that does not seem quite reason enough for saying I have a previous engagement at home, though I meant to make it do. Now, if you would come, my conscience would be quite at ease, and luckily the note is not written yet.'

I saw Miss Pole's countenance change while Miss Matty was speaking.

'Don't you mean to go then?' asked she.

'Oh, no!' said, Miss Matty quietly. 'You don't either, I suppose?'

'I don't know,' replied Miss Pole. 'Yes, I think I do,' said she, rather briskly; and on seeing Miss Matty look surprised, she added, 'You see, one would not like Mrs Jamieson to think that anything she could do, or say, was of consequence enough to give offence; it would be a kind of letting down of ourselves, that I, for one, should not like. It would be too flattering to Mrs Jamieson if we allowed her to suppose that what she had said affected us a week, nay ten days afterwards.'

'Well! I suppose it is wrong to be hurt and annoyed so long about anything; and, perhaps, after all, she did not mean to vex us. But I must say, I could not have brought myself to say the things Mrs Jamieson did about our not calling. I really don't think I shall go.'

'Oh, come! Miss Matty, you must go; you know our friend Mrs Jamieson is much more phlegmatic than most people, and does not enter into the little delicacies of feeling which you possess in so remarkable a degree.'

'I thought you possessed them, too, that day Mrs Jamieson called to tell us not to go,' said Miss Matty innocently.

But Miss Pole, in addition to her delicacies of feeling, possessed a very smart cap, which she was anxious to show to an admiring world; and so she seemed to forget all her angry words uttered not a fortnight before, and to be ready to act on what she called the great Christian principle of 'Forgive and forget'; and she lectured dear Miss Matty so long on this head that she absolutely ended by assuring her it was her duty, as a deceased rector's daughter, to buy a new cap and go to the party at Mrs Jamieson's. So 'we were most happy to accept', instead of 'regretting that we were obliged to decline'.

The expenditure on dress in Cranford was principally in that one article referred to. If the heads were buried in smart new caps, the ladies were like ostriches, and cared not what became of their bodies. Old gowns, white and venerable collars, any number of brooches, up and down and everywhere (some with dogs' eyes painted in them; some that were like small picture frames with mausoleums and weeping willows neatly executed in hair inside; some, again, with miniatures of ladies and gentlemen sweetly smiling out of a nest of stiff muslin), old brooches for a permanent ornament, and new caps to suit the fashion of the day – the ladies of Cranford always dressed with chaste elegance and propriety, as Miss Barker once prettily expressed it.

And with three new caps, and a greater array of brooches than had ever been seen together at one time since Cranford was a town, did Mrs Forrester, and Miss Matty, and Miss Pole appear on that memorable Tuesday evening. I counted seven brooches myself on Miss Pole's dress.

Two were fixed negligently in her cap (one was a butterfly made of
Scotch pebbles, which a vivid imagination might believe to be the real
insect); one fastened her net neckerchief; one her collar; one ornamented
the front of her gown, midway between her throat and waist; and another
adorned the point of her stomacher. Where the seventh was I have
forgotten, but it was somewhere about her, I am sure.

But I am getting on too fast, in describing the dresses of the company.
I should first relate the gathering on the way to Mrs Jamieson's. That
lady lived in a large house just outside the town. A road which had
known what it was to be a street ran right before the house, which
opened out upon it without any intervening garden or court. Whatever
the sun was about, he never shone on the front of that house. To be
sure, the living-rooms were at the back, looking on to a pleasant garden;
the front windows only belonged to kitchens and housekeepers' rooms,
and pantries, and in one of them Mr Mulliner was reported to sit. Indeed,
looking askance, we often saw the back of a head covered with hair
powder, which also extended itself over his coat-collar down to his very
waist; and this imposing back was always engaged in reading the *St
James's Chronicle*, opened wide, which, in some degree, accounted for
the length of time the said newspaper was in reaching us – equal
subscribers with Mrs Jamieson, though, in right of her honourableness,
she always had the reading of it first. This very Tuesday, the delay in
forwarding the last number had been particularly aggravating; just when
both Miss Pole and Miss Matty, the former more especially, had been
wanting to see it, in order to coach up the Court news ready for the
evening's interview with aristocracy. Miss Pole told us she had absolutely
taken time by the forelock, and been dressed by five o'clock, in order
to be ready if the *St James's Chronicle* should come in at the last
moment – the very *St James's Chronicle* which the powdered head was
tranquilly and composedly reading as we passed the accustomed window
this evening.

'The impudence of the man!' said Miss Pole, in a low indignant
whisper. 'I should like to ask him whether his mistress pays her quarter-
share for his exclusive use.'

We looked at her in admiration of the courage of her thought; for
Mr Mulliner was an object of great awe to all of us. He seemed never
to have forgotten his condescension in coming to live at Cranford.
Miss Jenkyns, at times, had stood forth as the undaunted champion of

her sex, and spoken to him on terms of equality; but even Miss Jenkyns could get no higher. In his pleasantest and most gracious moods he looked like a sulky cockatoo. He did not speak except in gruff mono-syllables. He would wait in the hall when we begged him not to wait, and then look deeply offended because we had kept him there, while, with trembling, hasty hands we prepared ourselves for appearing in company.

Miss Pole ventured on a small joke as we went upstairs, intended, though addressed to us, to afford Mr Mulliner some slight amusement. We all smiled, in order to seem as if we felt at our ease, and timidly looked for Mr Mulliner's sympathy. Not a muscle of that wooden face had relaxed; and we were grave in an instant.

Mrs Jamieson's drawing-room was cheerful; the evening sun came streaming into it, and the large square window was clustered round with flowers. The furniture was white and gold; not the later style, Louis Quatorze, I think they call it, all shells and twirls; no, Mrs Jamieson's chairs and tables had not a curve or bend about them. The chair and table legs diminished as they neared the ground, and were straight and square in all their corners. The chairs were all a-row against the walls, with the exception of four or five which stood in a circle round the fire. They were railed with white bars across the back and knobbed with gold; neither the railings nor the knobs invited to ease. There was a japanned table devoted to literature, on which lay a Bible, a Peerage, and a Prayer-Book. There was another square Pembroke table dedicated to the Fine Arts, on which were a kaleidoscope, conversation-cards, puzzle-cards (tied together to an interminable length with faded pink satin ribbon), and a box painted in fond imitation of the drawings which decorate tea-chests. Carlo lay on the worsted-worked rug, and ungraciously barked at us as we entered. Mrs Jamieson stood up, giving us each a torpid smile of welcome, and looking helplessly beyond us at Mr Mulliner, as if she hoped he would place us in chairs, for, if he did not, she never could. I suppose he thought we could find our way to the circle round the fire, which reminded me of Stonehenge, I don't know why. Lady Glenmire came to the rescue of our hostess, and, somehow or other, we found ourselves for the first time placed agreeably, and not formally, in Mrs Jamieson's house. Lady Glenmire, now we had time to look at her, proved to be a bright little woman of middle age, who had been very pretty in the days of her youth, and who was even yet very pleasant-looking. I saw Miss Pole appraising her dress in the first five minutes, and I take her word when she said the next day –

'My dear! ten pounds would have purchased every stitch she had on – lace and all.'

It was pleasant to suspect that a peeress could be poor, and partly reconciled us to the fact that her husband had never sat in the House of Lords; which, when we first heard of it, seemed a kind of swindling us out of our prospects on false pretences; a sort of 'A Lord and No Lord' business.

We were all very silent at first. We were thinking what we could talk about, that should be high enough to interest My Lady. There had been a rise in the price of sugar, which, as preserving-time was near, was a piece of intelligence to all our housekeeping hearts, and would have been the natural topic if Lady Glenmire had not been by. But we were not sure if the peerage ate preserves – much less knew how they were made. At last, Miss Pole, who had always a great deal of courage and *savoir faire*, spoke to Lady Glenmire, who on her part had seemed just as much puzzled to know how to break the silence as we were.

'Has your ladyship been to Court lately?' asked she; and then gave a little glance round at us, half timid and half triumphant, as much as to say, 'See how judiciously I have chosen a subject befitting the rank of the stranger.'

'I never was there in my life,' said Lady Glenmire, with a broad Scotch accent, but in a very sweet voice. And then, as if she had been too abrupt, she added: 'We very seldom went to London – only twice, in fact, during all my married life; and before I was married my father had far too large a family' (fifth daughter of Mr Campbell was in all our minds, I am sure) 'to take us often from our home, even to Edinburgh. Ye'll have been in Edinburgh, maybe?' said she, suddenly brightening up with the hope of a common interest. We had none of us been there; but Miss Pole had an uncle who once had passed a night there, which was very pleasant.

Mrs Jamieson, meanwhile, was absorbed in wonder why Mr Mulliner did not bring the tea; and at length the wonder oozed out of her mouth.

'I had better ring the bell, my dear, had not I?' said Lady Glenmire briskly.

'No – I think not – Mulliner does not like to be hurried.'

We should have liked our tea, for we dined at an earlier hour than Mrs Jamieson. I suspect Mr Mulliner had to finish the *St James's Chronicle* before he chose to trouble himself about tea. His mistress fidgeted and fidgeted, and kept saying, 'I can't think why Mulliner does not bring tea. I can't think what he can be about.' And Lady Glenmire at last grew quite impatient, but it was a pretty kind of impatience after all; and she rang the bell rather sharply, on receiving a half-permission from her sister-in-law to do so. Mr Mulliner appeared in dignified surprise. 'Oh!' said Mrs Jamieson, 'Lady Glenmire rang the bell; I believe it was for tea.'

In a few minutes tea was brought. Very delicate was the china, very old the plate, very thin the bread and butter, and very small the lumps of sugar. Sugar was evidently Mrs Jamieson's favourite economy. I question if the little filigree sugar-tongs, made something like scissors, could have opened themselves wide enough to take up an honest, vulgar good-sized piece; and when I tried to seize two little minnikin pieces at once, so as not to be detected in too many returns to the sugar-basin, they absolutely dropped one, with a little sharp clatter, quite in a malicious and unnatural manner. But before this happened we had had a slight disappointment. In the little silver jug was cream, in the larger one was milk. As soon as Mr Mulliner came in, Carlo began to beg, which was a thing our manners forebade us to do, though I am sure we were just as hungry; and Mrs Jamieson said she was certain we would excuse her if she gave her poor dumb Carlo his tea first. She accordingly mixed a saucerful for him, and put it down for him to lap; and then she told us how intelligent and sensible the dear little fellow was; he knew cream quite well, and constantly refused tea with only milk in it: so the milk was left for us; but we silently thought we were quite as intelligent and sensible as Carlo, and felt as if insult were added to injury when we were called upon to admire the gratitude evinced by his wagging his tail for the cream which should have been ours.

After tea we thawed down into common-life subjects. We were thankful to Lady Glenmire for having proposed some more bread and butter, and this mutual want made us better acquainted with her than we should ever have been with talking about the Court, though Miss Pole did say she had hoped to know how the dear Queen was from someone who had seen her.

The friendship begun over bread and butter extended on to cards. Lady Glenmire played Preference to admiration, and was a complete authority as to Ombre and Quadrille. Even Miss Pole quite forgot to say 'my lady', and 'your ladyship', and said 'Basto! ma'am'; 'you have Spadille, I believe', just as quietly as if we had never held the great Cranford Parliament on the subject of the proper mode of addressing a peeress.

As a proof of how thoroughly we had forgotten that we were in the presence of one who might have sat down to tea with a coronet, instead of a cap, on her head, Mrs Forrester related a curious little fact to Lady Glenmire – an anecdote known to the circle of her intimate friends, but of which even Mrs Jamieson was not aware. It related to some fine old lace, the sole relic of better days, which Lady Glenmire was admiring on Mrs Forrester's collar.

'Yes,' said that lady, 'such lace cannot be got now for either love or money; made by the nuns abroad, they tell me. They say that they can't make it now even there. But perhaps they can, now they've passed the Catholic Emancipation Bill. I should not wonder. But, in the meantime, I treasure up my lace very much. I daren't even trust the washing of it to my maid' (the little charity schoolgirl I have named before, but who sounded well as 'my maid'). 'I always wash it myself. And once it had a narrow escape. Of course, your ladyship knows that such lace must never be starched or ironed. Some people wash it in sugar and water, and some in coffee, to make it the right yellow colour; but I myself have a very good receipt for washing it in milk, which stiffens it enough, and gives it a very good creamy colour. Well, ma'am, I had tacked it together (and the beauty of this fine lace is that, when it is wet, it goes into a very little space), and put it to soak in milk, when, unfortunately, I left the room; on my return, I found pussy on the table, looking very like a thief, but gulping very uncomfortably, as if she was half-chocked with something she wanted to swallow and could not. And, would you believe it? At first I pitied her, and said "Poor pussy! poor pussy!" till, all at once, I looked and saw the cup of milk empty – cleaned out! "You naughty cat!" said I, and I believe I was provoked enough to give her a slap, which did no good, but only helped the lace down – just as one slaps a choking child on the back. I could have cried, I was so vexed; but I determined I would not give the lace up without a struggle for it. I hoped the lace might disagree with her, at any rate; but it would have been too much for Job, if he had seen, as I did, that cat come in, quite placid and purring, not a quarter of an hour after, and almost expecting to be stroked. "No, pussy!" said I, "if you have any conscience you ought not to expect that!" And then a thought struck me; and I rang the bell for my maid, and sent her to Mr Hoggins, with my compliments, and would he be kind enough to lend me one of his top-boots for an hour? I did not think there was anything odd in the message; but Jenny said the young men in the surgery laughed as if they would be ill at my wanting a top-boot. When it came, Jenny and I put pussy in, with her forefeet straight down, so that they were fastened, and could not scratch, and we gave her a teaspoonful of currant-jelly in which (your ladyship must excuse me) I had mixed some tartar emetic. I shall never forget how anxious I was for the next half-hour. I took pussy to my own room, and spread a clean towel on the floor. I could have kissed her when she returned the lace to sight, very much as it had gone down. Jenny had boiling water ready, and we soaked it and soaked it, and spread it on a lavender-bush in the sun before I could touch it again, even to put it in milk. But now your ladyship would never guess that it had been in pussy's inside.'

We found out, in the course of the evening, that Lady Glenmire was going to pay Mrs Jamieson a long visit, as she had given up her apartments in Edinburgh, and had no ties to take her back there in a hurry. On the whole, we were rather glad to hear this, for she had made a pleasant impression upon us; and it was also very comfortable to find, from things which dropped out in the course of conversation, that, in addition to many other genteel qualities, she was far removed from the 'vulgarity of wealth'.

'Don't you find it very unpleasant walking?' asked Mrs Jamieson, as our respective servants were announced. It was a pretty regular question from Mrs Jamieson, who had her own carriage in the coach-house, and always went out in a sedan-chair to the very shortest distances. The answers were nearly as much a matter of course.

'Oh dear, no! it is so pleasant and still at night!' 'Such a refreshment after the excitement of a party!' 'The stars are so beautiful!' This last was from Miss Matty.

'Are you fond of astronomy?' Lady Glenmire asked.

'Not very,' replied Miss Matty, rather confused at the moment to remember which was astronomy and which was astrology – but the answer was true under either circumstance, for she read, and was slightly alarmed at Francis Moore's astrological predictions; and, as to astronomy, in a private and confidential conversation, she had told me she never could believe that the earth was moving constantly, and that she would not believe it if she could, it made her feel so tired and dizzy whenever she thought about it.

In our pattens, we picked our way home with extra care that night, so refined and delicate were our perceptions after drinking tea with 'my lady'.

CHAPTER IX

SIGNOR BRUNONI

Soon after the events of which I gave an account in my last paper, I was summoned home by my father's illness; and for a time I forgot, in anxiety about him, to wonder how my dear friends at Cranford were getting on, or how Lady Glenmire could reconcile herself to the dullness of the long visit which she was still paying to her sister-in-law, Mrs Jamieson. When my father grew a little stronger I accompanied him to the seaside, so that altogether I seemed banished from Cranford, and was deprived of the opportunity of hearing any chance intelligence of the dear little town for the greater part of that year.

Late in November – when we had returned home again, and my father was once more in good health – I received a letter from Miss Matty; and a very mysterious letter it was. She began many sentences without ending them, running them one into another, in much the same confused sort of way in which written words run together on blotting-paper. All I could make out was that, if my father was better (which she hoped he was), and would take warning and wear a great-coat from Michaelmas to Lady Day, if turbans were in fashion, could I tell her? Such a piece of gaiety was going to happen as had not been seen or known of since Wombwell's lions came, when one of them ate a little child's arm; and she was, perhaps, too old to care about dress, but a new cap she must have; and, having heard that turbans were worn, and some of the county families likely to come, she would like to look tidy, if I would bring her a cap from the milliner I employed; and oh, dear! how careless of her to forget that she wrote to beg I would come and pay her a visit next Tuesday; when she hoped to have something to offer me in the way of amusement, which she would not now more particularly describe, only sea-green was her favourite colour. So she ended her letter; but in a P.S. she added, she thought she might as well tell me what was the peculiar attraction to Cranford just now; Signor Brunoni was going to exhibit his wonderful magic in the Cranford Assembly Rooms on Wednesday and Friday evening in the following week.

I was very glad to accept the invitation from my dear Miss Matty, independently of the conjuror, and most particularly anxious to prevent

her from disfiguring her small, gentle, mousey face with a great
Saracen's head turban; and accordingly, I bought her a pretty, neat,
middle-aged cap, which, however, was rather a disappointment to her
when, on my arrival, she followed me into my bedroom, ostensibly to
poke the fire, but in reality, I do believe, to see if the sea-green turban
was not inside the cap-box with which I had travelled. It was in vain
that I twirled the cap round on my hand to exhibit back and side fronts:
her heart had been set upon a turban, and all she could do was to say,
with resignation in her look and voice –

'I am sure you did your best, my dear. It is just like the caps all
the ladies in Cranford are wearing, and they have had theirs for a year,
I dare say. I should have liked something newer, I confess – something
more like the turbans Miss Betty Barker tells me Queen Adelaide
wears; but it is very pretty, my dear. And I dare say lavender will wear
better than sea-green. Well, after all, what is dress, that we should care
anything about it? You'll tell me if you want anything, my dear. Here
is the bell. I suppose turbans have not got down to Drumble yet?'

So saying, the dear old lady gently bemoaned herself out of the room,
leaving me to dress for the evening, when, as she informed me, she
expected Miss Pole and Mrs Forrester, and she hoped I should not feel
myself too much tired to join the party. Of course I should not; and I
made some haste to unpack and arrange my dress; but, with all my
speed, I heard the arrivals and the buzz of conversation in the next room
before I was ready. Just as I opened the door, I caught the words, 'I was
foolish to expect anything very genteel out of the Drumble shops; poor
girl! she did her best, I've no doubt.' But, for all that, I had rather that
she blamed Drumble and me than disfigured herself with a turban.

Miss Pole was always the person, in the trio of Cranford ladies now
assembled, to have had adventures. She was in the habit of spending the
morning in rambling from shop to shop, not to purchase anything (except
an occasional reel of cotton or a piece of tape), but to see the new articles
and report upon them, and to collect all the stray pieces of intelligence
in the town. She had a way, too, of demurely popping hither and thither
into all sorts of places to gratify her curiosity on any point – a way which,
if she had not looked so very genteel and prim, might have been considered impertinent. And now, by the expressive way in which she cleared
her throat, and waited for all minor subjects (such as caps and turbans)
to be cleared off the course, we knew she had something very particular

to relate, when the due pause came – and I defy any people possessed of common modesty to keep up a conversation long, where one among them sits up aloft in silence, looking down upon all the things they chance to say as trivial and contemptible compared to what they could disclose, if properly entreated. Miss Pole began –

'As I was stepping out of Gordon's shop today, I chanced to go into the "George" (my Betty has a second-cousin who is chambermaid there, and I thought Betty would like to hear how she was), and, not seeing anyone about, I strolled up the staircase, and found myself in the passage leading to the Assembly Room (you and I remember the Assembly Room, I am sure, Miss Matty! and the *minuets de la cour*!); so I went on, not thinking of what I was about, when, all at once, I perceived that I was in the middle of the preparations for tomorrow night – the room being divided with great clothes-maids, over which Crosby's men were tacking red flannel; very dark and odd it seemed; it quite bewildered me, and I was going on behind the screens, in my absence of mind, when a gentleman (quite the gentleman, I can assure you) stepped forwards and asked if I had any business he could arrange for me. He spoke such pretty broken English, I could not help thinking of *Thaddeus of Warsaw*, and the *Hungarian Brothers*, and *Santo Sebastiani*; and while I was busy picturing his past life to myself, he had bowed me out of the room. But wait a minute! You have not heard half my story yet! I was going downstairs, when who should I meet but Betty's second cousin. So, of course, I stopped to speak to her for Betty's sake; and she told me that I had really seen the conjuror – the gentleman who spoke broken English was Signor Brunoni himself. Just at this moment he passed us on the stairs, making such a graceful bow! in reply to which I dropped a curtsey – all foreigners have such polite manners, one catches something of it. But when he had gone downstairs, I bethought me that I had dropped my glove in the Assembly Room (it was safe in my muff all the time, but I never found it till afterwards); so I went back, and, just as I was creeping up the passage left on one side of the great screen that goes nearly across the room, who should I see but the very same gentleman that had met me before, and passed me on the stairs, coming now forwards from the inner part of the room, to which there is no entrance – you remember, Miss Matty – and just repeating, in his pretty broken English, the inquiry if I had any business there – I don't mean that he put it quite so bluntly, but he seemed very determined that I should not pass the screen – so, of course, I explained about my glove, which, curiously enough, I found at that very moment.'

Miss Pole, then, had seen the conjuror – the real, live conjuror! and numerous were the questions we all asked her. 'Had he a beard?' 'Was he young, or old?' 'Fair, or dark?' 'Did he look' – (unable to shape my question prudently, I put it in another form) – 'How did he look?' In short, Miss Pole was the heroine of the evening, owing to her morning's encounter. If she was not the rose (that is to say the conjuror) she had been near it.

Conjuration, sleight of hand, magic, witchcraft, were the subjects of the evening. Miss Pole was slightly sceptical, and inclined to think there might be a scientific solution found for even the proceedings of the Witch of Endor. Mrs Forrester believed everything, from ghosts to death-watches. Miss Matty ranged between the two – always convinced by the last speaker. I think she was naturally more inclined to Mrs Forrester's side, but a desire of proving herself a worthy sister to Miss Jenkyns kept her equally balanced – Miss Jenkyns, who would never allow a servant to call the little rolls of tallow that formed themselves round candles 'winding-sheets', but insisted on their being spoken of as 'roley-poleys'! A sister of hers to be superstitious! It would never do.

After tea, I was despatched downstairs into the dining-parlour for that volume of the old Encyclopædia which contained the nouns beginning with C, in order that Miss Pole might prime herself with scientific explanations for the tricks of the following evening. It spoilt the pool at Preference which Miss Matty and Mrs Forrester had been looking forward to, for Miss Pole became so much absorbed in her subject, and the plates by which it was illustrated, that we felt it would be cruel to disturb her otherwise than by one or two well-timed yawns, which I threw in now and then, for I was really touched by the meek way in which the two ladies were bearing their disappointment. But Miss Pole only read the more zealously, imparting to us no more information than this –

'Ah! I see; I comprehend perfectly. A represents the ball. Put A between B and D – no! between C and F, and turn the second joint of the third finger of your left hand over the wrist of your right H. Very clear indeed! My dear Mrs Forrester, conjuring and witchcraft is a mere affair of the alphabet. Do let me read you this one passage?'

Mrs Forrester implored Miss Pole to spare her, saying, from a child upwards, she never could understand being read aloud to; and I dropped the pack of cards, which I had been shuffling very audibly, and by this discreet movement I obliged Miss Pole to perceive that Preference was to have been the order of the evening, and to propose, rather unwillingly, that the pool should commence. The pleasant brightness that stole over the other two ladies' faces on this! Miss Matty had one or two twinges of self-reproach for having interrupted Miss Pole in her studies: and did not remember her cards well, or give her full attention to the game, until she had soothed her conscience by offering to lend the volume of the Encyclopædia to Miss Pole, who accepted it thankfully, and said Betty should take it home when she came with the lantern.

The next evening we were all in a little gentle flutter at the idea of the gaiety before us. Miss Matty went up to dress betimes, and hurried me until I was ready, when we found we had an hour-and-a-half to wait before the 'doors opened at seven precisely'. And we had only twenty yards to go! However, as Miss Matty said, it would not do to get too much absorbed in anything, and forget the time; so she thought we had better sit quietly, without lighting the candles, till five minutes to seven. So Miss Matty dozed, and I knitted.

At length we set off; and at the door under the carriage-way at the 'George', we met Mrs Forrester and Miss Pole: the latter was discussing the subject of the evening with more vehemence than ever, and throwing X's and B's at our heads like hailstones. She had even copied one or two of the 'receipts' – as she called them – for the different tricks, on backs of letters, ready to explain and to detect Signor Brunoni's arts.

We went into the cloakroom adjoining the Assembly Room; Miss Matty gave a sigh or two to her departed youth, and the remembrance of the last time she had been there, as she adjusted her pretty new cap before the strange, quaint old mirror in the cloakroom. The Assembly Room had been added to the inn, about a hundred years before, by the different county families, who met together there once a month during the winter to dance and play at cards. Many a county beauty had first swung through the minuet that she afterwards danced before Queen Charlotte in this very room. It was said that one of the Gunnings had graced the apartment with her beauty; it was certain that a rich and beautiful widow, Lady Williams, had here been smitten with the noble figure of a young artist, who was staying with some family in the neighbourhood for professional purposes, and accompanied his patrons to the Cranford Assembly. And a pretty bargain poor Lady Williams had of her handsome husband, if all tales were true. Now, no beauty blushed and dimpled along the sides of the Cranford Assembly Room; no handsome artist won hearts by his bow, *chapeau bras* in hand; the old room was dingy; the salmon-coloured paint had faded into a drab; great pieces of plaster had chipped off from the fine wreaths and festoons on its walls; but still a mouldy odour of aristocracy lingered about the place, and a dusty recollection of the days that were gone made Miss Matty and Mrs Forrester bridle up as they entered, and walk mincingly up the room, as if there were a number of genteel observers, instead of two little boys with a stick of toffee between them with which to beguile the time.

We stopped short at the second front row; I could hardly understand why, until I heard Miss Pole ask a stray waiter if any of the county families were expected; and when he shook his head, and believed not, Mrs Forrester and Miss Matty moved forwards, and our party represented a conversational square. The front row was soon augmented and enriched by Lady Glenmire and Mrs Jamieson. We six occupied the two front rows, and our aristocratic seclusion was respected by the groups of shopkeepers who strayed in from time to time and huddled together on the back benches. At least I conjectured so, from the noise they made, and the sonorous bumps they gave in sitting down; but when, in weariness of the obstinate green curtain that would not draw up, but would stare at me with two odd eyes, seen through holes, as in the old tapestry story, I would fain have looked round at the merry chattering people behind me, Miss Pole clutched my arm, and begged me not to turn, for 'it was not the thing'. What 'the thing' was, I never could find out, but it must have been something eminently dull and tiresome. However, we all sat eyes right, square front, gazing at the tantalising curtain, and hardly speaking intelligibly, we were so afraid of being caught in the vulgarity of making any noise in a place of public amusement. Mrs Jamieson was the most fortunate, for she fell asleep.

At length the eyes disappeared – the curtain quivered – one side went up before the other, which stuck fast; it was dropped again, and, with a fresh effort, and a vigorous pull from some unseen hand, it flew up, revealing to our sight a magnificent gentleman in the Turkish costume, seated before a little table, gazing at us (I should have said with the same eyes that I had last seen through the hole in the curtain) with calm and condescending dignity, 'like a being of another sphere', as I heard a sentimental voice ejaculate behind me.

'That's not Signor Brunoni!' said Miss Pole decidedly; and so audibly that I am sure he heard, for he glanced down over his flowing beard at our party with an air of mute reproach. 'Signor Brunoni had no beard – but perhaps he'll come soon.' So she lulled herself into patience. Meanwhile, Miss Matty had reconnoitred through her eye-glass, wiped it, and looked again. Then she turned round, and said to me, in a kind, mild, sorrowful tone –

'You see, my dear, turbans *are* worn.'

But we had no time for more conversation. The Grand Turk, as Miss Pole chose to call him, arose and announced himself as Signor Brunoni.

'I don't believe him!' exclaimed Miss Pole, in a defiant manner. He looked at her again, with the same dignified upbraiding in his countenance. 'I don't!' she repeated more positively than ever. 'Signor Brunoni had not got that muffy sort of thing about his chin, but looked like a close-shaved Christian gentleman.'

Miss Pole's energetic speeches had the good effect of wakening up Mrs Jamieson, who opened her eyes wide, in sign of the deepest attention – a proceeding which silenced Miss Pole and encouraged the Grand Turk to proceed, which he did in very broken English – so broken that there was no cohesion between the parts of his sentences; a fact which he himself perceived at last, and so left off speaking and proceeded to action.

Now we *were* astonished. How he did his tricks I could not imagine; no, not even when Miss Pole pulled out her pieces of paper and began reading aloud – or at least in a very audible whisper – the separate 'receipts' for the most common of his tricks. If ever I saw a man frown and look enraged, I saw the Grand Turk frown at Miss Pole; but, as she said, what could be expected but unchristian looks from a Mussulman? If Miss Pole were sceptical, and more engrossed with her receipts and diagrams than with his tricks, Miss Matty and Mrs Forrester were mystified and perplexed to the highest degree. Mrs Jamieson kept taking her spectacles off and wiping them, as if she thought it was something defective in them which made the legerdemain; and Lady Glenmire, who had seen many curious sights in Edinburgh, was very much struck with the tricks, and would not at all agree with Miss Pole, who declared that anybody could do them with a little practice, and that she would, herself, undertake to do all he did, with two hours given to study the Encyclopædia and make her third finger flexible.

At last Miss Matty and Mrs Forrester became perfectly awestricken.

They whispered together. I sat just behind them, so I could not help hearing what they were saying. Miss Matty asked Mrs Forrester 'if she thought it was quite right to have come to see such things? She could not help fearing they were lending encouragement to something that was not quite' – A little shake of the head filled up the blank. Mrs Forrester replied, that the same thought had crossed her mind; she too was feeling very uncomfortable, it was so very strange. She was quite certain that it was her pocket-handkerchief which was in that loaf just now; and it had been in her own hand not five minutes before. She wondered who had furnished the bread? She was sure it could not be Dakin, because he was the church-warden. Suddenly Miss Matty half-turned towards me –

'Will you look, my dear – you are a stranger in the town, and it won't give rise to unpleasant reports – will you just look round and see if the rector is here? If he is, I think we may conclude that this wonderful man is sanctioned by the Church, and that will be a great relief to my mind.'

I looked, and I saw the tall, thin, dry, dusty rector, sitting surrounded by National School boys, guarded by troops of his own sex from any approach of the many Cranford spinsters. His kind face was all agape with broad smiles, and the boys around him were in chinks of laughing. I told Miss Matty that the Church was smiling approval, which set her mind at ease.

I have never named Mr Hayter, the rector, because I, as a well-to-do and happy young woman, never came in contact with him. He was an old bachelor, but as afraid of matrimonial reports getting abroad about him as any girl of eighteen: and he would rush into a shop or dive down an entry, sooner than encounter any of the Cranford ladies in the street; and, as for the Preference parties, I did not wonder at his not accepting invitations to them. To tell the truth, I always suspected Miss Pole of having given very vigorous chase to Mr Hayter when he first came to Cranford; and not the less, because now she appeared to share so vividly in his dread lest her name should ever be coupled with his. He found all his interests among the poor and helpless; he had treated the National School boys this very night to the performance; and virtue was for once its own reward, for they guarded him right and left, and clung round him as if he had been the queen-bee and they the swarm. He felt so safe in their environment that he could even afford to give our party a bow as we filed out. Miss Pole ignored his presence, and pretended to be absorbed in convincing us that we had been cheated, and had not seen Signor Brunoni after all.

CHAPTER X
THE PANIC

I think a series of circumstances dated from Signor Brunoni's visit to Cranford, which seemed at the time connected in our minds with him, though I don't know that he had anything really to do with them. All at once all sorts of uncomfortable rumours got afloat in the town. There were one or two robberies – real *bonâ fide* robberies; men had up before the magistrates and committed for trial – and that seemed to make us all afraid of being robbed; and for a long time, at Miss Matty's, I know, we used to make a regular expedition all round the kitchens and cellars every night, Miss Matty leading the way, armed with the poker, I following with the hearth-brush, and Martha carrying the shovel and fire-irons with which to sound the alarm; and by the accidental hitting together of them she often frightened us so much that we bolted ourselves up, all three together, in the back kitchen, or storeroom, or wherever we happened to be, till, when our affright was over, we recollected ourselves and set out afresh with double valiance. By day we heard strange stories from the shopkeepers and cottagers, of carts that went about in the dead of night, drawn by horses shod with felt, and guarded by men in dark clothes, going round the town, no doubt in search of some unwatched house or some unfastened door.

Miss Pole, who affected great bravery herself, was the principal person to collect and arrange these reports so as to make them assume their most fearful aspect. But we discovered that she had begged one of Mr Hoggins's worn-out hats to hang up in her lobby, and we (at least I) had doubts as to whether she really would enjoy the little adventure of having her house broken into, as she protested she should. Miss Matty made no secret of being an arrant coward, but she went regularly through her housekeeper's duty of inspection – only the hour for this became earlier and earlier, till at last we went the rounds at half-past six, and Miss Matty adjourned to bed soon after seven, 'in order to get the night over the sooner'.

Cranford had so long piqued itself on being an honest and moral town that it had grown to fancy itself too genteel and well-bred to be otherwise, and felt the stain upon its character at this time doubly. But we comforted ourselves with the assurance which we gave to each other that the robberies could never have been committed by any Cranford person; it must have been a stranger or strangers who brought this disgrace upon the town, and occasioned as many precautions as if we were living among the Red Indians or the French.

This last comparison of our nightly state of defence and fortification was made by Mrs Forrester, whose father had served under General Burgoyne in the American war, and whose husband had fought the French in Spain. She indeed inclined to the idea that, in some way, the French were connected with the small thefts, which were ascertained facts, and the burglaries and highway robberies, which were rumours. She had been deeply impressed with the idea of French spies at some time in her life; and the notion could never be fairly eradicated, but sprang up again from time to time. And now her theory was this: – The Cranford people respected themselves too much, and were too grateful to the aristocracy who were so kind as to live near the town, ever to disgrace their bringing up by being dishonest or immoral; therefore, we must believe that the robbers were strangers – if strangers, why not foreigners? – if foreigners, who so likely as the French? Signor Brunoni spoke broken English like a Frenchman; and, though he wore a turban like a Turk, Mrs Forrester had seen a print of Madame de Staël with a turban on, and another of Mr Denon in just such a dress as that in which the conjuror had made his appearance, showing clearly that the French, as well as the Turks, wore turbans. There could be no doubt Signor Brunoni was a Frenchman – a French spy come to discover the weak and undefended places of England, and doubtless he had his accomplices. For her part, she, Mrs Forrester, had always had her own opinion of Miss Pole's adventure at the 'George Inn' – seeing two men where only one was believed to be. French people had ways and means which, she was thankful to say, the English knew nothing about; and she had never felt quite easy in her mind about going to see that conjuror – it was rather too much like a forbidden thing, though the rector was there. In short, Mrs Forrester grew more excited than we had ever known her before, and, being an officer's daughter and widow, we looked up to her opinion, of course.

Really I do not know how much was true or false in the reports which flew about like wildfire just at this time; but it seemed to me then that there was every reason to believe that at Mardon (a small town about eight miles from Cranford) houses and shops were entered by holes made in the walls, the bricks being silently carried away in the dead of the night, and all done so quietly that no sound was heard either in or out of the house. Miss Matty gave it up in despair when she heard of this. 'What was the use,' said she, 'of locks and bolts, and bells to the windows, and going round the house every night? That last trick was fit for a conjuror. Now she did believe that Signor Brunoni was at the bottom of it.'

One afternoon, about five o'clock, we were startled by a hasty knock at the door. Miss Matty bade me run and tell Martha on no account to open the door till she (Miss Matty) had reconnoitred through the window; and she armed herself with a footstool to drop down on the head of the visitor, in case he should show a face covered with black crape, as he looked up in answer to her inquiry of who was there. But it was nobody but Miss Pole and Betty. The former came upstairs, carrying a little hand-basket, and she was evidently in a state of great agitation.

'Take care of that!' said she to me, as I offered to relieve her of her basket. 'It's my plate. I am sure there is a plan to rob my house tonight. I am come to throw myself on your hospitality, Miss Matty. Betty is going to sleep with her cousin at the 'George'. I can sit up here all night if you will allow me; but my house is so far from any neighbours, and I don't believe we could be heard if we screamed ever so!'

'But,' said Miss Matty, 'what has alarmed you so much? Have you seen any men lurking about the house?'

'Oh, yes!' answered Miss Pole. 'Two very bad-looking men have gone three times past the house, very slowly; and an Irish beggar-woman came not half an hour ago, and all but forced herself in past Betty, saying her children were starving, and she must speak to the mistress. You see, she said "mistress", though there was a hat hanging up in the hall, and it would have been more natural to have said "master". But Betty shut the door in her face, and came up to me, and we got the spoons together, and sat in the parlour window watching till we saw Thomas Jones going from his work, when we called to him and asked him to take care of us into the town.'

We might have triumphed over Miss Pole, who had professed such bravery until she was frightened; but we were too glad to perceive that she shared in the weaknesses of humanity to exult over her; and I gave up my room to her very willingly, and shared Miss Matty's bed for the night. But before we retired, the two ladies rummaged up, out of the recesses of their memory, such horrid stories of robbery and murder that I quite quaked in my shoes. Miss Pole was evidently anxious to prove that such terrible events had occurred within her experience that she was justified in her sudden panic; and Miss Matty did not like to be outdone, and capped every story with one yet more horrible, till it reminded me oddly enough, of an old story I had read somewhere, of a nightingale and a musician, who strove one against the other which could produce the most admirable music, till poor Philomel dropped down dead.

One of the stories that haunted me for a long time afterwards was of a girl who was left in charge of a great house in Cumberland on some particular fair-day, when the other servants all went off to the gaieties. The family were away in London, and a pedlar came by, and asked to leave his large and heavy pack in the kitchen, saying he would call for it again at night; and the girl (a gamekeeper's daughter), roaming about in search of amusement, chanced to hit upon a gun hanging up in the hall, and took it down to look at the chasing; and it went off through the open kitchen door, hit the pack, and a slow dark thread of blood came oozing out. (How Miss Pole enjoyed this part of the story, dwelling on each word as if she loved it!) She rather hurried over the further account of the girl's bravery, and I have but a confused idea that, somehow, she baffled the robbers with Italian irons, heated red-hot, and then restored to blackness by being dipped in grease.

We parted for the night with an awe-stricken wonder as to what we should hear of in the morning – and, on my part, with a vehement desire for the night to be over and gone: I was so afraid lest the robbers should have seen, from some dark lurking-place, that Miss Pole had carried off her plate, and thus have a double motive for attacking our house.

But until Lady Glenmire came to call next day we heard of nothing unusual. The kitchen fire-irons were in exactly the same position against the back door as when Martha and I had skilfully piled them up, like spillikins, ready to fall with an awful clatter if only a cat had touched the outside panels. I had wondered what we should all do if thus awakened and alarmed, and had proposed to Miss Matty that we should cover up our faces under the bedclothes so that there should be no

danger of the robbers thinking that we could identify them; but Miss
Matty, who was trembling very much, scouted this idea, and said we
owed it to society to apprehend them, and that she should certainly do
her best to lay hold of them and lock them up in the garret till morning.

When Lady Glenmire came, we almost felt jealous of her. Mrs
Jamieson's house had really been attacked; at least there were men's
footsteps to be seen on the flower borders, underneath the kitchen
windows, 'where nae men should be'; and Carlo had barked all through
the night as if strangers were abroad. Mrs Jamieson had been awakened
by Lady Glenmire, and they had rung the bell which communicated
with Mr Mulliner's room in the third storey, and when his night-capped
head had appeared over the bannisters, in answer to the summons, they
had told him of their alarm, and the reasons for it; whereupon he
retreated into his bedroom, and locked the door (for fear of draughts,
as he informed them in the morning), and opened the window, and
called out valiantly to say, if the supposed robbers would come to him
he would fight them; but, as Lady Glenmire observed, that was but
poor comfort, since they would have to pass by Mrs Jamieson's room
and her own before they could reach him, and must be of a very
pugnacious disposition indeed if they neglected the opportunities of
robbery presented by the unguarded lower storeys, to go up to a garret,
and there force a door in order to get at the champion of the house.
Lady Glenmire, after waiting and listening for some time in the drawing-
room, had proposed to Mrs Jamieson that they should go to bed; but
that lady said she should not feel comfortable unless she sat up and
watched; and, accordingly, she packed herself warmly up on the sofa,
where she was found by the housemaid, when she came into the room
at six o'clock, fast asleep; but Lady Glenmire went to bed, and kept
awake all night.

When Miss Pole heard of this, she nodded her head in great satisfaction. She had been sure we should hear of something happening in
Cranford that night; and we had heard. It was clear enough they had
first proposed to attack her house; but when they saw that she and Betty
were on their guard, and had carried off the plate, they had changed
their tactics and gone to Mrs Jamieson's, and no one knew what might
have happened if Carlo had not barked, like a good dog as he was!

Poor Carlo! his barking days were nearly over. Whether the gang
who infested the neighbourhood were afraid of him, or whether they

were revengeful enough, for the way in which he had baffled them on the night in question, to poison him; or whether, as some among the more uneducated people thought, he died of apoplexy, brought on by too much feeding and too little exercise; at any rate, it is certain that, two days after this eventful night, Carlo was found dead, with his poor legs stretched out stiff in the attitude of running, as if by such unusual exertion he could escape the sure pursuer, Death.

We were all sorry for Carlo, the old familiar friend who had snapped at us for so many years; and the mysterious mode of his death made us very uncomfortable. Could Signor Brunoni be at the bottom of this? He had apparently killed a canary with only a word of command; his will seemed of deadly force; who knew but what he might yet be lingering in the neighbourhood willing all sorts of awful things!

We whispered these fancies among ourselves in the evenings; but in the mornings our courage came back with the daylight, and in a week's time we had got over the shock of Carlo's death; all but Mrs Jamieson. She, poor thing, felt it as she had felt no event since her husband's death; indeed, Miss Pole said, that as the Honourable Mr Jamieson drank a good deal, and occasioned her much uneasiness, it was possible that Carlo's death might be the greater affliction. But there was always a tinge of cynicism in Miss Pole's remarks. However, one thing was clear and certain – it was necessary for Mrs Jamieson to have some change of scene; and Mr Mulliner was very impressive on this point, shaking his head whenever we inquired after his mistress, and speaking of her loss of appetite and bad nights very ominously; and with justice too, for if she had two characteristics in her natural state of health they were a facility of eating and sleeping. If she could neither eat nor sleep, she must be indeed out of spirits and out of health.

Lady Glenmire (who had evidently taken very kindly to Cranford) did not like the idea of Mrs Jamieson's going to Cheltenham, and more than once insinuated pretty plainly that it was Mr Mulliner's doing, who had been much alarmed on the occasion of the house being attacked, and since had said, more than once, that he felt it a very responsible charge to have to defend so many women. Be that as it might, Mrs Jamieson went to Cheltenham, escorted by Mr Mulliner; and Lady Glenmire remained in possession of the house, her ostensible office being to take care that the maidservants did not pick up followers.

She made a very pleasant-looking dragon; and, as soon as it was arranged for her stay in Cranford, she found out that Mrs Jamieson's visit to Cheltenham was just the best thing in the world. She had let her house in Edinburgh, and was for the time houseless, so the charge of her sister-in-law's comfortable abode was very convenient and acceptable.

Miss Pole was very much inclined to instal herself as a heroine, because of the decided steps she had taken in flying from the two men and one woman, whom she entitled 'that murderous gang'. She described their appearance in glowing colours, and I noticed that every time she went over the story some fresh trait of villainy was added to their appearance. One was tall – he grew to be gigantic in height before we had done with him; he of course had black hair – and by-and-by it hung in elf-locks over his forehead and down his back. The other was short and broad – and a hump sprouted out on his shoulder before we heard the last of him; he had red hair – which deepened into carroty; and she was almost sure he had a cast in the eye – a decided squint. As for the woman, her eyes glared, and she was masculine-looking – a perfect virago; most probably a man dressed in woman's clothes; afterwards, we heard of a beard on her chin, and a manly voice and a stride.

If Miss Pole was delighted to recount the events of that afternoon to all inquirers, others were not so proud of their adventures in the robbery line. Mr Hoggins, the surgeon, had been attacked at his own door by two ruffians, who were concealed in the shadow of the porch, and so effectually silenced him that he was robbed in the interval between ringing his bell and the servant's answering it. Miss Pole was sure it would turn out that this robbery had been committed by 'her men', and went the very day she heard the report to have her teeth examined, and to question Mr Hoggins. She came to us afterwards; so we heard what she had heard, straight and direct from the source, while we were yet in the excitement and flutter of the agitation caused by the first intelligence; for the event had only occurred the night before.

'Well!' said Miss Pole, sitting down with the decision of a person who has made up her mind as to the nature of life and the world (and such people never tread lightly, or seat themselves without a bump), 'well, Miss Matty! men will be men. Every mother's son of them wishes to be considered Samson and Solomon rolled into one – too strong ever to be beaten or discomfited – too wise ever to be outwitted. If you will notice, they have always foreseen events, though they never tell one for one's warning before the events happen. My father was a man, and I know the sex pretty well.'

She had talked herself out of breath, and we should have been very glad to fill up the necessary pause as chorus, but we did not exactly know what to say, or which man had suggested this diatribe against the sex; so we only joined in generally, with a grave shake of the head, and a soft murmur of 'They are very incomprehensible, certainly!'

'Now, only think,' said she. 'There, I have undergone the risk of having one of my remaining teeth drawn (for one is terribly at the mercy of any surgeon-dentist; and I, for one, always speak them fair till I have got my mouth out of their clutches), and, after all, Mr Hoggins is too much of a man to own that he was robbed last night.'

'Not robbed!' exclaimed the chorus.

'Don't tell me!' Miss Pole exclaimed, angry that we could be for a moment imposed upon. 'I believe he was robbed, just as Betty told me, and he is ashamed to own it; and, to be sure, it was very silly of him to be robbed just at his own door; I dare say he feels that such a thing won't raise him in the eyes of Cranford society, and is anxious to conceal it – but he need not have tried to impose upon me, by saying I must have heard an exaggerated account of some petty theft of a neck of mutton, which, it seems, was stolen out of the safe in his yard last week; he had the impertinence to add, he believed that that was taken by the cat. I have no doubt, if I could get at the bottom of it, it was that Irishman dressed up in woman's clothes, who came spying about my house, with the story about the starving children.'

After we had duly condemned the want of candour which Mr Hoggins had evinced, and abused men in general, taking him for the representative and type, we got round to the subject about which we had been talking when Miss Pole came in; namely, how far, in the present disturbed state of the country, we could venture to accept an invitation which Miss Matty had just received from Mrs Forrester, to come as usual and keep the anniversary of her wedding day by drinking tea with her at five o'clock, and playing a quiet pool afterwards. Mrs Forrester had said that she asked us with some diffidence, because the roads were, she feared, very unsafe. But she suggested that perhaps one of us would not object to take the sedan, and that the others, by walking briskly, might keep up with the long trot of the chairmen, and so we might all arrive safely at Over Place, a suburb of the town. (No; that is too large an expression: a small cluster of houses separated from Cranford by about two hundred yards of a dark and lonely lane.) There was no doubt but that a similar note was awaiting Miss Pole at home; so her call was a very fortunate affair, as it enabled us to consult together. We would all much rather have declined this invitation; but we felt that it would not be quite kind to Mrs Forrester, who would otherwise be left to a solitary retrospect of her not very happy or fortunate life. Miss Matty and Miss Pole had been visitors on this occasion for many years, and now they gallantly determined to nail their colours to the mast, and to go through Darkness Lane rather than fail in loyalty to their friend.

But when the evening came, Miss Matty (for it was she who was voted into the chair, as she had a cold), before being shut down in the sedan, like jack-in-a-box, implored the chairmen, whatever might befall, not to run away and leave her fastened up there, to be murdered; and even after they had promised, I saw her tighten her features into the stern determination of a martyr, and she gave me a melancholy and ominous shake of the head through the glass. However, we got there safely, only rather out of breath, for it was who could trot hardest through Darkness Lane, and I am afraid poor Miss Matty was sadly jolted.

Mrs Forrester had made extra preparations, in acknowledgement of our exertion in coming to see her through such dangers. The usual forms of genteel ignorance as to what her servants might send up were all gone through; and harmony and Preference seemed likely to be the order of the evening, but for an interesting conversation that began I don't know how, but which had relation, of course, to the robbers who infested the neighbourhood of Cranford.

Having braved the dangers of Darkness Lane, and thus having a little stock of reputation for courage to fall back upon; and also, I dare say, desirous of proving ourselves superior to men (*videlicet* Mr Hoggins) in the article of candour, we began to relate our individual fears, and the private precautions we each of us took. I owned that my pet apprehension was eyes – eyes looking at me, and watching me, glittering out from some dull, flat, wooden surface; and that if I dared to go up to my looking-glass when I was panic-stricken, I should certainly turn it round, with its back towards me, for fear of seeing eyes behind me looking out of the darkness. I saw Miss Matty nerving herself up for a confession; and at last out it came. She owned that, ever since she had been a girl, she had dreaded being caught by her last leg, just as she was getting into her bed, by someone concealed under it. She said, when she was younger and more active, she used to take a flying leap from a distance, and so bring both her legs up safely into bed at once; but that this had always annoyed Deborah, who piqued herself upon getting into bed gracefully, and she had given it up in consequence. But now the old terror would often come over her, especially since Miss Pole's house had been attacked (we had got quite to believe in the fact of the attack having taken place), and yet it was very unpleasant to think of looking under a bed, and seeing a man concealed, with a great, fierce face staring out at you; so she had bethought herself of something – perhaps I had noticed that she had told Martha to buy her a penny ball, such as children play with – and now she rolled this ball under the bed every night: if it came out on the other side, well and good; if not she always took care to have her hand on the bell-rope, and meant to call out John and Harry, just as if she expected men-servants to answer her ring.

We all applauded this ingenious contrivance, and Miss Matty sank back into satisfied silence, with a look at Mrs Forrester as if to ask for *her* private weakness.

Mrs Forrester looked askance at Miss Pole, and tried to change the subject a little by telling us that she had borrowed a boy from one of the neighbouring cottages and promised his parents a hundredweight of coals at Christmas, and his supper every evening, for the loan of him at nights. She had instructed him in his possible duties when he first came; and, finding him sensible, she had given him the Major's sword (the Major was her late husband), and desired him to put it very carefully behind his pillow at night, turning the edge towards the head of the pillow. He was a sharp lad, she was sure; for, spying out the Major's cocked hat, he had said, if he might have that to wear, he was sure he could frighten two Englishmen, or four Frenchmen any day. But she had impressed upon him anew that he was to lose no time in putting on hats or anything else; but, if he heard any noise, he was to run at it with his drawn sword. On my suggesting that some accident might occur from such slaughterous and indiscriminate directions, and that he might rush on Jenny getting up to wash, and have spitted her before he had discovered that she was not a Frenchman, Mrs Forrester said she did not think that that was likely, for he was a very sound sleeper, and generally had to be well shaken or cold-pigged in a morning before they could rouse him. She sometimes thought such dead sleep must be owing to the hearty suppers the poor lad ate, for he was half-starved at home, and she told Jenny to see that he got a good meal at night.

Still this was no confession of Mrs Forrester's peculiar timidity, and we urged her to tell us what she thought would frighten her more than anything. She paused, and stirred the fire, and snuffed the candles, and then she said, in a sounding whisper –

'Ghosts!'

She looked at Miss Pole, as much as to say, she had declared it, and would stand by it. Such a look was a challenge in itself. Miss Pole came down upon her with indigestion, spectral illusions, optical delusions, and a great deal out of Dr Ferrier and Dr Hibbert besides. Miss Matty had rather a leaning to ghosts, as I have mentioned before, and what little she did say was all on Mrs Forrester's side, who, emboldened by sympathy, protested that ghosts were a part of her religion; that surely she, the widow of a major in the army, knew what to be frightened at, and what not; in short, I never saw Mrs Forrester so warm either before or since, for she was a gentle, meek, enduring old lady in most things. Not all the elder-wine that ever was mulled could this night wash out the remembrance of this difference between Miss Pole and her hostess. Indeed, when the elder-wine was brought in, it gave rise to a new burst of discussion; for Jenny, the little maiden who staggered under the tray, had to give evidence of having seen a ghost with her own eyes, not so many nights ago, in Darkness Lane, the very lane we were to go through on our way home.

In spite of the uncomfortable feeling which this last consideration gave me, I could not help being amused at Jenny's position, which was exceedingly like that of a witness being examined and cross-examined by two counsel who are not at all scrupulous about asking leading questions. The conclusion I arrived at was, that Jenny had certainly seen something beyond what a fit of indigestion would have caused. A lady all in white, and without her head, was what she deposed and adhered to, supported by a consciousness of the secret sympathy of her mistress under the withering scorn with which Miss Pole regarded her. And not only she, but many others, had seen this headless lady, who sat by the roadside wringing her hands as in deep grief. Mrs Forrester looked at us from time to time with an air of conscious triumph; but then she had not to pass through Darkness Lane before she could bury herself beneath her own familiar bedclothes.

We preserved a discreet silence as to the headless lady while we were putting on our things to go home, for there was no knowing how near the ghostly head and ears might be, or what spiritual connection they might be keeping up with the unhappy body in Darkness Lane; and, therefore, even Miss Pole felt that it was as well not to speak lightly on such subjects, for fear of vexing or insulting that woebegone trunk. At least, so I conjecture; for, instead of the busy clatter usual in the operation, we tied on our cloaks as sadly as mutes at a funeral. Miss Matty drew the curtains round the windows of the chair to shut out disagreeable sights, and the men (either because they were in spirits that their labours were so nearly ended, or because they were going down hill), set off at such a round and merry pace, that it was all Miss Pole and I could do to keep up with them. She had breath for nothing beyond an imploring 'Don't leave me!' uttered as she clutched my arm so tightly that I could not have quitted her, ghost or no ghost. What a relief it was when the men, weary of their burden and their quick trot, stopped just where Headingley Causeway branches off from Darkness Lane! Miss Pole unloosed me and caught at one of the men –

'Could not you – could not you take Miss Matty round by Headingley Causeway? – the pavement in Darkness Lane jolts so, and she is not very strong.'

A smothered voice was heard from the inside of the chair –

'Oh! pray go on! What is the matter? What is the matter? I will give you sixpence more to go on very fast; pray don't stop here.'

'And I'll give you a shilling,' said Miss Pole, with tremulous dignity, 'if you'll go by Headingley Causeway.'

The two men grunted acquiescence and took up the chair, and went along the causeway, which certainly answered Miss Pole's kind purpose of saving Miss Matty's bones; for it was covered with soft, thick mud, and even a fall there would have been easy till the getting-up came, when there might have been some difficulty in extrication.

CHAPTER XI

SAMUEL BROWN

The next morning I met Lady Glenmire and Miss Pole setting out on a long walk to find some old woman who was famous in the neighbourhood for her skill in knitting woollen stockings. Miss Pole said to me, with a smile half-kindly and half-contemptuous upon her countenance, 'I have been just telling Lady Glenmire of our poor friend Mrs Forrester, and her terror of ghosts. It comes from living so much alone, and listening to the bug-a-boo stories of that Jenny of hers.' She was so calm and so much above superstitious fears herself that I was almost ashamed to say how glad I had been of her Headingley Causeway proposition the night before, and turned off the conversation to something else.

In the afternoon Miss Pole called on Miss Matty to tell her of the adventure – the real adventure they had met with on their morning's walk. They had been perplexed about the exact path which they were to take across the fields in order to find the knitting old woman, and had stopped to inquire at a little wayside public house, standing on the high road to London, about three miles from Cranford. The good woman had asked them to sit down and rest themselves while she fetched her husband, who could direct them better than she could; and, while they were sitting in the sanded parlour, a little girl came in. They thought that she belonged to the landlady, and began some trifling conversation with her; but, on Mrs Roberts's return, she told them that the little thing was the only child of a couple who were staying in the house. And then she began a long story, out of which Lady Glenmire and Miss Pole could only gather one or two decided facts, which were that, about six weeks ago, a light spring-cart had broken down just before their door, in which there were two men, one woman, and this child. One of the men was seriously hurt – no bones broken, only 'shaken', the landlady called it; but he had probably sustained some severe internal injury, for he had languished in their house ever since, attended by his wife, the mother of this little girl. Miss Pole had asked what he was, what he looked like. And Mrs Roberts had made answer that he was not like a gentleman, nor yet like a common person; if it had not been that he and his wife were such decent, quiet people, she could almost have thought he was a mountebank, or something of that kind, for they had a great box in the cart, full of she did not know what. She had helped to unpack it, and take out their linen and clothes, when the other man – his twin-brother, she believed he was – had gone off with the horse and cart.

Miss Pole had begun to have her suspicions at this point, and expressed her idea that it was rather strange that the box and cart and horse and all should have disappeared; but good Mrs Roberts seemed to have become quite indignant at Miss Pole's implied suggestion; in fact, Miss Pole said she was as angry as if Miss Pole had told her that she herself was a swindler. As the best way of convincing the ladies, she bethought her of begging them to see the wife; and, as Miss Pole said, there was no doubting the honest, worn, bronzed face of the woman, who at the first tender word from Lady Glenmire, burst into tears, which she was too weak to check until some word from the landlady made her swallow down her sobs, in order that she might testify to the Christian kindness shown by Mr and Mrs Roberts. Miss Pole came round with a swing to as vehement a belief in the sorrowful tale as she had been sceptical before; and, as a proof of this, her energy in the poor sufferer's behalf was nothing daunted when she found out that he, and no other, was our Signor Brunoni, to whom all Cranford had been attributing all manner of evil this six weeks past! Yes! his wife said his proper name was Samuel Brown – 'Sam', she called him – but to the last we preferred calling him 'the Signor'; it sounded so much better.

The end of their conversation with the Signora Brunoni was that it was agreed that he should be placed under medical advice, and for any expense incurred in procuring this Lady Glenmire promised to hold herself responsible, and had accordingly gone to Mr Hoggins to beg him to ride over to the 'Rising Sun' that very afternoon, and examine into the signor's real state; and, as Miss Pole said, if it was desirable to remove him to Cranford to be more immediately under Mr Hoggins's eye, she would undertake to see for lodgings and arrange about the rent. Mrs Roberts had been as kind as could be all throughout, but it was evident that their long residence there had been a slight inconvenience.

Before Miss Pole left us, Miss Matty and I were as full of the morning's adventure as she was. We talked about it all the evening, turning it in every possible light, and we went to bed anxious for the morning, when we should surely hear from someone what Mr Hoggins thought and recommended; for, as Miss Matty observed, though Mr Hoggins did say 'Jack's up', 'a fig for his heels', and called Preference 'Pref.' she believed he was a very worthy man and a very clever surgeon. Indeed, we were rather proud of our doctor at Cranford, as a doctor. We often wished, when we heard of Queen Adelaide or the Duke of Wellington being ill, that they would send for Mr Hoggins; but, on consideration, we were rather glad they did not, for, if we were ailing, what should we do if Mr Hoggins had been appointed physician-in-ordinary to the Royal Family? As a surgeon we were proud of him; but as a man – or rather, I should say, as a gentleman – we could only shake our heads over his name and himself, and wished that he had read Lord Chesterfield's Letters in the days when his manners were susceptible of improvement. Nevertheless, we all regarded his dictum in the signor's case as infallible, and when he said that with care and attention he might rally, we had no more fear for him.

But, although we had no more fear, everybody did as much as if there was great cause for anxiety – as indeed there was until Mr Hoggins took charge of him. Miss Pole looked out clean and comfort-able, if homely, lodgings; Miss Matty sent the sedan-chair for him, and Martha and I aired it well before it left Cranford by holding a warming-pan full of red-hot coals in it, and then shutting it up close, smoke and all, until the time when he should get into it at the 'Rising Sun'. Lady Glenmire undertook the medical department under Mr Hoggins's directions, and rummaged up all Mrs Jamieson's medicine glasses, and spoons, and bed-tables, in a free-and-easy way, that made Miss Matty feel a little anxious as to what that lady and Mr Mulliner might say, if they knew. Mrs Forrester made some of the bread-jelly, for which she was so famous, to have ready as a refreshment in the lodgings when he should arrive. A present of this bread-jelly was the highest mark of favour dear Mrs Forrester could confer. Miss Pole had once asked her for the receipt, but she had met with a very decided rebuff; that lady told her that she could not part with it to anyone during her life, and that after her death it was bequeathed, as her executors would find, to Miss Matty. What Miss Matty, or, as Mrs Forrester called her (remembering the clause in her will and the dignity of the occasion), Miss Matilda Jenkyns – might choose to do with the receipt when it came into her possession – whether to make it public, or to hand it down as an heirloom – she did not know, nor would she dictate. And a mould of this admirable, digestible, unique bread-jelly was sent by Mrs Forrester to our poor sick conjuror. Who says that the aristocracy are proud? Here was a lady by birth a Tyrrell, and descended from the great Sir Walter that shot King Rufus, and in whose veins ran the blood of him who murdered the little princes in the Tower, going every day to see what dainty dishes she could prepare for Samuel Brown, a mountebank! But, indeed, it was wonderful to see what kind feelings were called out by this poor man's coming amongst us. And also wonderful to see how the great Cranford panic, which had been occasioned by his first coming in his Turkish dress, melted away into thin air on his second coming – pale and feeble, and with his heavy, filmy eyes, that only brightened a very little when they fell upon the countenance of his faithful wife, or their pale and sorrowful little girl.

Somehow we all forgot to be afraid. I dare say it was that finding out that he, who had first excited our love of the marvellous by his unprecedented arts, had not sufficient everyday gifts to manage a shying horse, made us feel as if we were ourselves again. Miss Pole came with her little basket at all hours of the evening, as if her lonely house and the unfrequented road to it had never been infested by that 'murderous gang'; Mrs Forrester said she thought that neither Jenny nor she need mind the headless lady who wept and wailed in Darkness Lane, for surely the power was never given to such beings to harm those who went about to try to do what little good was in their power, to which Jenny tremblingly assented; but the mistress's theory had little effect on the maid's practice until she had sewn two pieces of red flannel in the shape of a cross on her inner garment.

I found Miss Matty covering her penny ball – the ball that she used to roll under her bed – with gay-coloured worsted in rainbow stripes.

'My dear,' said she, 'my heart is sad for that little careworn child. Although her father is a conjuror, she looks as if she had never had a good game of play in her life. I used to make very pretty balls in this way when I was a girl, and I thought I would try if I could not make this one smart and take it to Phoebe this afternoon. I think 'the gang' must have left the neighbourhood, for one does not hear any more of their violence and robbery now.'

We were all of us far too full of the signor's precarious state to talk either about robbers or ghosts. Indeed, Lady Glenmire said she never had heard of any actual robberies, except that two little boys had stolen some apples from Farmer Benson's orchard, and that some eggs had been missed on a market-day off Widow Hayward's stall. But that was expecting too much of us; we could not acknowledge that we had only had this small foundation for all our panic. Miss Pole drew herself up at this remark of Lady Glenmire's, and said 'that she wished she could agree with her as to the very small reason we had had for alarm, but with the recollection of a man disguised as a woman who had endeavoured to force himself into her house while his confederates waited outside; with the knowledge gained from Lady Glenmire herself, of the footprints seen on Mrs Jamieson's flower borders; with the fact before her of the audacious robbery committed on Mr Hoggins at his own door' – But here Lady Glenmire broke in with a very strong expression of doubt as to whether this last story was not an entire fabrication founded upon the theft of a cat; she grew so red while she was saying all this that I was not surprised at Miss Pole's manner of bridling up, and I am certain, if Lady Glenmire had not been 'her ladyship', we should have had a more emphatic contradiction than the 'Well, to be sure!' and similar fragmentary ejaculations, which were all that she ventured upon in my lady's presence. But when she was gone Miss Pole began a long congratulation to Miss Matty that so far they had escaped marriage, which she noticed always made people credulous to the last degree; indeed, she thought it argued great natural credulity in a woman if she could not keep herself from being married; and in what Lady Glenmire had said about Mr Hoggins's robbery we had a specimen of what people came to if they gave way to such a weakness; evidently Lady Glenmire would swallow anything if she could believe the poor vamped-up story about a neck of mutton and a pussy with which he had tried to impose on Miss Pole, only she had always been on her guard against believing too much of what men said.

We were thankful, as Miss Pole desired us to be, that we had never been married; but I think, of the two, we were even more thankful that the robbers had left Cranford; at least I judge so from a speech of Miss Matty's that evening, as we sat over the fire, in which she evidently looked upon a husband as a great protector against thieves, burglars, and ghosts; and said that she did not think that she should dare to be always warning young people against matrimony, as Miss Pole did continually; to be sure, marriage was a risk, as she saw, now she had had some experience; but she remembered the time when she had looked forward to being married as much as anyone.

'Not to any particular person, my dear,' said she, hastily checking herself up, as if she were afraid of having admitted too much; 'only the old story, you know, of ladies always saying, "*When* I marry", and gentlemen, "*If* I marry".' It was a joke spoken in rather a sad tone, and I doubt if either of us smiled; but I could not see Miss Matty's face by the flickering firelight. In a little while she continued –

'But, after all, I have not told you the truth. It is so long ago, and no one ever knew how much I thought of it at the time, unless, indeed, my dear mother guessed; but I may say that there was a time when I did not think I should have been only Miss Matty Jenkyns all my life; for even if I did meet with anyone who wished to marry me now (and, as Miss Pole says, one is never too safe), I could not take him – I hope he would not take it too much to heart, but I could *not* take him – or anyone but the person I once thought I should be married to; and he is dead and gone, and he never knew how it all came about that I said "No," when I had thought many and many a time – Well, it's no matter what I thought. God ordains it all, and I am very happy, my dear. No one has such kind friends as I,' continued she, taking my hand and holding it in hers.

If I had never known of Mr Holbrook, I could have said something in this pause, but as I had, I could not think of anything that would come in naturally, and so we both kept silence for a little time.

'My father once made us,' she began, 'keep a diary, in two columns; on one side we were to put down in the morning what we thought would be the course and events of the coming day, and at night we were to put down on the other side what really had happened. It would be to some people rather a sad way of telling their lives,' (a tear dropped upon my hand at these words) – 'I don't mean that mine has been sad, only so very different to what I expected. I remember, one winter's evening, sitting over our bedroom fire with Deborah – I remember it as if it were yesterday – and we were planning our future lives, both of us were planning, though only she talked about it. She said she should like to marry an archdeacon, and write his charges; and you know, my dear, she never was married, and, for aught I know, she never spoke to an unmarried archdeacon in her life. I never was ambitious, nor could I have written charges, but I thought I could manage a house (my mother used to call me her right hand), and I was always so fond of little children – the shyest babies would stretch out their little arms to come to me; when I was a girl, I was half my leisure time nursing in the neighbouring cottages; but I don't know how it was, when I grew sad and grave – which I did a year or two after this time – the little things drew back from me, and I am afraid I lost the knack, though I am just as fond of children as ever, and have a strange yearning at my heart whenever I see a mother with her baby in her arms. Nay, my dear' (and by a sudden blaze which sprang up from a fall of the unstirred coals, I saw that her eyes were full of tears – gazing intently on some vision of what might have been), 'do you know I dream sometimes that I have a little child – always the same – a little girl of about two years old; she never grows older, though I have dreamt about her for many years. I don't think I ever dream of any words or sound she makes; she is very noiseless and still, but she comes to me when she is very sorry or very glad, and I have wakened with the clasp of her dear little arms round my neck. Only last night – perhaps because I had gone to sleep thinking of this ball for Phoebe – my little darling came in my dream, and put up her mouth to be kissed, just as I have seen real babies do to real mothers before going to bed. But all this is nonsense, dear! only don't be frightened by Miss Pole from being married. I can fancy it may be a very happy state, and a little credulity helps one on through life very smoothly – better than always doubting and doubting and seeing difficulties and disagreeables in everything.'

If I had been inclined to be daunted from matrimony, it would not have been Miss Pole to do it; it would have been the lot of poor Signor Brunoni and his wife. And yet again, it was an encouragement to see how, through all their cares and sorrows, they thought of each other and not of themselves; and how keen were their joys, if they only passed through each other, or through the little Phoebe.

The signora told me, one day, a good deal about their lives up to this period. It began by my asking her whether Miss Pole's story of the twin-brothers were true; it sounded so wonderful a likeness, that I should have had my doubts, if Miss Pole had not been unmarried.

But the signora, or (as we found out she preferred to be called) Mrs Brown, said it was quite true; that her brother-in-law was by many taken for her husband, which was of great assistance to them in their profession; 'though,' she continued, 'how people can mistake Thomas for the real Signor Brunoni, I can't conceive; but he says they do; so I suppose I must believe him. Not but what he is a very good man; I am sure I don't know how we should have paid our bill at the "Rising Sun" but for the money he sends; but people must know very little about art if they can take him for my husband. Why, Miss, in the ball trick, where my husband spreads his fingers wide, and throws out his little finger with quite an air and a grace, Thomas just clumps up his hand like a fist, and might have ever so many balls hidden in it. Besides, he has never been in India, and knows nothing of the proper sit of a turban.'

'Have you been in India?' said I, rather astonished.

'Oh, yes! many a year, ma'am. Sam was a sergeant in the 31st; and when the regiment was ordered to India, I drew a lot to go, and I was more thankful than I can tell; for it seemed as if it would only be a slow death to me to part from my husband. But, indeed, ma'am, if I had known all, I don't know whether I would not rather have died there and then than gone through what I have done since. To be sure, I've been able to comfort Sam, and to be with him; but, ma'am, I've lost six children,' said she, looking up at me with those strange eyes that I've never noticed but in mothers of dead children – with a kind of wild look in them, as if seeking for what they never more might find. 'Yes! Six children died off, like little buds nipped untimely, in that cruel India. I thought, as each died, I never could – I never would – love a child again; and when the next came, it had not only its own love, but the deeper love that came from the thoughts of its little dead brothers and sisters. And when Phoebe was coming, I said to my husband, "Sam, when the child is born, and I am strong, I shall leave you; it will cut my heart cruel; but if this baby dies too, I shall go mad; the madness is in me now; but if you let me go down to Calcutta, carrying my baby step by step, it will, maybe, work itself off; and I will save, and I will hoard, and I will beg – and I will die, to get a passage home to England, where our baby may live?" God bless him! he said I might go; and he saved up his pay, and I saved every pice I could get for washing or any way; and when Phoebe came, and I grew strong again, I set off. It was very lonely; through the thick forests, dark again with their heavy trees – along by the river's side (but I had been brought up near the Avon in Warwickshire, so that flowing noise sounded like home) – from station to station, from Indian village to village, I went along, carrying my child. I had seen one of the officer's ladies with a little picture, ma'am – done by a Catholic foreigner, ma'am – of the Virgin and the little Saviour, ma'am. She had him on her arm, and her form was softly curled round him, and their cheeks touched. Well, when I went to bid goodbye to this lady, for whom I had washed, she cried sadly; for she, too, had lost her children, but she had not another to save, like me; and I was bold enough to ask her would she give me that print. And she cried the more, and said her children were with that little blessed Jesus; and gave it me, and told me that she had heard it had been painted on the bottom of a cask, which made it have that round shape. And when my body was very weary, and my heart was sick (for there were times when I misdoubted if I could ever reach my home, and there were times when I thought of my husband, and one time when I thought my baby was dying), I took out that picture and looked at it, till I could have thought the mother spoke to me, and comforted me. And the natives were very kind. We could not understand one another; but they saw my baby on my breast, and they came out to me, and brought me rice and milk, and sometimes flowers – I have got some of the flowers dried. Then, the next morning, I was so tired; and they wanted me to stay with them – I could tell that – and tried to frighten me from going into the deep woods, which, indeed, looked very strange and dark; but it seemed to me as if Death was following me to take my baby away from me; and as if I must go on, and on – and I thought how God had cared for mothers ever since the world was made, and would care for me; so I bade them goodbye, and set off afresh. And once when my baby was ill, and both she and I needed rest, He led me to a place where I found a kind Englishman lived, right in the midst of the natives.'

'And you reached Calcutta safely at last?'

'Yes, safely! Oh! when I knew I had only two days' journey more before me, I could not help it, ma'am – it might be idolatry, I cannot tell – but I was near one of the native temples, and I went into it with my baby to thank God for His great mercy; for it seemed to me that where others had prayed before to their God, in their joy or in their agony, was of itself a sacred place. And I got as servant to an invalid lady, who grew quite fond of my baby aboard-ship; and, in two years' time, Sam earned his discharge, and came home to me, and to our child. Then he had to fix on a trade; but he knew of none; and once, once upon a time, he had learnt some tricks from an Indian juggler; so he set up conjuring, and it answered so well that he took Thomas to help him – as his man, you know, not as another conjuror, though Thomas has set it up now on his own hook. But it has been a great help to us that likeness between the twins, and made a good many tricks go off well that they made up together. And Thomas is a good brother, only he has not the fine carriage of my husband, so that I can't think how he can be taken for Signor Brunoni himself, as he says he is.'

'Poor little Phoebe!' said I, my thoughts going back to the baby she carried all those hundred miles.

'Ah! you may say so! I never thought I should have reared her, though, when she fell ill at Chunderabaddad; but that good, kind Aga Jenkyns took us in, which I believe was the very saving of her.'

'Jenkyns!' said I.

'Yes, Jenkyns. I shall think all people of that name are kind; for here is that nice old lady who comes every day to take Phoebe a walk!'

But an idea had flashed through my head; could the Aga Jenkyns be the lost Peter? True he was reported by many to be dead. But, equally true, some had said that he had arrived at the dignity of Great Lama of Thibet. Miss Matty thought he was alive. I would make further inquiry.

CHAPTER XII

ENGAGED TO BE MARRIED

Was the 'poor Peter' of Cranford the Aga Jenkyns of Chunderabaddad, or was he not? As somebody says, that was the question.

In my own home, whenever people had nothing else to do, they blamed me for want of discretion. Indiscretion was my bug-bear fault. Everybody has a bug-bear fault, a sort of standing characteristic – a *pièce de résistance* for their friends to cut at; and in general they cut and come again. I was tired of being called indiscreet and incautious; and I determined for once to prove myself a model of prudence and wisdom. I would not even hint my suspicions respecting the Aga. I would collect evidence and carry it home to lay before my father, as the family friend of the two Miss Jenkynses.

In my search after facts, I was often reminded of a description my father had once given of a ladies' committee that he had had to preside over. He said he could not help thinking of a passage in Dickens, which spoke of a chorus in which every man took the tune he knew best, and sang it to his own satisfaction. So, at this charitable committee, every lady took the subject uppermost in her mind, and talked about it to her own great contentment, but not much to the advancement of the subject they had met to discuss. But even that committee could have been nothing to the Cranford ladies when I attempted to gain some clear and definite information as to poor Peter's height, appearance, and when and where he was seen and heard of last. For instance, I remember asking Miss Pole (and I thought the question was very opportune, for I put it when I met her at a call at Mrs Forrester's, and both the ladies had known Peter, and I imagined that they might refresh each other's memories) – I asked Miss Pole what was the very last thing they had ever heard about him; and then she named the absurd report to which I have alluded, about his having been elected Great Lama of Thibet; and this was a signal for each lady to go off on her separate idea. Mrs Forrester's start was made on the veiled prophet in 'Lalla Rookh' – whether I thought he was meant for the Great Lama, though Peter was not so ugly, indeed rather handsome, if he had not been freckled. I was thankful to see her double upon Peter; but, in a moment, the delusive lady was off upon Rowland's Kalydor, and the merits of cosmetics and hair oils in general, and holding forth so fluently that I turned to listen to Miss Pole, who (through the llamas, the beasts of burden) had got to Peruvian bonds, and the share market, and her poor opinion of joint-stock banks in general, and of that one in particular in which Miss Matty's money was invested. In vain I put in 'When was it – in what year was it that you heard that Mr Peter was the Great Lama?' They only joined issue to dispute whether llamas were carnivorous animals or not; in which dispute they were not quite on fair grounds, as Mrs Forrester (after they had grown warm and cool again) acknowledged that she always confused carnivorous and gramini-vorous together, just as she did horizontal and perpendicular; but then she apologised for it very prettily, by saying that in her day the only use people made of four-syllabled words was to teach how they should be spelt.

The only fact I gained from this conversation was that certainly Peter had last been heard of in India, 'or that neighbourhood'; and that this scanty intelligence of his whereabouts had reached Cranford in the year when Miss Pole had brought her Indian muslin gown, long since worn out (we washed it and mended it, and traced its decline and fall into a window-blind before we could go on); and in a year when Wombwell came to Cranford, because Miss Matty had wanted to see an elephant in order that she might the better imagine Peter riding on one; and had seen a boa-constrictor too, which was more than she wished to imagine in her fancy-pictures of Peter's locality; and in a year when Miss Jenkyns had learnt some piece of poetry off by heart, and used to say, at all the Cranford parties, how Peter was 'surveying mankind from China to Peru', which everybody had thought very grand, and rather appropriate, because India was between China and Peru, if you took care to turn the globe to the left instead of the right.

I suppose all these inquiries of mine, and the consequent curiosity excited in the minds of my friends, made us blind and deaf to what was going on around us. It seemed to me as if the sun rose and shone, and as if the rain rained on Cranford, just as usual, and I did not notice any sign of the times that could be considered as a prognostic of any uncommon event; and, to the best of my belief, not only Miss Matty and Mrs Forrester, but even Miss Pole herself, whom we looked upon as a kind of prophetess, from the knack she had of foreseeing things before they came to pass – although she did not like to disturb her friends by telling them her foreknowledge – even Miss Pole herself was breathless with astonishment when she came to tell us of the astounding piece of news. But I must recover myself; the contemplation of it, even at this distance of time, has taken away my breath and my grammar, and unless I subdue my emotion, my spelling will go too.

We were sitting – Miss Matty and I – much as usual, she in the blue chintz easy-chair, with her back to the light, and her knitting in her hand, I reading aloud the *St James's Chronicle*. A few minutes more, and we should have gone to make the little alterations in dress usual before calling-time (twelve o'clock) in Cranford. I remember the scene and the date well. We had been talking of the signor's rapid recovery since the warmer weather had set in, and praising Mr Hoggins's skill, and lamenting his want of refinement and manner (it seems a curious coincidence that this should have been our subject, but so it was), when a knock was heard – a caller's knock – three distinct taps – and we were flying (that is to say, Miss Matty could not walk very fast, having had a touch of rheumatism) to our rooms, to change cap and collars, when Miss Pole arrested us by calling out, as she came up the stairs, 'Don't go – I can't wait – it is not twelve, I know – but never mind your dress – I must speak to you.' We did our best to look as if it was not we who had made the hurried movement, the sound of which she had heard; for, of course, we did not like to have it supposed that we had any old clothes that it was convenient to wear out in the 'sanctuary of home', as Miss Jenkyns once prettily called the back parlour, where she was tying up preserves. So we threw our gentility with double force into our manners, and very genteel we were for two minutes while Miss Pole recovered breath, and excited our curiosity strongly by lifting up her hands in amazement, and bringing them down in silence, as if what she had to say was too big for words, and could only be expressed by pantomime.

'What do you think, Miss Matty? What *do* you think? Lady Glenmire is to marry – is to be married, I mean – Lady Glenmire – Mr Hoggins – Mr Hoggins is going to marry Lady Glenmire!'

'Marry!' said we. 'Marry! Madness!'

'Marry!' said Miss Pole, with the decision that belonged to her character. '*I* said marry! as you do; and I also said, "What a fool my lady is going to make of herself!" I could have said "Madness!" but I controlled myself, for it was in a public shop that I heard of it. Where feminine delicacy is gone to, I don't know! You and I, Miss Matty, would have been ashamed to have known that our marriage was spoken of in a grocer's shop, in the hearing of shopmen!'

'But,' said Miss Matty, sighing as one recovering from a blow, 'perhaps it is not true. Perhaps we are doing her injustice.'

'No,' said Miss Pole. 'I have taken care to ascertain that. I went straight to Mrs Fitz-Adam, to borrow a cookery-book which I knew she had; and I introduced my congratulations *à propos* of the difficulty gentlemen must have in housekeeping; and Mrs Fitz-Adam bridled up, and said that she believed it was true, though how and where I could have heard it she did not know. She said her brother and Lady Glenmire had come to an understanding at last. "Understanding"! such a coarse word! But my lady will have to come down to many a want of refinement. I have reason to believe Mr Hoggins sups on bread and cheese and beer every night.'

'Marry!' said Miss Matty once again. 'Well! I never thought of it. Two people that we know going to be married. It's coming very near!'

'So near that my heart stopped beating when I heard of it, while you might have counted twelve,' said Miss Pole.

'One does not know whose turn may come next. Here, in Cranford, poor Lady Glenmire might have thought herself safe,' said Miss Matty, with a gentle pity in her tones.

'Bah!' said Miss Pole, with a toss of her head. 'Don't you remember poor dear Captain Brown's song "Tibbie Fowler," and the line –

'Set her on the Tintock tap, The wind will blaw a man till her.'

'That was because "Tibbie Fowler" was rich, I think.'

'Well! there was a kind of attraction about Lady Glenmire that I, for one, should be ashamed to have.'

I put in my wonder. 'But how can she have fancied Mr Hoggins? I am not surprised that Mr Hoggins has liked her.'

'Oh! I don't know. Mr Hoggins is rich, and very pleasant-looking,' said Miss Matty, 'and very good-tempered and kind-hearted.'

'She has married for an establishment, that's it. I suppose she takes the surgery with it,' said Miss Pole, with a little dry laugh at her own joke. But, like many people who think they have made a severe and sarcastic speech, which yet is clever of its kind, she began to relax in her grimness from the moment when she made this allusion to the surgery; and we turned to speculate on the way in which Mrs Jamieson would receive the news. The person whom she had left in charge of her house to keep off followers from her maids to set up a follower of her own! And that follower a man whom Mrs Jamieson had tabooed as vulgar, and inadmissible to Cranford society, not merely on account of his name, but because of his voice, his complexion, his boots, smelling of the stable, and himself, smelling of drugs. Had he ever been to see Lady Glenmire at Mrs Jamieson's? Chloride of lime would not purify the house in its owner's estimation if he had. Or had their interviews been confined to the occasional meetings in the chamber of the poor sick conjuror, to whom, with all our sense of the *mésalliance*, we could not help allowing that they had both been exceedingly kind? And now it turned out that a servant of Mrs Jamieson's had been ill, and Mr Hoggins had been attending her for some weeks. So the wolf had got into the fold, and now he was carrying off the shepherdess. What would Mrs Jamieson say? We looked into the darkness of futurity as a child gazes after a rocket up in the cloudy sky, full of wondering expectation of the rattle, the discharge, and the brilliant shower of sparks and light. Then we brought ourselves down to earth and the present time by questioning each other (being all equally ignorant, and all equally without the slightest data to build any conclusions upon) as to when *it* would take place? Where? How much a year Mr Hoggins had? Whether she would drop her title? And how Martha and the other correct servants in Cranford would ever be brought to announce a married couple as Lady Glenmire and Mr Hoggins? But would they be visited? Would Mrs Jamieson let us? Or must we choose between the Honourable Mrs Jamieson and the degraded Lady Glenmire? We all liked Lady Glenmire the best. She was bright, and kind, and sociable, and agreeable; and Mrs Jamieson was dull, and inert, and pompous, and tiresome. But we had acknowledged the sway of the latter so long, that it seemed like a kind of disloyalty now even to meditate disobedience to the prohibition we anticipated.

Mrs Forrester surprised us in our darned caps and patched collars; and we forgot all about them in our eagerness to see how she would bear the information, which we honourably left to Miss Pole, to impart, although, if we had been inclined to take unfair advantage, we might have rushed in ourselves, for she had a most out-of-place fit of coughing for five minutes after Mrs Forrester entered the room. I shall never forget the imploring expression of her eyes, as she looked at us over her pocket-handkerchief. They said, as plain as words could speak, 'Don't let Nature deprive me of the treasure which is mine, although for a time I can make no use of it.' And we did not.

Mrs Forrester's surprise was equal to ours; and her sense of injury rather greater, because she had to feel for her Order, and saw more fully than we could do how such conduct brought stains on the aristocracy.

When she and Miss Pole left us we endeavoured to subside into calmness; but Miss Matty was really upset by the intelligence she had heard. She reckoned it up, and it was more than fifteen years since she had heard of any of her acquaintance going to be married, with the one exception of Miss Jessie Brown; and, as she said, it gave her quite a shock, and made her feel as if she could not think what would happen next.

I don't know whether it is a fancy of mine, or a real fact, but I have noticed that, just after the announcement of an engagement in any set, the unmarried ladies in that set flutter out in an unusual gaiety and newness of dress, as much as to say, in a tacit and unconscious manner, 'We also are spinsters.' Miss Matty and Miss Pole talked and thought more about bonnets, gowns, caps, and shawls, during the fortnight that succeeded this call, than I had known them do for years before. But it might be the spring weather, for it was a warm and pleasant March; and merinoes and beavers, and woollen materials of all sorts were but ungracious receptacles of the bright sun's glancing rays. It had not been Lady Glenmire's dress that had won Mr Hoggins's heart, for she went about on her errands of kindness more shabby than ever. Although in the hurried glimpses I caught of her at church or elsewhere she appeared rather to shun meeting any of her friends, her face seemed to have almost something of the flush of youth in it; her lips looked redder and more trembling full than in their old compressed state, and her eyes dwelt on all things with a lingering light, as if she was learning to love Cranford and its belongings. Mr Hoggins looked broad and radiant, and creaked up the middle aisle at church in a brand-new pair of top-boots – an audible, as well as visible, sign of his purposed change of state; for the tradition went, that the boots he had worn till now were the identical pair in which he first set out on his rounds in Cranford twenty-five years ago; only they had been new-pieced, high and low, top and bottom, heel and sole, black leather and brown leather, more times than anyone could tell.

None of the ladies in Cranford chose to sanction the marriage by congratulating either of the parties. We wished to ignore the whole affair until our liege lady, Mrs Jamieson, returned. Till she came back to give us our cue, we felt that it would be better to consider the engagement in the same light as the Queen of Spain's legs – facts which certainly existed, but the less said about the better. This restraint upon our tongues – for you see if we did not speak about it to any of the parties concerned, how could we get answers to the questions that we longed to ask? – was beginning to be irksome, and our idea of the dignity of silence was paling before our curiosity, when another direction was given to our thoughts, by an announcement on the part of the principal shopkeeper of Cranford, who ranged the trades from grocer and cheesemonger to man-milliner, as occasion required, that the spring fashions were arrived, and would be exhibited on the following Tuesday at his rooms in High Street. Now Miss Matty had been only waiting for this before buying herself a new silk gown. I had offered, it is true, to send to Drumble for patterns, but she had rejected my proposal, gently implying that she had not forgotten her disappointment about the sea-green turban. I was thankful that I was on the spot now, to counteract the dazzling fascination of any yellow or scarlet silk.

I must say a word or two here about myself. I have spoken of my father's old friendship for the Jenkyns family; indeed, I am not sure if there was not some distant relationship. He had willingly allowed me to remain all the winter at Cranford, in consideration of a letter which Miss Matty had written to him about the time of the panic, in which I suspect she had exaggerated my powers and my bravery as a defender of the house. But now that the days were longer and more cheerful, he was beginning to urge the necessity of my return; and I only delayed in a sort of odd forlorn hope that if I could obtain any clear information, I might make the account given by the signora of the Aga Jenkyns tally with that of 'poor Peter', his appearance and disappearance, which I had winnowed out of the conversation of Miss Pole and Mrs Forrester.

CHAPTER XIII
STOPPED PAYMENT

The very Tuesday morning on which Mr Johnson was going to show the fashions, the post-woman brought two letters to the house. I say the post-woman, but I should say the postman's wife. He was a lame shoe-maker, a very clean, honest man, much respected in the town; but he never brought the letters round except on unusual occasions, such as Christmas Day or Good Friday; and on those days the letters, which should have been delivered at eight in the morning, did not make their appearance until two or three in the afternoon, for everyone liked poor Thomas, and gave him a welcome on these festive occasions. He used to say, 'He was welly stawed wi' eating, for there were three or four houses where nowt would serve 'em but he must share in their break-fast;' and by the time he had done his last breakfast, he came to some other friend who was beginning dinner; but come what might in the way of temptation, Tom was always sober, civil, and smiling; and, as Miss Jenkyns used to say, it was a lesson in patience, that she doubted not would call out that precious quality in some minds, where, but for Thomas, it might have lain dormant and undiscovered. Patience was certainly very dormant in Miss Jenkyns's mind. She was always expecting letters, and always drumming on the table till the post-woman had called or gone past. On Christmas Day and Good Friday she drummed from breakfast till church, from church-time till two o'clock – unless when the fire wanted stirring, when she invariably knocked down the fire-irons, and scolded Miss Matty for it. But equally certain was the hearty welcome and the good dinner for Thomas; Miss Jenkyns standing over him like a bold dragoon, questioning him as to his chil-dren – what they were doing – what school they went to; upbraiding him if another was likely to make its appearance, but sending even the little babies the shilling and the mince-pie which was her gift to all the children, with half-a-crown in addition for both father and mother. The post was not half of so much consequence to dear Miss Matty; but not for the world would she have diminished Thomas's welcome and his dole, though I could see that she felt rather shy over the ceremony, which had been regarded by Miss Jenkyns as a glorious

opportunity for giving advice and benefiting her fellow-creatures. Miss
Matty would steal the money all in a lump into his hand, as if she
were ashamed of herself. Miss Jenkyns gave him each individual coin
separate, with a 'There! that's for yourself; that's for Jenny,' etc. Miss
Matty would even beckon Martha out of the kitchen while he ate his
food: and once, to my knowledge, winked at its rapid disappearance
into a blue cotton pocket-handkerchief. Miss Jenkyns almost scolded
him if he did not leave a clean plate, however heaped it might have
been, and gave an injunction with every mouthful.

I have wandered a long way from the two letters that awaited us
on the breakfast-table that Tuesday morning. Mine was from my father.
Miss Matty's was printed. My father's was just a man's letter; I mean
it was very dull, and gave no information beyond that he was well,
that they had had a good deal of rain, that trade was very stagnant,
and there were many disagreeable rumours afloat. He then asked me
if I knew whether Miss Matty still retained her shares in the Town and
County Bank, as there were very unpleasant reports about it; though
nothing more than he had always foreseen, and had prophesied to Miss
Jenkyns years ago, when she would invest their little property in it –
the only unwise step that clever woman had ever taken, to his knowledge
(the only time she ever acted against his advice, I knew). However, if
anything had gone wrong, of course I was not to think of leaving Miss
Matty while I could be of any use, etc.

'Who is your letter from, my dear? Mine is a very civil invitation,
signed "Edwin Wilson", asking me to attend an important meeting of
the shareholders of the Town and County Bank, to be held in Drumble,
on Thursday the twenty-first. I am sure, it is very attentive of them to
remember me.'

I did not like to hear of this 'important meeting', for, though I did
not know much about business, I feared it confirmed what my father
said: however, I thought, ill news always came fast enough, so I resolved
to say nothing about my alarm, and merely told her that my father was
well, and sent his kind regards to her. She kept turning over and
admiring her letter. At last she spoke –

'I remember their sending one to Deborah just like this; but that I
did not wonder at, for everybody knew she was so clear-headed. I am
afraid I could not help them much; indeed, if they came to accounts, I
should be quite in the way, for I never could do sums in my head.

Deborah, I know, rather wished to go, and went so far as to order a new bonnet for the occasion: but when the time came she had a bad cold; so they sent her a very polite account of what they had done. Chosen a director, I think it was. Do you think they want me to help them to choose a director? I am sure I should choose your father at once!'

'My father has no shares in the bank,' said I.

'Oh, no! I remember. He objected very much to Deborah's buying any, I believe. But she was quite the woman of business, and always judged for herself; and here, you see, they have paid eight per cent all these years.'

It was a very uncomfortable subject to me, with my half-knowledge; so I thought I would change the conversation, and I asked at what time she thought we had better go and see the fashions. 'Well, my dear,' she said, 'the thing is this: it is not etiquette to go till after twelve; but then, you see, all Cranford will be there, and one does not like to be too curious about dress and trimmings and caps with all the world looking on. It is never genteel to be over-curious on these occasions. Deborah had the knack of always looking as if the latest fashion was nothing new to her; a manner she had caught from Lady Arley, who did see all the new modes in London, you know. So I thought we would just slip down – for I do want this morning, soon after breakfast half-a-pound of tea – and then we could go up and examine the things at our leisure, and see exactly how my new silk gown must be made; and then, after twelve, we could go with our minds disengaged, and free from thoughts of dress.'

We began to talk of Miss Matty's new silk gown. I discovered that it would be really the first time in her life that she had had to choose anything of consequence for herself: for Miss Jenkyns had always been the more decided character, whatever her taste might have been; and it is astonishing how such people carry the world before them by the mere force of will. Miss Matty anticipated the sight of the glossy folds with as much delight as if the five sovereigns, set apart for the purchase, could buy all the silks in the shop; and (remembering my own loss of two hours in a toyshop before I could tell on what wonder to spend a silver threepence) I was very glad that we were going early, that dear Miss Matty might have leisure for the delights of perplexity.

If a happy sea-green could be met with, the gown was to be sea-green: if not, she inclined to maize, and I to silver grey; and we discussed the requisite number of breadths until we arrived at the shop-door. We were to buy the tea, select the silk, and then clamber up the iron corkscrew stairs that led into what was once a loft, though now a fashion showroom.

The young men at Mr Johnson's had on their best looks; and their best cravats, and pivoted themselves over the counter with surprising activity. They wanted to show us upstairs at once; but on the principle of business first and pleasure afterwards, we stayed to purchase the tea. Here Miss Matty's absence of mind betrayed itself. If she was made aware that she had been drinking green tea at any time, she always thought it her duty to lie awake half through the night afterward (I have known her take it in ignorance many a time without such effects), and consequently green tea was prohibited the house; yet today she herself asked for the obnoxious article, under the impression that she was talking about the silk. However, the mistake was soon rectified; and then the silks were unrolled in good truth. By this time the shop was pretty well filled, for it was Cranford market-day, and many of the farmers and country people from the neighbourhood round came in, sleeking down their hair, and glancing shyly about, from under their eyelids, as anxious to take back some notion of the unusual gaiety to the mistress or the lasses at home, and yet feeling that they were out of place among the smart shopmen and gay shawls and summer prints. One honest-looking man, however, made his way up to the counter at which we stood, and boldly asked to look at a shawl or two. The other country folk confined themselves to the grocery side; but our neighbour was evidently too full of some kind intention towards mistress, wife or daughter, to be shy; and it soon became a question with me, whether he or Miss Matty would keep their shopmen the longest time. He thought each shawl more beautiful than the last; and, as for Miss Matty, she smiled and sighed over each fresh bale that was brought out; one colour set off another, and the heap together would, as she said, make even the rainbow look poor.

'I am afraid,' said she, hesitating, 'Whichever I choose I shall wish I had taken another. Look at this lovely crimson! it would be so warm in winter. But spring is coming on, you know. I wish I could have a gown for every season,' said she, dropping her voice – as we all did in Cranford whenever we talked of anything we wished for but could not afford. 'However,' she continued in a louder and more cheerful tone, 'it would give me a great deal of trouble to take care of them if I had them; so, I think, I'll only take one. But which must it be, my dear?'

And now she hovered over a lilac with yellow spots, while I pulled out a quiet sage-green that had faded into insignificance under the more brilliant colours, but which was nevertheless a good silk in its humble way. Our attention was called off to our neighbour. He had chosen a shawl of about thirty shillings' value; and his face looked broadly happy, under the anticipation, no doubt, of the pleasant surprise he would give to some Molly or Jenny at home; he had tugged a leathern purse out of his breeches pocket, and had offered a five-pound note in payment for the shawl, and for some parcels which had been brought round to him from the grocery counter; and it was just at this point that he attracted our notice. The shopman was examining the note with a puzzled, doubtful air.

'Town and County Bank! I am not sure, sir, but I believe we have received a warning against notes issued by this bank only this morning. I will just step and ask Mr Johnson, sir; but I'm afraid I must trouble you for payment in cash, or in a note of a different bank.'

I never saw a man's countenance fall so suddenly into dismay and bewilderment. It was almost piteous to see the rapid change.

'Dang it!' said he, striking his fist down on the table, as if to try which was the harder, 'the chap talks as if notes and gold were to be had for the picking up.'

Miss Matty had forgotten her silk gown in her interest for the man. I don't think she had caught the name of the bank, and in my nervous cowardice I was anxious that she should not; and so I began admiring the yellow-spotted lilac gown that I had been utterly condemning only a minute before. But it was of no use.

'What bank was it? I mean, what bank did your note belong to?'

'Town and County Bank.'

'Let me see it,' said she quietly to the shopman, gently taking it out of his hand, as he brought it back to return it to the farmer.

Mr Johnson was very sorry, but, from information he had received, the notes issued by that bank were little better than waste paper.

'I don't understand it,' said Miss Matty to me in a low voice. 'That is our bank, is it not? – the Town and County Bank?'

'Yes,' said I. 'This lilac silk will just match the ribbons in your new cap, I believe,' I continued, holding up the folds so as to catch the light, and wishing that the man would make haste and be gone, and yet having a new wonder, that had only just sprung up, how far it was wise or right in me to allow Miss Matty to make this expensive purchase, if the affairs of the bank were really so bad as the refusal of the note implied.

But Miss Matty put on the soft dignified manner, peculiar to her, rarely used, and yet which became her so well, and laying her hand gently on mine, she said –

'Never mind the silks for a few minutes, dear. I don't understand you, sir,' turning now to the shopman, who had been attending to the farmer. 'Is this a forged note?'

'Oh, no, ma'am. It is a true note of its kind; but you see, ma'am, it is a joint-stock bank, and there are reports out that it is likely to break. Mr Johnson is only doing his duty, ma'am, as I am sure Mr Dobson knows.'

But Mr Dobson could not respond to the appealing bow by any answering smile. He was turning the note absently over in his fingers, looking gloomily enough at the parcel containing the lately-chosen shawl.

'It's hard upon a poor man,' said he, 'as earns every farthing with the sweat of his brow. However, there's no help for it. You must take back your shawl, my man; Lizzie must go on with her cloak for a while. And yon figs for the little ones – I promised them to 'em – I'll take them; but the 'bacco, and the other things' –

'I will give you five sovereigns for your note, my good man,' said Miss Matty. 'I think there is some great mistake about it, for I am one of the shareholders, and I'm sure they would have told me if things had not been going on right.'

The shopman whispered a word or two across the table to Miss Matty. She looked at him with a dubious air.

'Perhaps so,' said she. 'But I don't pretend to understand business; I only know that if it is going to fail, and if honest people are to lose their money because they have taken our notes – I can't explain myself,' said she, suddenly becoming aware that she had got into a long sentence with four people for audience; 'only I would rather exchange my gold for the note, if you please,' turning to the farmer, 'and then you can take your wife the shawl. It is only going without my gown a few days longer,' she continued, speaking to me. 'Then, I have no doubt, everything will be cleared up.'

'But if it is cleared up the wrong way?' said I.

'Why, then it will only have been common honesty in me, as a shareholder, to have given this good man the money. I am quite clear about it in my own mind; but, you know, I can never speak quite as comprehensibly as others can, only you must give me your note, Mr Dobson, if you please, and go on with your purchases with these sovereigns.'

The man looked at her with silent gratitude – too awkward to put his thanks into words; but he hung back for a minute or two, fumbling with his note.

'I'm loth to make another one lose instead of me, if it is a loss; but, you see, five pounds is a deal of money to a man with a family; and, as you say, ten to one in a day or two the note will be as good as gold again.'

'No hope of that, my friend,' said the shopman.

'The more reason why I should take it,' said Miss Matty quietly. She pushed her sovereigns towards the man, who slowly laid his note down in exchange. 'Thank you. I will wait a day or two before I purchase any of these silks; perhaps you will then have a greater choice. My dear, will you come upstairs?'

We inspected the fashions with as minute and curious an interest as if the gown to be made after them had been bought. I could not see that the little event in the shop below had in the least damped Miss Matty's curiosity as to the make of sleeves or the sit of skirts. She once or twice exchanged congratulations with me on our private and leisurely view of the bonnets and shawls; but I was, all the time, not so sure that our examination was so utterly private, for I caught glimpses of a figure dodging behind the cloaks and mantles; and, by a dexterous move, I came face to face with Miss Pole, also in morning costume (the principal feature of which was her being without teeth, and wearing a veil to conceal the deficiency), come on the same errand as ourselves. But she quickly took her departure, because, as she said, she had a bad headache, and did not feel herself up to conversation.

As we came down through the shop, the civil Mr Johnson was awaiting us; he had been informed of the exchange of the note for gold, and with much good feeling and real kindness, but with a little want of tact, he wished to condole with Miss Matty, and impress upon her the true state of the case. I could only hope that he had heard an exaggerated rumour for he said that her shares were worse than nothing, and that the bank could not pay a shilling in the pound. I was glad that Miss Matty seemed still a little incredulous; but I could not tell how much of this was real or assumed, with that self-control which seemed habitual to ladies of Miss Matty's standing in Cranford, who would have thought their dignity compromised by the slightest expression of surprise, dismay, or any similar feeling to an inferior in station, or in a public shop. However, we walked home very silently. I am ashamed to say, I believe I was rather vexed and annoyed at Miss Matty's conduct in taking the note to herself so decidedly. I had so set my heart upon her having a new silk gown, which she wanted sadly; in general she was so undecided anybody might turn her round; in this case I had felt that it was no use attempting it, but I was not the less put out at the result.

Somehow, after twelve o'clock, we both acknowledged to a sated curiosity about the fashions, and to a certain fatigue of body (which was, in fact, depression of mind) that indisposed us to go out again. But still we never spoke of the note; till, all at once, something possessed me to ask Miss Matty if she would think it her duty to offer sovereigns for all the notes of the Town and County Bank she met with? I could have bitten my tongue out the minute I had said it. She looked up rather sadly, and as if I had thrown a new perplexity into her already distressed mind; and for a minute or two she did not speak. Then she said – my own dear Miss Matty – without a shade of reproach in her voice –

'My dear, I never feel as if my mind was what people call very strong; and it's often hard enough work for me to settle what I ought to do with the case right before me. I was very thankful to – I was very thankful, that I saw my duty this morning, with the poor man standing by me; but its rather a strain upon me to keep thinking and thinking what I should do if such and such a thing happened; and, I believe, I had rather wait and see what really does come; and I don't doubt I shall be helped then if I don't fidget myself, and get too anxious beforehand. You know, love, I'm not like Deborah. If Deborah had lived, I've no doubt she would have seen after them, before they had got themselves into this state.'

We had neither of us much appetite for dinner, though we tried to talk cheerfully about indifferent things. When we returned into the drawing-room, Miss Matty unlocked her desk and began to look over her account-books. I was so penitent for what I had said in the morning, that I did not choose to take upon myself the presumption to suppose that I could assist her; I rather left her alone, as, with puzzled brow, her eye followed her pen up and down the ruled page. By-and-by she shut the book, locked the desk, and came and drew a chair to mine, where I sat in moody sorrow over the fire. I stole my hand into hers; she clasped it, but did not speak a word. At last she said, with forced composure in her voice, 'If that bank goes wrong, I shall lose one hundred and forty-nine pounds thirteen shillings and fourpence a year; I shall only have thirteen pounds a year left.' I squeezed her hand hard and tight. I did not know what to say. Presently (it was too dark to see her face) I felt her fingers work convulsively in my grasp; and I knew she was going to speak again. I heard the sobs in her voice as she said, 'I hope it's not wrong – not wicked – but, oh! I am so glad poor Deborah is spared this. She could not have borne to come down in the world – she had such a noble, lofty spirit.'

This was all she said about the sister who had insisted upon investing their little property in that unlucky bank. We were later in lighting the candle than usual that night, and until that light shamed us into speaking, we sat together very silently and sadly.

However, we took to our work after tea with a kind of forced cheerfulness (which soon became real as far as it went), talking of that never-ending wonder, Lady Glenmire's engagement. Miss Matty was almost coming round to think it a good thing.

'I don't mean to deny that men are troublesome in a house. I don't judge from my own experience, for my father was neatness itself, and wiped his shoes on coming in as carefully as any woman; but still a man has a sort of knowledge of what should be done in difficulties, that it is very pleasant to have one at hand ready to lean upon. Now, Lady Glenmire, instead of being tossed about, and wondering where she is to settle, will be certain of a home among pleasant and kind people, such as our good Miss Pole and Mrs Forrester. And Mr Hoggins is really a very personable man; and as for his manners, why, if they are not very polished, I have known people with very good hearts and very clever minds too, who were not what some people reckoned refined, but who were both true and tender.'

She fell off into a soft reverie about Mr Holbrook, and I did not interrupt her, I was so busy maturing a plan I had had in my mind for some days, but which this threatened failure of the bank had brought to a crisis. That night, after Miss Matty went to bed, I treacherously lighted the candle again, and sat down in the drawing-room to compose a letter to the Aga Jenkyns, a letter which should affect him if he were Peter, and yet seem a mere statement of dry facts if he were a stranger. The church clock pealed out two before I had done.

The next morning news came, both official and otherwise, that the Town and County Bank had stopped payment. Miss Matty was ruined.

She tried to speak quietly to me; but when she came to the actual fact that she would have but about five shillings a week to live upon, she could not restrain a few tears.

'I am not crying for myself, dear,' said she, wiping them away; 'I believe I am crying for the very silly thought of how my mother would grieve if she could know; she always cared for us so much more than for herself. But many a poor person has less, and I am not very extravagant, and, thank God, when the neck of mutton, and Martha's wages, and the rent are paid, I have not a farthing owing. Poor Martha! I think she'll be sorry to leave me.'

Miss Matty smiled at me through her tears, and she would fain have had me see only the smile, not the tears.

CHAPTER XIV
FRIENDS IN NEED

It was an example to me, and I fancy it might be to many others, to see how immediately Miss Matty set about the retrenchment which she knew to be right under her altered circumstances. While she went down to speak to Martha, and break the intelligence to her, I stole out with my letter to the Aga Jenkyns, and went to the signor's lodgings to obtain the exact address. I bound the signora to secrecy; and indeed her military manners had a degree of shortness and reserve in them which made her always say as little as possible, except when under the pressure of strong excitement. Moreover (which made my secret doubly sure), the signor was now so far recovered as to be looking forward to travelling and conjuring again in the space of a few days, when he, his wife, and little Phoebe would leave Cranford. Indeed, I found him looking over a great black and red placard, in which the Signor Brunoni's accomplishments were set forth, and to which only the name of the town where he would next display them was wanting. He and his wife were so much absorbed in deciding where the red letters would come in with most effect (it might have been the Rubric for that matter), that it was some time before I could get my question asked privately, and not before I had given several decisions, the which I questioned afterwards with equal wisdom of sincerity as soon as the signor threw in his doubts and reasons on the important subject. At last I got the address, spelt by sound, and very queer it looked. I dropped it in the post on my way home, and then for a minute I stood looking at the wooden pane with a gaping slit which divided me from the letter but a moment ago in my hand. It was gone from me like life, never to be recalled. It would get tossed about on the sea, and stained with sea-waves perhaps, and be carried among palm-trees, and scented with all tropical fragrance; the little piece of paper, but an hour ago so familiar and commonplace, had set out on its race to the strange wild countries beyond the Ganges! But I could not afford to lose much time on this speculation. I hastened home, that Miss Matty might not miss me. Martha opened the door to me, her face swollen with crying. As soon as she saw me she burst out afresh, and taking hold of my arm she pulled me in, and banged the door to, in order to ask me if indeed it was all true that Miss Matty had been saying.

'I'll never leave her! No; I won't. I told her so, and said I could not think how she could find in her heart to give me warning. I could not have had the face to do it, if I'd been her. I might ha' been just as good for nothing as Mrs Fitz-Adam's Rosy, who struck for wages after living seven years and a half in one place. I said I was not one to go and serve Mammon at that rate; that I knew when I'd got a good missus, if she didn't know when she'd got a good servant' –

'But, Martha,' said I, cutting in while she wiped her eyes.

'Don't "but Martha" me,' she replied to my deprecatory tone.

'Listen to reason' –

'I'll not listen to reason,' she said, now in full possession of her voice, which had been rather choked with sobbing. 'Reason always means what someone else has got to say. Now I think what I've got to say is good enough reason; but reason or not, I'll say it, and I'll stick to it. I've money in the Savings Bank, and I've a good stock of clothes, and I'm not going to leave Miss Matty. No, not if she gives me warning every hour in the day!'

She put her arms akimbo, as much as to say she defied me; and, indeed, I could hardly tell how to begin to remonstrate with her, so much did I feel that Miss Matty, in her increasing infirmity, needed the attendance of this kind and faithful woman.

'Well' – said I at last.

'I'm thankful you begin with "well"! If you'd have begun with "but", as you did afore, I'd not ha' listened to you. Now you may go on.'

'I know you would be a great loss to Miss Matty, Martha' –

'I told her so. A loss she'd never cease to be sorry for,' broke in Martha triumphantly.

'Still, she will have so little – so very little – to live upon, that I don't see just now how she could find you food – she will even be pressed for her own. I tell you this, Martha, because I feel you are like a friend to dear Miss Matty, but you know she might not like to have it spoken about.'

Apparently this was even a blacker view of the subject than Miss Matty had presented to her, for Martha just sat down on the first chair that came to hand, and cried out loud (we had been standing in the kitchen).

At last she put her apron down, and looking me earnestly in the face, asked, 'Was that the reason Miss Matty wouldn't order a pudding today? She said she had no great fancy for sweet things, and you and she would just have a mutton chop. But I'll be up to her. Never you tell, but I'll make her a pudding, and a pudding she'll like, too, and I'll pay for it myself; so mind you see she eats it. Many a one has been comforted in their sorrow by seeing a good dish come upon the table.'

I was rather glad that Martha's energy had taken the immediate and practical direction of pudding-making, for it staved off the quarrelsome discussion as to whether she should or should not leave Miss Matty's service. She began to tie on a clean apron, and otherwise prepare herself for going to the shop for the butter, eggs, and what else she might require. She would not use a scrap of the articles already in the house for her cookery, but went to an old teapot in which her private store of money was deposited, and took out what she wanted.

I found Miss Matty very quiet, and not a little sad; but by-and-by she tried to smile for my sake. It was settled that I was to write to my father, and ask him to come over and hold a consultation, and as soon as this letter was despatched we began to talk over future plans. Miss Matty's idea was to take a single room, and retain as much of her furniture as would be necessary to fit up this, and sell the rest, and there to quietly exist upon what would remain after paying the rent. For my part, I was more ambitious and less contented. I thought of all the things by which a woman, past middle age, and with the education common to ladies fifty years ago, could earn or add to a living without materially losing caste; but at length I put even this last clause on one side, and wondered what in the world Miss Matty could do.

Teaching was, of course, the first thing that suggested itself. If Miss Matty could teach children anything, it would throw her among the little elves in whom her soul delighted. I ran over her accomplishments. Once upon a time I had heard her say she could play '*Ah! vous dirai-je, maman?*' on the piano, but that was long, long ago; that faint shadow of musical acquirement had died out years before. She had also once been able to trace out patterns very nicely for muslin embroidery, by dint of placing a piece of silver paper over the design to be copied, and holding both against the window-pane while she marked the scollop and eyelet-holes. But that was her nearest approach to the accomplishment of drawing, and I did not think it would go very far. Then again, as to the branches of a solid English education – fancy work and the use of the globes – such as the mistress of the Ladies' Seminary, to which all the tradespeople in Cranford sent their daughters, professed to teach. Miss Matty's eyes were failing her, and I doubted if she could discover the number of threads in a worsted-work pattern, or rightly appreciate the different shades required for Queen Adelaide's face in the loyal wool-work now fashionable in Cranford. As for the use of the globes, I had never been able to find it out myself, so perhaps I was not a good judge of Miss Matty's capability of instructing in this branch of education; but it struck me that equators and tropics, and such mystical circles, were very imaginary lines indeed to her, and that she looked upon the signs of the Zodiac as so many remnants of the Black Art.

What she piqued herself upon, as arts in which she excelled, was making candle-lighters, or 'spills' (as she preferred calling them), of coloured paper, cut so as to resemble feathers, and knitting garters in a variety of dainty stitches. I had once said, on receiving a present of an elaborate pair, that I should feel quite tempted to drop one of them in the street, in order to have it admired; but I found this little joke (and it was a very little one) was such a distress to her sense of propriety, and was taken with such anxious, earnest alarm, lest the temptation might some day prove too strong for me, that I quite regretted having ventured upon it. A present of these delicately-wrought garters, a bunch of gay 'spills', or a set of cards on which sewing-silk was wound in a mystical manner, were the well-known tokens of Miss Matty's favour. But would anyone pay to have their children taught these arts? or, indeed, would Miss Matty sell, for filthy lucre, the knack and the skill with which she made trifles of value to those who loved her?

I had to come down to reading, writing, and arithmetic; and, in reading the chapter every morning, she always coughed before coming to long words. I doubted her power of getting through a genealogical chapter, with any number of coughs. Writing she did well and delicately – but spelling! She seemed to think that the more out-of-the-way this was, and the more trouble it cost her, the greater the compliment she paid to her correspondent; and words that she would spell quite correctly in her letters to me became perfect enigmas when she wrote to my father.

No! there was nothing she could teach to the rising generation of Cranford, unless they had been quick learners and ready imitators of her patience, her humility, her sweetness, her quiet contentment with all that she could not do. I pondered and pondered until dinner was announced by Martha, with a face all blubbered and swollen with crying.

Miss Matty had a few little peculiarities which Martha was apt to regard as whims below her attention, and appeared to consider as childish fancies of which an old lady of fifty-eight should try and cure herself. But today everything was attended to with the most careful regard. The bread was cut to the imaginary pattern of excellence that existed in Miss Matty's mind, as being the way which her mother had preferred, the curtain was drawn so as to exclude the dead brick wall of a neighbour's stable, and yet left so as to show every tender leaf of the poplar which was bursting into spring beauty. Martha's tone to Miss Matty was just such as that good, rough-spoken servant usually kept sacred for little children, and which I had never heard her use to any grown-up person.

I had forgotten to tell Miss Matty about the pudding, and I was afraid she might not do justice to it, for she had evidently very little appetite this day; so I seized the opportunity of letting her into the secret while Martha took away the meat. Miss Matty's eyes filled with tears, and she could not speak, either to express surprise or delight, when Martha returned bearing it aloft, made in the most wonderful representation of a lion *couchant* that ever was moulded. Martha's face gleamed with triumph as she set it down before Miss Matty with an exultant 'There!' Miss Matty wanted to speak her thanks, but could not; so she took Martha's hand and shook it warmly, which set Martha off crying, and I myself could hardly keep up the necessary composure. Martha burst out of the room, and Miss Matty had to clear her voice once or twice before she could speak. At last she said, 'I should like to keep this pudding under a glass shade, my dear!' and the notion of the lion *couchant*, with his currant eyes, being hoisted up to the place of honour on a mantelpiece, tickled my hysterical fancy, and I began to laugh, which rather surprised Miss Matty.

'I am sure, dear, I have seen uglier things under a glass shade before now,' said she.

So had I, many a time and oft, and I accordingly composed my countenance (and now I could hardly keep from crying), and we both fell to upon the pudding, which was indeed excellent – only every morsel seemed to choke us, our hearts were so full.

We had too much to think about to talk much that afternoon. It passed over very tranquilly. But when the tea-urn was brought in a new thought came into my head. Why should not Miss Matty sell tea – be an agent to the East India Tea Company which then existed? I could see no objections to this plan, while the advantages were many – always supposing that Miss Matty could get over the degradation of condescending to anything like trade. Tea was neither greasy nor sticky – grease and stickiness being two of the qualities which Miss Matty could not endure. No shop-window would be required. A small, genteel notification of her being licensed to sell tea would, it is true, be necessary, but I hoped that it could be placed where no one would see it. Neither was tea a heavy article, so as to tax Miss Matty's fragile strength. The only thing against my plan was the buying and selling involved.

While I was giving but absent answers to the questions Miss Matty was putting – almost as absently – we heard a clumping sound on the stairs, and a whispering outside the door, which indeed once opened and shut as if by some invisible agency. After a little while Martha came in, dragging after her a great tall young man, all crimson with shyness, and finding his only relief in perpetually sleeking down his hair.

'Please, ma'am, he's only Jem Hearn,' said Martha, by way of an introduction; and so out of breath was she that I imagine she had had some bodily struggle before she could overcome his reluctance to be presented on the courtly scene of Miss Matilda Jenkyns's drawing-room.

'And please, ma'am, he wants to marry me off-hand. And please, ma'am, we want to take a lodger – just one quiet lodger, to make our two ends meet; and we'd take any house conformable; and, oh dear Miss Matty, if I may be so bold, would you have any objections to lodging with us? Jem wants it as much as I do.' [To Jem] – 'You great oaf! why can't you back me! – But he does want it all the same, very bad – don't you, Jem? – only, you see, he's dazed at being called on to speak before quality.'

'It's not that,' broke in Jem. 'It's that you've taken me all on a sudden, and I didn't think for to get married so soon – and such quick words does flabbergast a man. It's not that I'm against it, ma'am' (addressing Miss Matty), 'only Martha has such quick ways with her

when once she takes a thing into her head; and marriage, ma'am –
marriage nails a man, as one may say. I dare say I shan't mind it after
it's once over.'

'Please, ma'am,' said Martha – who had plucked at his sleeve, and
nudged him with her elbow, and otherwise tried to interrupt him all the
time he had been speaking – 'don't mind him, he'll come to; 'twas only
last night he was an-axing me, and an-axing me, and all the more because
I said I could not think of it for years to come, and now he's only taken
aback with the suddenness of the joy; but you know, Jem, you are just
as full as me about wanting a lodger.' (Another great nudge.)

'Ay! if Miss Matty would lodge with us – otherwise I've no mind
to be cumbered with strange folk in the house,' said Jem, with a want
of tact which I could see enraged Martha, who was trying to represent
a lodger as the great object they wished to obtain, and that, in fact,
Miss Matty would be smoothing their path and conferring a favour, if
she would only come and live with them.

Miss Matty herself was bewildered by the pair; their, or rather
Martha's sudden resolution in favour of matrimony staggered her, and
stood between her and the contemplation of the plan which Martha
had at heart. Miss Matty began –

'Marriage is a very solemn thing, Martha.'

'It is indeed, ma'am,' quoth Jem. 'Not that I've no objections to
Martha.'

'You've never let me a-be for asking me for to fix when I would
be married,' said Martha – her face all a-fire, and ready to cry with
vexation – 'and now you're shaming me before my missus and all.'

'Nay, now! Martha don't ee! don't ee! only a man likes to have
breathing-time,' said Jem, trying to possess himself of her hand, but
in vain. Then seeing that she was more seriously hurt than he had
imagined, he seemed to try to rally his scattered faculties, and with
more straightforward dignity than, ten minutes before, I should have
thought it possible for him to assume, he turned to Miss Matty, and
said, 'I hope, ma'am, you know that I am bound to respect everyone
who has been kind to Martha. I always looked on her as to be my wife
– some time; and she has often and often spoken of you as the kindest
lady that ever was; and though the plain truth is, I would not like to
be troubled with lodgers of the common run, yet if, ma'am, you'd
honour us by living with us, I'm sure Martha would do her best to

make you comfortable; and I'd keep out of your way as much as I could, which I reckon would be the best kindness such an awkward chap as me could do.'

Miss Matty had been very busy with taking off her spectacles, wiping them, and replacing them; but all she could say was, 'Don't let any thought of me hurry you into marriage: pray don't. Marriage is such a very solemn thing!'

'But Miss Matilda will think of your plan, Martha,' said I, struck with the advantages that it offered, and unwilling to lose the opportunity of considering about it. 'And I'm sure neither she nor I can ever forget your kindness; nor your's either, Jem.'

'Why, yes, ma'am! I'm sure I mean kindly, though I'm a bit fluttered by being pushed straight ahead into matrimony, as it were, and mayn't express myself conformable. But I'm sure I'm willing enough, and give me time to get accustomed; so, Martha, wench, what's the use of crying so, and slapping me if I come near?'

This last was *sotto voce*, and had the effect of making Martha bounce out of the room, to be followed and soothed by her lover. Whereupon Miss Matty sat down and cried very heartily, and accounted for it by saying that the thought of Martha being married so soon gave her quite a shock, and that she should never forgive herself if she thought she was hurrying the poor creature. I think my pity was more for Jem, of the two; but both Miss Matty and I appreciated to the full the kindness of the honest couple, although we said little about this, and a good deal about the chances and dangers of matrimony.

The next morning, very early, I received a note from Miss Pole, so mysteriously wrapped up, and with so many seals on it to secure secrecy, that I had to tear the paper before I could unfold it. And when I came to the writing I could hardly understand the meaning, it was so involved and oracular. I made out, however, that I was to go to Miss Pole's at eleven o'clock; the number *eleven* being written in full length as well as in numerals, and *a.m.* twice dashed under, as if I were very likely to come at eleven at night, when all Cranford was usually a-bed and asleep by ten. There was no signature except Miss Pole's initials reversed, P.E.; but as Martha had given me the note, 'with Miss Pole's kind regards', it needed no wizard to find out who sent it; and if the writer's name was to be kept secret, it was very well that I was alone when Martha delivered it.

I went as requested to Miss Pole's. The door was opened to me by her little maid Lizzy in Sunday trim, as if some grand event was impending over this work-day. And the drawing-room upstairs was arranged in accordance with this idea. The table was set out with the best green card-cloth, and writing materials upon it. On the little chiffonier was a tray with a newly-decanted bottle of cowslip wine, and some ladies'-finger biscuits. Miss Pole herself was in solemn array, as if to receive visitors, although it was only eleven o'clock. Mrs Forrester was there, crying quietly and sadly, and my arrival seemed only to call forth fresh tears. Before we had finished our greetings, performed with lugubrious mystery of demeanour, there was another rat-tat-tat, and Mrs Fitz-Adam appeared, crimson with walking and excitement. It seemed as if this was all the company expected; for now Miss Pole made several demonstrations of being about to open the business of the meeting, by stirring the fire, opening and shutting the door, and coughing and blowing her nose. Then she arranged us all round the table, taking care to place me opposite to her; and last of all, she inquired of me if the sad report was true, as she feared it was, that Miss Matty had lost all her fortune?

Of course, I had but one answer to make; and I never saw more unaffected sorrow depicted on any countenances than I did there on the three before me.

'I wish Mrs Jamieson was here!' said Mrs Forrester at last; but to judge from Mrs Fitz-Adam's face, she could not second the wish.

'But without Mrs Jamieson,' said Miss Pole, with just a sound of offended merit in her voice, 'we, the ladies of Cranford, in my drawing-room assembled, can resolve upon something. I imagine we are none of us what may be called rich, though we all possess a genteel competency, sufficient for tastes that are elegant and refined, and would not, if they could, be vulgarly ostentatious.' (Here I observed Miss Pole refer to a small card concealed in her hand, on which I imagine she had put down a few notes.)

'Miss Smith,' she continued, addressing me (familiarly known as 'Mary' to all the company assembled, but this was a state occasion), 'I have conversed in private – I made it my business to do so yesterday afternoon – with these ladies on the misfortune which has happened to our friend, and one and all of us have agreed that while we have a superfluity, it is not only a duty, but a pleasure – a true pleasure, Mary!'

– her voice was rather choked just here, and she had to wipe her spectacles before she could go on – 'to give what we can to assist her – Miss Matilda Jenkyns. Only in consideration of the feelings of delicate independence existing in the mind of every refined female' – I was sure she had got back to the card now – 'we wish to contribute our mites in a secret and concealed manner, so as not to hurt the feelings I have referred to. And our object in requesting you to meet us this morning is that, believing you are the daughter – that your father is, in fact, her confidential adviser, in all pecuniary matters, we imagined that, by consulting with him, you might devise some mode in which our contribution could be made to appear the legal due which Miss Matilda Jenkyns ought to receive from —. Probably your father, knowing her investments, can fill up the blank.'

Miss Pole concluded her address, and looked round for approval and agreement.

'I have expressed your meaning, ladies, have I not? And while Miss Smith considers what reply to make, allow me to offer you some little refreshment.'

I had no great reply to make: I had more thankfulness at my heart for their kind thoughts than I cared to put into words; and so I only mumbled out something to the effect 'that I would name what Miss Pole had said to my father, and that if anything could be arranged for dear Miss Matty', – and here I broke down utterly, and had to be refreshed with a glass of cowslip wine before I could check the crying which had been repressed for the last two or three days. The worst was, all the ladies cried in concert. Even Miss Pole cried, who had said a hundred times that to betray emotion before anyone was a sign of weakness and want of self-control. She recovered herself into a slight degree of impatient anger, directed against me, as having set them all off; and, moreover, I think she was vexed that I could not make a speech back in return for hers; and if I had known beforehand what was to be said, and had a card on which to express the probable feelings that would rise in my heart, I would have tried to gratify her. As it was, Mrs Forrester was the person to speak when we had recovered our composure.

'I don't mind, among friends, stating that I – no! I'm not poor exactly, but I don't think I'm what you may call rich; I wish I were, for dear Miss Matty's sake – but, if you please, I'll write down in a sealed paper what I can give. I only wish it was more; my dear Mary, I do indeed.'

Now I saw why paper, pens, and ink were provided. Every lady wrote down the sum she could give annually, signed the paper, and sealed it mysteriously. If their proposal was acceded to, my father was to be allowed to open the papers, under pledge of secrecy. If not, they were to be returned to their writers.

When the ceremony had been gone through, I rose to depart; but each lady seemed to wish to have a private conference with me. Miss Pole kept me in the drawing-room to explain why, in Mrs Jamieson's absence, she had taken the lead in this 'movement', as she was pleased to call it, and also to inform me that she had heard from good sources that Mrs Jamieson was coming home directly in a state of high displeasure against her sister-in-law, who was forthwith to leave her house, and was, she believed, to return to Edinburgh that very afternoon. Of course this piece of intelligence could not be communicated before Mrs Fitz-Adam, more especially as Miss Pole was inclined to think that Lady Glenmire's engagement to Mr Hoggins could not possibly hold against the blaze of Mrs Jamieson's displeasure. A few hearty inquiries after Miss Matty's health concluded my interview with Miss Pole.

On coming downstairs I found Mrs Forrester waiting for me at the entrance to the dining-parlour; she drew me in, and when the door was shut, she tried two or three times to begin on some subject, which was so unapproachable apparently, that I began to despair of our ever getting to a clear understanding. At last out it came; the poor old lady trembling all the time as if it were a great crime which she was exposing to daylight, in telling me how very, very little she had to live upon; a confession which she was brought to make from a dread lest we should think that the small contribution named in her paper bore any proportion to her love and regard for Miss Matty. And yet that sum which she so eagerly relinquished was, in truth, more than a twentieth part of what she had to live upon, and keep house, and a little serving-maid, all as became one born a Tyrrell. And when the whole income does not nearly amount to a hundred pounds, to give up a twentieth of it will necessitate many careful economies, and many pieces of self-denial, small and insignificant in the world's account, but bearing a different value in another account-book that I have heard of. She did so wish she was rich, she said, and this wish she kept repeating, with no thought of herself in it, only with a longing, yearning desire to be able to heap up Miss Matty's measure of comforts.

It was some time before I could console her enough to leave her; and then, on quitting the house, I was waylaid by Mrs Fitz-Adam, who had also her confidence to make of pretty nearly the opposite description. She had not liked to put down all that she could afford and was ready to give. She told me she thought she never could look Miss Matty in the face again if she presumed to be giving her so much as she should like to do. 'Miss Matty!' continued she, 'that I thought was such a fine young lady when I was nothing but a country girl, coming to market with eggs and butter and such like things. For my father, though well-to-do, would always make me go on as my mother had done before me, and I had to come into Cranford every Saturday, and see after sales, and prices, and what not. And one day, I remember, I met Miss Matty in the lane that leads to Combehurst; she was walking on the footpath, which, you know, is raised a good way above the road, and a gentleman rode beside her, and was talking to her, and she was looking down at some primroses she had gathered, and pulling them all to pieces, and I do believe she was crying. But after she had passed, she turned round and ran after me to ask – oh, so kindly – about my poor mother, who lay on her death-bed; and when I cried she took hold of my hand to comfort me – and the gentleman waiting for her all the time – and her poor heart very full of something, I am sure; and I thought it such an honour to be spoken to in that pretty way by the rector's daughter, who visited at Arley Hall. I have loved her ever since, though perhaps I'd no right to do it; but if you can think of any way in which I might be allowed to give a little more without anyone knowing it, I should be so much obliged to you, my dear. And my brother would be delighted to doctor her for nothing – medicines, leeches, and all. I know that he and her ladyship (my dear, I little thought in the days I was telling you of that I should ever come to be sister-in-law to a ladyship!) would do anything for her. We all would.'

I told her I was quite sure of it, and promised all sorts of things in my anxiety to get home to Miss Matty, who might well be wondering what had become of me – absent from her two hours without being able to account for it. She had taken very little note of time, however, as she had been occupied in numberless little arrangements preparatory to the great step of giving up her house. It was evidently a relief to her to be doing something in the way of retrenchment, for, as she said, whenever she paused to think, the recollection of the poor fellow with his bad five-pound note came over her, and she felt quite dishonest; only if it made her so uncomfortable, what must it not be doing to the directors of the bank, who must know so much more of the misery consequent upon this failure? She almost made me angry by dividing her sympathy between these directors (whom she imagined over-whelmed by self-reproach for the mismanagement of other people's affairs) and those who were suffering like her. Indeed, of the two, she seemed to think poverty a lighter burden than self-reproach; but I privately doubted if the directors would agree with her.

Old hoards were taken out and examined as to their money value which luckily was small, or else I don't know how Miss Matty would have prevailed upon herself to part with such things as her mother's wedding-ring, the strange, uncouth brooch with which her father had disfigured his shirt-frill, &c. However, we arranged things a little in order as to their pecuniary estimation, and were all ready for my father when he came the next morning.

I am not going to weary you with the details of all the business we went through; and one reason for not telling about them is, that I did not understand what we were doing at the time, and cannot recollect it now. Miss Matty and I sat assenting to accounts, and schemes, and reports, and documents, of which I do not believe we either of us understood a word; for my father was clear-headed and decisive, and a capital man of business, and if we made the slightest inquiry, or expressed the slightest want of comprehension, he had a sharp way of saying, 'Eh? eh? it's as clear as daylight. What's your objection?' And as we had not comprehended anything of what he had proposed, we found it rather difficult to shape our objections; in fact, we never were sure if we had any. So presently Miss Matty got into a nervously acquiescent state, and said 'Yes,' and 'Certainly,' at every pause, whether required or not; but when I once joined in as chorus to a 'Decidedly,' pronounced by Miss Matty in a tremblingly dubious tone, my father fired round at me and asked me 'What there was to decide?' And I am sure to this day I have never known. But, in justice to him, I must say he had come over from Drumble to help Miss Matty when he could

ill spare the time, and when his own affairs were in a very anxious
state.

While Miss Matty was out of the room giving orders for luncheon
– and sadly perplexed between her desire of honouring my father by
a delicate, dainty meal, and her conviction that she had no right, now
that all her money was gone, to indulge this desire – I told him of the
meeting of the Cranford ladies at Miss Pole's the day before. He kept
brushing his hand before his eyes as I spoke – and when I went back
to Martha's offer the evening before, of receiving Miss Matty as a
lodger, he fairly walked away from me to the window, and began
drumming with his fingers upon it. Then he turned abruptly round,
and said, 'See, Mary, how a good, innocent life makes friends all
around. Confound it! I could make a good lesson out of it if I were a
parson; but, as it is, I can't get a tail to my sentences – only I'm sure
you feel what I want to say. You and I will have a walk after lunch
and talk a bit more about these plans.'

The lunch – a hot savoury mutton-chop, and a little of the cold loin
sliced and fried – was now brought in. Every morsel of this last dish
was finished, to Martha's great gratification. Then my father bluntly
told Miss Matty he wanted to talk to me alone, and that he would
stroll out and see some of the old places, and then I could tell her
what plan we thought desirable. Just before we went out, she called
me back and said, 'Remember, dear, I'm the only one left – I mean,
there's no one to be hurt by what I do. I'm willing to do anything
that's right and honest; and I don't think, if Deborah knows where she
is, she'll care so very much if I'm not genteel; because, you see, she'll
know all, dear. Only let me see what I can do, and pay the poor people
as far as I'm able.'

I gave her a hearty kiss, and ran after my father. The result of our
conversation was this. If all parties were agreeable, Martha and Jem
were to be married with as little delay as possible, and they were to
live on in Miss Matty's present abode; the sum which the Cranford
ladies had agreed to contribute annually being sufficient to meet the
greater part of the rent, and leaving Martha free to appropriate what
Miss Matty should pay for her lodgings to any little extra comforts
required. About the sale, my father was dubious at first. He said the
old rectory furniture, however carefully used and reverently treated,
would fetch very little; and that little would be but as a drop in the

sea of the debts of the Town and County Bank. But when I represented how Miss Matty's tender conscience would be soothed by feeling that she had done what she could, he gave way; especially after I had told him the five-pound note adventure, and he had scolded me well for allowing it. I then alluded to my idea that she might add to her small income by selling tea; and, to my surprise (for I had nearly given up the plan), my father grasped at it with all the energy of a tradesman. I think he reckoned his chickens before they were hatched, for he immediately ran up the profits of the sales that she could effect in Cranford to more than twenty pounds a year. The small dining-parlour was to be converted into a shop, without any of its degrading characteristics; a table was to be the counter; one window was to be retained unaltered, and the other changed into a glass door. I evidently rose in his estimation for having made this bright suggestion. I only hoped we should not both fall in Miss Matty's.

But she was patient and content with all our arrangements. She knew, she said, that we should do the best we could for her; and she only hoped, only stipulated, that she should pay every farthing that she could be said to owe, for her father's sake, who had been so respected in Cranford. My father and I had agreed to say as little as possible about the bank, indeed never to mention it again, if it could be helped. Some of the plans were evidently a little perplexing to her; but she had seen me sufficiently snubbed in the morning for want of comprehension to venture on too many inquiries now; and all passed over well with a hope on her part that no one would be hurried into marriage on her account. When we came to the proposal that she should sell tea, I could see it was rather a shock to her; not on account of any personal loss of gentility involved, but only because she distrusted her own powers of action in a new line of life, and would timidly have preferred a little more privation to any exertion for which she feared she was unfitted. However, when she saw my father was bent upon it, she sighed, and said she would try; and if she did not do well, of course she might give it up. One good thing about it was, she did not think men ever bought tea; and it was of men particularly she was afraid. They had such sharp loud ways with them; and did up accounts, and counted their change so quickly! Now, if she might only sell comfits to children, she was sure she could please them!

CHAPTER XV

A HAPPY RETURN

Before I left Miss Matty at Cranford everything had been comfortably arranged for her. Even Mrs Jamieson's approval of her selling tea had been gained. That oracle had taken a few days to consider whether by so doing Miss Matty would forfeit her right to the privileges of society in Cranford. I think she had some little idea of mortifying Lady Glenmire by the decision she gave at last; which was to this effect: that whereas a married woman takes her husband's rank by the strict laws of precedence, an unmarried woman retains the station her father occupied. So Cranford was allowed to visit Miss Matty; and, whether allowed or not, it intended to visit Lady Glenmire.

But what was our surprise – our dismay – when we learnt that Mr and *Mrs Hoggins* were returning on the following Tuesday! Mrs Hoggins! Had she absolutely dropped her title, and so, in a spirit of bravado, cut the aristocracy to become a Hoggins! She, who might have been called Lady Glenmire to her dying day! Mrs Jamieson was pleased. She said it only convinced her of what she had known from the first, that the creature had a low taste. But 'the creature' looked very happy on Sunday at church; nor did we see it necessary to keep our veils down on that side of our bonnets on which Mr and Mrs Hoggins sat, as Mrs Jamieson did; thereby missing all the smiling glory of his face, and all the becoming blushes of hers. I am not sure if Martha and Jem looked more radiant in the afternoon, when they, too, made their first appearance. Mrs Jamieson soothed the turbulence of her soul by having the blinds of her windows drawn down, as if for a funeral, on the day when Mr and Mrs Hoggins received callers; and it was with some difficulty that she was prevailed upon to continue the *St James's Chronicle*, so indignant was she with its having inserted the announcement of the marriage.

Miss Matty's sale went off famously. She retained the furniture of her sitting-room and bedroom; the former of which she was to occupy till Martha could meet with a lodger who might wish to take it; and into this sitting-room and bedroom she had to cram all sorts of things, which were (the auctioneer assured her) bought in for her at the sale by an unknown friend. I always suspected Mrs Fitz-Adam of this; but she must have had an accessory, who knew what articles were particularly regarded by Miss Matty on account of their associations with her early days. The rest of the house looked rather bare, to be sure; all except one tiny bedroom, of which my father allowed me to purchase the furniture for my occasional use in case of Miss Matty's illness.

I had expended my own small store in buying all manner of comfits and lozenges, in order to tempt the little people whom Miss Matty loved so much to come about her. Tea in bright green canisters, and comfits in tumblers – Miss Matty and I felt quite proud as we looked round us on the evening before the shop was to be opened. Martha had scoured the boarded floor to a white cleanness, and it was adorned with a brilliant piece of oil-cloth, on which customers were to stand before the table-counter. The wholesome smell of plaster and whitewash pervaded the apartment. A very small 'Matilda Jenkyns, licensed to sell tea', was hidden under the lintel of the new door, and two boxes of tea, with cabalistic inscriptions all over them, stood ready to disgorge their contents into the canisters.

Miss Matty, as I ought to have mentioned before, had had some scruples of conscience at selling tea when there was already Mr Johnson in the town, who included it among his numerous commodities; and, before she could quite reconcile herself to the adoption of her new business, she had trotted down to his shop, unknown to me, to tell him of the project that was entertained, and to inquire if it was likely to injure his business. My father called this idea of hers 'great nonsense', and 'wondered how tradespeople were to get on if there was to be a continual consulting of each other's interests, which would put a stop to all competition directly'. And, perhaps, it would not have done in Drumble, but in Cranford it answered very well; for not only did Mr Johnson kindly put at rest all Miss Matty's scruples and fear of injuring his business, but I have reason to know he repeatedly sent customers to her, saying that the teas he kept were of a common kind, but that Miss Jenkyns had all the choice sorts. And expensive tea is a very favourite luxury with well-to-do tradespeople and rich farmers' wives, who turn up their noses at the Congou and Souchong prevalent at many tables of gentility, and will have nothing else than Gunpowder and Pekoe for themselves.

But to return to Miss Matty. It was really very pleasant to see how her unselfishness and simple sense of justice called out the same good qualities in others. She never seemed to think anyone would impose upon her, because she should be so grieved to do it to them. I have heard her put a stop to the asseverations of the man who brought her coals by quietly saying, 'I am sure you would be sorry to bring me wrong weight'; and if the coals were short measure that time, I don't believe they ever were again. People would have felt as much ashamed of presuming on her good faith as they would have done on that of a child. But my father says 'such simplicity might be very well in Cranford, but would never do in the world'. And I fancy the world must be very bad, for with all my father's suspicion of everyone with whom he has dealings, and in spite of all his many precautions, he lost upwards of a thousand pounds by roguery only last year.

I just stayed long enough to establish Miss Matty in her new mode of life, and to pack up the library, which the rector had purchased. He had written a very kind letter to Miss Matty, saying 'how glad he should be to take a library, so well selected as he knew that the late Mr Jenkyns's must have been, at any valuation put upon them'. And when she agreed to this, with a touch of sorrowful gladness that they would go back to the rectory and be arranged on the accustomed walls once more, he sent word that he feared that he had not room for them all, and perhaps Miss Matty would kindly allow him to leave some volumes on her shelves. But Miss Matty said that she had her Bible and Johnson's *Dictionary*, and should not have much time for reading, she was afraid; still, I retained a few books out of consideration for the rector's kindness.

The money which he had paid, and that produced by the sale, was partly expended in the stock of tea, and part of it was invested against a rainy day – *i.e.* old age or illness. It was but a small sum, it is true; and it occasioned a few evasions of truth and white lies (all of which I think very wrong indeed – in theory – and would rather not put them in practice), for we knew Miss Matty would be perplexed as to her duty if she were aware of any little reserve-fund being made for her while the debts of the bank remained unpaid. Moreover, she had never been told of the way in which her friends were contributing to pay the rent. I should have liked to tell her this, but the mystery of the affair gave a piquancy to their deed of kindness which the ladies were unwilling to give up; and at first Martha had to shirk many a perplexed question as to her ways and means of living in such a house, but

by-and-by Miss Matty's prudent uneasiness sank down into acquiescence with the existing arrangement.

I left Miss Matty with a good heart. Her sales of tea during the first
two days had surpassed my most sanguine expectations. The whole
country round seemed to be all out of tea at once. The only alteration
I could have desired in Miss Matty's way of doing business was, that
she should not have so plaintively entreated some of her customers
not to buy green tea – running it down as a slow poison, sure to destroy
the nerves, and produce all manner of evil. Their pertinacity in taking
it, in spite of all her warnings, distressed her so much that I really
thought she would relinquish the sale of it, and so lose half her custom;
and I was driven to my wits' end for instances of longevity entirely
attributable to a persevering use of green tea. But the final argument,
which settled the question, was a happy reference of mine to the train-
oil and tallow candles which the Esquimaux not only enjoy but digest.
After that she acknowledged that 'one man's meat might be another
man's poison,' and contented herself thence-forward with an occasional
remonstrance when she thought the purchaser was too young and
innocent to be acquainted with the evil effects green tea produced on
some constitutions, and an habitual sigh when people old enough to
choose more wisely would prefer it.

I went over from Drumble once a quarter at least to settle the
accounts, and see after the necessary business letters. And, speaking
of letters, I began to be very much ashamed of remembering my letter
to the Aga Jenkyns, and very glad I had never named my writing to
anyone. I only hoped the letter was lost. No answer came. No sign
was made.

About a year after Miss Matty set up shop, I received one of Martha's
hieroglyphics, begging me to come to Cranford very soon. I was afraid
that Miss Matty was ill, and went off that very afternoon, and took
Martha by surprise when she saw me on opening the door. We went
into the kitchen as usual, to have our confidential conference, and then
Martha told me she was expecting her confinement very soon – in a
week or two; and she did not think Miss Matty was aware of it, and
she wanted me to break the news to her, 'for indeed, miss,' continued
Martha, crying hysterically, 'I'm afraid she won't approve of it, and
I'm sure I don't know who is to take care of her as she should be
taken care of when I am laid up.'

I comforted Martha by telling her I would remain till she was about again, and only wished she had told me her reason for this sudden summons, as then I would have brought the requisite stock of clothes. But Martha was so tearful and tender-spirited, and unlike her usual self, that I said as little as possible about myself, and endeavoured rather to comfort Martha under all the probable and possible misfortunes which came crowding upon her imagination.

I then stole out of the house-door, and made my appearance as if I were a customer in the shop, just to take Miss Matty by surprise, and gain an idea of how she looked in her new situation. It was warm May weather, so only the little half-door was closed; and Miss Matty sat behind the counter, knitting an elaborate pair of garters; elaborate they seemed to me, but the difficult stitch was no weight upon her mind, for she was singing in a low voice to herself as her needles went rapidly in and out. I call it singing, but I dare say a musician would not use that word to the tuneless yet sweet humming of the low worn voice. I found out from the words, far more than from the attempt at the tune, that it was the Old Hundredth she was crooning to herself; but the quiet continuous sound told of content, and gave me a pleasant feeling, as I stood in the street just outside the door, quite in harmony with that soft May morning. I went in. At first she did not catch who it was, and stood up as if to serve me; but in another minute watchful pussy had clutched her knitting, which was dropped in eager joy at seeing me. I found, after we had had a little conversation, that it was as Martha said, and that Miss Matty had no idea of the approaching household event. So I thought I would let things take their course, secure that when I went to her with the baby in my arms, I should obtain that forgiveness for Martha which she was needlessly frightening herself into believing that Miss Matty would withhold, under some notion that the new claimant would require attentions from its mother that it would be faithless treason to Miss Matty to render.

But I was right. I think that must be an hereditary quality, for my father says he is scarcely ever wrong. One morning, within a week after I arrived, I went to call Miss Matty, with a little bundle of flannel in my arms. She was very much awestruck when I showed her what it was, and asked for her spectacles off the dressing-table, and looked at it curiously, with a sort of tender wonder at its small perfection of parts. She could not banish the thought of the surprise all day, but

went about on tiptoe, and was very silent. But she stole up to see
Martha and they both cried with joy, and she got into a complimentary
speech to Jem, and did not know how to get out of it again, and was
only extricated from her dilemma by the sound of the shop-bell, which
was an equal relief to the shy, proud, honest Jem, who shook my hand
so vigorously when I congratulated him, that I think I feel the pain of
it yet.

I had a busy life while Martha was laid up. I attended on Miss
Matty, and prepared her meals; I cast up her accounts, and examined
into the state of her canisters and tumblers. I helped her, too, occasionally, in the shop; and it gave me no small amusement, and sometimes
a little uneasiness, to watch her ways there. If a little child came in to
ask for an ounce of almond-comfits (and four of the large kind which
Miss Matty sold weighed that much), she always added one more by
'way of make-weight', as she called it, although the scale was hand-
somely turned before; and when I remonstrated against this, her reply
was, 'The little things like it so much!' There was no use in telling
her that the fifth comfit weighed a quarter of an ounce, and made every
sale into a loss to her pocket. So I remembered the green tea, and
winged my shaft with a feather out of her own plumage. I told her
how unwholesome almond-comfits were, and how ill excess in them
might make the little children. This argument produced some effect;
for, henceforward, instead of the fifth comfit, she always told them to
hold out their tiny palms, into which she shook either peppermint or
ginger lozenges, as a preventive to the dangers that might arise from
the previous sale. Altogether the lozenge trade, conducted on these
principles, did not promise to be remunerative; but I was happy to find
she had made more than twenty pounds during the last year by her
sales of tea; and, moreover, that now she was accustomed to it, she
did not dislike the employment, which brought her into kindly intercourse with many of the people round about. If she gave them good
weight, they, in their turn, brought many a little country present to the
'old rector's daughter'; a cream cheese, a few new-laid eggs, a little
fresh ripe fruit, a bunch of flowers. The counter was quite loaded with
these offerings sometimes, as she told me.

As for Cranford in general, it was going on much as usual. The
Jamieson and Hoggins feud still raged, if a feud it could be called,
when only one side cared much about it. Mr and Mrs Hoggins were

very happy together, and, like most very happy people, quite ready to be friendly; indeed, Mrs Hoggins was really desirous to be restored to Mrs Jamieson's good graces, because of the former intimacy. But Mrs Jamieson considered their very happiness an insult to the Glenmire family, to which she had still the honour to belong, and she doggedly refused and rejected every advance. Mr Mulliner, like a faithful clansman, espoused his mistress' side with ardour. If he saw either Mr or Mrs Hoggins, he would cross the street, and appear absorbed in the contemplation of life in general, and his own path in particular, until he had passed them by. Miss Pole used to amuse herself with wondering what in the world Mrs Jamieson would do, if either she, or Mr Mulliner, or any other member of her household was taken ill; she could hardly have the face to call in Mr Hoggins after the way she had behaved to them. Miss Pole grew quite impatient for some indisposition or accident to befall Mrs Jamieson or her dependants, in order that Cranford might see how she would act under the perplexing circumstances.

Martha was beginning to go about again, and I had already fixed a limit, not very far distant, to my visit, when one afternoon, as I was sitting in the shop-parlour with Miss Matty – I remember the weather was colder now than it had been in May, three weeks before, and we had a fire and kept the door fully closed – we saw a gentleman go slowly past the window, and then stand opposite to the door, as if looking out for the name which we had so carefully hidden. He took out a double eyeglass and peered about for some time before he could discover it. Then he came in. And, all on a sudden, it flashed across me that it was the Aga himself! For his clothes had an out-of-the-way foreign cut about them, and his face was deep brown, as if tanned and re-tanned by the sun. His complexion contrasted oddly with his plentiful snow-white hair, his eyes were dark and piercing, and he had an odd way of contracting them and puckering up his cheeks into innumerable wrinkles when he looked earnestly at objects. He did so to Miss Matty when he first came in. His glance had first caught and lingered a little upon me, but then turned, with the peculiar searching look I have described, to Miss Matty. She was a little fluttered and nervous, but no more so than she always was when any man came into her shop. She thought that he would probably have a note, or a sovereign at least, for which she would have to give change, which was an operation she very much disliked to perform. But the present customer stood opposite to her, without asking for anything, only looking fixedly at her as he drummed upon the table with his fingers, just for all the world as Miss Jenkyns used to do. Miss Matty was on the point of asking him what he wanted (as she told me afterwards), when he turned sharp to me: 'Is your name Mary Smith?'

'Yes!' said I.

All my doubts as to his identity were set at rest, and I only wondered what he would say or do next, and how Miss Matty would stand the joyful shock of what he had to reveal. Apparently he was at a loss how to announce himself, for he looked round at last in search of something to buy, so as to gain time, and, as it happened, his eye caught on the almond-comfits, and he boldly asked for a pound of 'those things'. I doubt if Miss Matty had a whole pound in the shop, and, besides the unusual magnitude of the order, she was distressed with the idea of the indigestion they would produce, taken in such unlimited quantities. She looked up to remonstrate. Something of tender relaxation in his face struck home to her heart. She said, 'It is – oh, sir! can you be Peter?' and trembled from head to foot. In a moment he was round the table and had her in his arms, sobbing the tearless cries of old age. I brought her a glass of wine, for indeed her colour had changed so as to alarm me and Mr Peter too. He kept saying, 'I have been too sudden for you, Matty – I have, my little girl.'

I proposed that she should go at once up into the drawing-room and lie down on the sofa there. She looked wistfully at her brother, whose hand she had held tight, even when nearly fainting; but on his assuring her that he would not leave her, she allowed him to carry her upstairs.

I thought that the best I could do was to run and put the kettle on the fire for early tea, and then to attend to the shop, leaving the brother and sister to exchange some of the many thousand things they must have to say. I had also to break the news to Martha, who received it with a burst of tears which nearly infected me. She kept recovering herself to ask if I was sure it was indeed Miss Matty's brother, for I had mentioned that he had grey hair, and she had always heard that he was a very handsome young man. Something of the same kind perplexed Miss Matty at tea-time, when she was installed in the great easy-chair opposite to Mr Jenkyns in order to gaze her fill. She could hardly drink for looking at him, and as for eating, that was out of the question.

'I suppose hot climates age people very quickly,' said she, almost to herself. 'When you left Cranford you had not a grey hair in your head.'

'But how many years ago is that?' said Mr Peter, smiling.

'Ah, true! yes, I suppose you and I are getting old. But still I did not think we were so very old! But white hair is very becoming to you, Peter,' she continued – a little afraid lest she had hurt him by revealing how his appearance had impressed her.

'I suppose I forgot dates too, Matty, for what do you think I have brought for you from India? I have an Indian muslin gown and a pearl necklace for you somewhere in my chest at Portsmouth.' He smiled as if amused at the idea of the incongruity of his presents with the appearance of his sister; but this did not strike her all at once, while the elegance of the articles did. I could see that for a moment her imagination dwelt complacently on the idea of herself thus attired; and instinctively she put her hand up to her throat – that little delicate throat which (as Miss Pole had told me) had been one of her youthful charms; but the hand met the touch of folds of soft muslin in which she was always swathed up to her chin, and the sensation recalled a sense of the unsuitableness of a pearl necklace to her age. She said, 'I'm afraid I'm too old; but it was very kind of you to think of it. They are just what I should have liked years ago – when I was young.'

'So I thought, my little Matty. I remembered your tastes; they were so like my dear mother's.' At the mention of that name the brother and sister clasped each other's hands yet more fondly, and, although they were perfectly silent, I fancied they might have something to say if they were unchecked by my presence, and I got up to arrange my room for Mr Peter's occupation that night, intending myself to share Miss Matty's bed. But at my movement, he started up. 'I must go and settle about a room at the "George". My carpet-bag is there too.'

'No!' said Miss Matty, in great distress – 'you must not go; please, dear Peter – pray, Mary – oh! you must not go!'

She was so much agitated that we both promised everything she wished. Peter sat down again and gave her his hand, which for better security she held in both of hers, and I left the room to accomplish my arrangements.

Long, long into the night, far, far into the morning, did Miss Matty and I talk. She had much to tell me of her brother's life and adventures,

which he had communicated to her as they had sat alone. She said all
was thoroughly clear to her; but I never quite understood the whole
story; and when in after days I lost my awe of Mr Peter enough to
question him myself, he laughed at my curiosity, and told me stories
that sounded so very much like Baron Munchausen's, that I was sure
he was making fun of me. What I heard from Miss Matty was that he
had been a volunteer at the siege of Rangoon; had been taken prisoner
by the Burmese; and somehow obtained favour and eventual freedom
from knowing how to bleed the chief of the small tribe in some case
of dangerous illness; that on his release from years of captivity he had
had his letters returned from England with the ominous word 'Dead'
marked upon them; and, believing himself to be the last of his race,
he had settled down as an indigo planter, and had proposed to spend
the remainder of his life in the country to whose inhabitants and modes
of life he had become habituated, when my letter had reached him;
and, with the odd vehemence which characterised him in age as it had
done in youth, he had sold his land and all his possessions to the first
purchaser, and come home to the poor old sister, who was more glad
and rich than any princess when she looked at him. She talked me to
sleep at last, and then I was awakened by a slight sound at the door,
for which she begged my pardon as she crept penitently into bed; but
it seems that when I could no longer confirm her belief that the long-
lost was really here – under the same roof – she had begun to fear lest
it was only a waking dream of hers; that there never had been a Peter
sitting by her all that blessed evening – but that the real Peter lay dead
far away beneath some wild sea-wave, or under some strange eastern
tree. And so strong had this nervous feeling of hers become, that she
was fain to get up and go and convince herself that he was really there
by listening through the door to his even, regular breathing – I don't
like to call it snoring, but I heard it myself through two closed doors
– and by-and-by it soothed Miss Matty to sleep.

I don't believe Mr Peter came home from India as rich as a nabob;
he even considered himself poor, but neither he nor Miss Matty cared
much about that. At any rate, he had enough to live upon 'very genteelly'
at Cranford; he and Miss Matty together. And a day or two after his
arrival, the shop was closed, while troops of little urchins gleefully
awaited the shower of comfits and lozenges that came from time to
time down upon their faces as they stood up-gazing at Miss Matty's

drawing-room windows. Occasionally Miss Matty would say to them (half-hidden behind the curtains), 'My dear children, don't make yourselves ill;' but a strong arm pulled her back, and a more rattling shower than ever succeeded. A part of the tea was sent in presents to the Cranford ladies; and some of it was distributed among the old people who remembered Mr Peter in the days of his frolicsome youth. The Indian muslin gown was reserved for darling Flora Gordon (Miss Jessie Brown's daughter). The Gordons had been on the Continent for the last few years, but were now expected to return very soon; and Miss Matty, in her sisterly pride, anticipated great delight in the joy of showing them Mr Peter. The pearl necklace disappeared; and about that time many handsome and useful presents made their appearance in the households of Miss Pole and Mrs Forrester; and some rare and delicate Indian ornaments graced the drawing-rooms of Mrs Jamieson and Mrs Fitz-Adam. I myself was not forgotten. Among other things, I had the handsomest-bound and best edition of Dr Johnson's works that could be procured; and dear Miss Matty, with tears in her eyes, begged me to consider it as a present from her sister as well as herself. In short, no one was forgotten; and, what was more, everyone, however insignificant, who had shown kindness to Miss Matty at any time, was sure of Mr Peter's cordial regard.

CHAPTER XVI

PEACE TO CRANFORD

It was not surprising that Mr Peter became such a favourite at Cranford. The ladies vied with each other who should admire him most; and no wonder, for their quiet lives were astonishingly stirred up by the arrival from India – especially as the person arrived told more wonderful stories than Sindbad the Sailor; and, as Miss Pole said, was quite as good as an Arabian Night any evening. For my own part, I had vibrated all my life between Drumble and Cranford, and I thought it was quite possible that all Mr Peter's stories might be true, although wonderful; but when I found that, if we swallowed an anecdote of tolerable magnitude one week, we had the dose considerably increased the next, I began to have my doubts; especially as I noticed that when his sister was present the accounts of Indian life were comparatively tame; not that she knew more than we did, perhaps less. I noticed also that when the rector came to call, Mr Peter talked in a different way about the countries he had been in. But I don't think the ladies in Cranford would have considered him such a wonderful traveller if they had only heard him talk in the quiet way he did to him. They liked him the better, indeed, for being what they called 'so very Oriental'.

One day, at a select party in his honour, which Miss Pole gave, and from which, as Mrs Jamieson honoured it with her presence, and had even offered to send Mr Mulliner to wait, Mr and Mrs Hoggins and Mrs Fitz-Adam were necessarily excluded – one day at Miss Pole's, Mr Peter said he was tired of sitting upright against the hard-backed uneasy chairs, and asked if he might not indulge himself in sitting cross-legged. Miss Pole's consent was eagerly given, and down he went with the utmost gravity. But when Miss Pole asked me, in an audible whisper, 'if he did not remind me of the Father of the Faithful?' I could not help thinking of poor Simon Jones, the lame tailor, and while Mrs Jamieson slowly commented on the elegance and convenience of the attitude, I remembered how we had all followed that lady's lead in condemning Mr Hoggins for vulgarity because he simply crossed his legs as he sat still on his chair. Many of Mr Peter's ways of eating were a little strange amongst such ladies as Miss Pole, and Miss Matty,

and Mrs Jamieson, especially when I recollected the untasted green
peas and two-pronged forks at poor Mr Holbrook's dinner.

The mention of that gentleman's name recalls to my mind a
conversation between Mr Peter and Miss Matty one evening in the
summer after he returned to Cranford. The day had been very hot,
and Miss Matty had been much oppressed by the weather, in the heat
of which her brother revelled. I remember that she had been unable
to nurse Martha's baby, which had become her favourite employment
of late, and which was as much at home in her arms as in its mother's,
as long as it remained a lightweight, portable by one so fragile as
Miss Matty. This day to which I refer, Miss Matty had seemed more
than usually feeble and languid, and only revived when the sun went
down, and her sofa was wheeled to the open window, through which,
although it looked into the principal street of Cranford, the fragrant
smell of the neighbouring hayfields came in every now and then,
borne by the soft breezes that stirred the dull air of the summer
twilight, and then died away. The silence of the sultry atmosphere
was lost in the murmuring noises which came in from many an open
window and door; even the children were abroad in the street, late
as it was (between ten and eleven), enjoying the game of play for
which they had not had spirits during the heat of the day. It was a
source of satisfaction to Miss Matty to see how few candles were
lighted, even in the apartments of those houses from which issued
the greatest signs of life. Mr Peter, Miss Matty, and I had all been
quiet, each with a separate reverie, for some little time, when Mr
Peter broke in –

'Do you know, little Matty, I could have sworn you were on the
high road to matrimony when I left England that last time! If anybody
had told me you would have lived and died an old maid then, I should
have laughed in their faces.'

Miss Matty made no reply, and I tried in vain to think of some
subject which should effectually turn the conversation; but I was very
stupid; and before I spoke he went on –

'It was Holbrook, that fine manly fellow who lived at Woodley, that
I used to think would carry off my little Matty. You would not think it
now, I dare say, Mary; but this sister of mine was once a very pretty
girl – at least, I thought so, and so I've a notion did poor Holbrook.
What business had he to die before I came home to thank him for all

his kindness to a good-for-nothing cub as I was? It was that that made me first think he cared for you; for in all our fishing expeditions it was Matty, Matty, we talked about. Poor Deborah! What a lecture she read me on having asked him home to lunch one day, when she had seen the Arley carriage in the town, and thought that my lady might call. Well, that's long years ago; more than half a lifetime, and yet it seems like yesterday! I don't know a fellow I should have liked better as a brother-in-law. You must have played your cards badly, my little Matty, somehow or another – wanted your brother to be a good go-between, eh, little one?' said he, putting out his hand to take hold of hers as she lay on the sofa. 'Why, what's this? you're shivering and shaking, Matty, with that confounded open window. Shut it, Mary, this minute!'

I did so, and then stooped down to kiss Miss Matty, and see if she really were chilled. She caught at my hand, and gave it a hard squeeze – but unconsciously, I think – for in a minute or two she spoke to us quite in her usual voice, and smiled our uneasiness away, although she patiently submitted to the prescriptions we enforced of a warm bed and a glass of weak negus. I was to leave Cranford the next day, and before I went I saw that all the effects of the open window had quite vanished. I had superintended most of the alterations necessary in the house and household during the latter weeks of my stay. The shop was once more a parlour: the empty resounding rooms again furnished up to the very garrets.

There had been some talk of establishing Martha and Jem in another house, but Miss Matty would not hear of this. Indeed, I never saw her so much roused as when Miss Pole had assumed it to be the most desirable arrangement. As long as Martha would remain with Miss Matty, Miss Matty was only too thankful to have her about her; yes, and Jem too, who was a very pleasant man to have in the house, for she never saw him from week's end to week's end. And as for the probable children, if they would all turn out such little darlings as her god-daughter, Matilda, she should not mind the number, if Martha didn't. Besides, the next was to be called Deborah – a point which Miss Matty had reluctantly yielded to Martha's stubborn determination that her first-born was to be Matilda. So Miss Pole had to lower her colours, and even her voice, as she said to me that, as Mr and Mrs Hearn were still to go on living in the same house with Miss Matty, we had certainly done a wise thing in hiring Martha's niece as an auxiliary.

I left Miss Matty and Mr Peter most comfortable and contented; the only subject for regret to the tender heart of the one, and the social friendly nature of the other, being the unfortunate quarrel between Mrs Jamieson and the plebeian Hogginses and their following. In joke, I prophesied one day that this would only last until Mrs Jamieson or Mr Mulliner were ill, in which case they would only be too glad to be friends with Mr Hoggins; but Miss Matty did not like my looking forward to anything like illness in so light a manner, and before the year was out all had come round in a far more satisfactory way.

I received two Cranford letters on one auspicious October morning. Both Miss Pole and Miss Matty wrote to ask me to come over and meet the Gordons, who had returned to England alive and well with their two children, now almost grown up. Dear Jessie Brown had kept her old kind nature, although she had changed her name and station; and she wrote to say that she and Major Gordon expected to be in Cranford on the fourteenth, and she hoped and begged to be remembered to Mrs Jamieson (named first, as became her honourable station), Miss Pole and Miss Matty – could she ever forget their kindness to her poor father and sister? – Mrs Forrester, Mr Hoggins (and here again came in an allusion to kindness shown to the dead long ago), his new wife, who as such must allow Mrs Gordon to desire to make her acquaintance, and who was, moreover, an old Scotch friend of her husband's. In short, everyone was named, from the rector – who had been appointed to Cranford in the interim between Captain Brown's death and Miss Jessie's marriage, and was now associated with the latter event – down to Miss Betty Barker. All were asked to the luncheon; all except Mrs Fitz-Adam, who had come to live in Cranford since Miss Jessie Brown's days, and whom I found rather moping on account of the omission. People wondered at Miss Betty Barker's being included in the honourable list; but, then, as Miss Pole said, we must remember the disregard of the genteel proprieties of life in which the poor captain had educated his girls, and for his sake we swallowed our pride. Indeed, Mrs Jamieson rather took it as a compliment, as putting Miss Betty (formerly *her* maid) on a level with 'those Hogginses'.

But when I arrived in Cranford, nothing was as yet ascertained of Mrs Jamieson's own intentions; would the honourable lady go, or would she not? Mr Peter declared that she should and she would; Miss Pole shook her head and desponded. But Mr Peter was a man of resources.

In the first place, he persuaded Miss Matty to write to Mrs Gordon, and to tell her of Mrs Fitz-Adam's existence, and to beg that one so kind, and cordial, and generous, might be included in the pleasant invitation. An answer came back by return of post, with a pretty little note for Mrs Fitz-Adam, and a request that Miss Matty would deliver it herself and explain the previous omission. Mrs Fitz-Adam was as pleased as could be, and thanked Miss Matty over and over again. Mr Peter had said: 'Leave Mrs Jamieson to me'; so we did; especially as we knew nothing that we could do to alter her determination if once formed.

I did not know, nor did Miss Matty, how things were going on, until Miss Pole asked me, just the day before Mrs Gordon came, if I thought there was anything between Mr Peter and Mrs Jamieson in the matrimonial line, for that Mrs Jamieson was really going to the lunch at the 'George'. She had sent Mr Mulliner down to desire that there might be a footstool put to the warmest seat in the room, as she meant to come, and knew that their chairs were very high. Miss Pole had picked this piece of news up, and from it she conjectured all sorts of things, and bemoaned yet more. 'If Peter should marry, what would become of poor dear Miss Matty? And Mrs Jamieson, of all people!' Miss Pole seemed to think there were other ladies in Cranford who would have done more credit to his choice, and I think she must have had someone who was unmarried in her head, for she kept saying, 'It was so wanting in delicacy in a widow to think of such a thing.'

When I got back to Miss Matty's I really did begin to think that Mr Peter might be thinking of Mrs Jamieson for a wife, and I was as unhappy as Miss Pole about it. He had the proof sheet of a great placard in his hand. 'Signor Brunoni, Magician to the King of Delhi, the Rajah of Oude, and the great Lama of Thibet', etc., was going to 'perform in Cranford for one night only', the very next night; and Miss Matty, exultant, showed me a letter from the Gordons, promising to remain over this gaiety, which Miss Matty said was entirely Peter's doing. He had written to ask the signor to come, and was to be at all the expenses of the affair. Tickets were to be sent gratis to as many as the room would hold. In short, Miss Matty was charmed with the plan, and said that tomorrow Cranford would remind her of the Preston Guild, to which she had been in her youth – a luncheon at the 'George', with the dear Gordons, and the signor in the Assembly Room in the evening. But I – I looked only at the fatal words: –

'*Under the Patronage of the* HONOURABLE MRS JAMIESON.'

She, then, was chosen to preside over this entertainment of Mr Peter's; she was perhaps going to displace my dear Miss Matty in his heart, and make her life lonely once more! I could not look forward to the morrow with any pleasure; and every innocent anticipation of Miss Matty's only served to add to my annoyance.

So, angry and irritated, and exaggerating every little incident which could add to my irritation, I went on till we were all assembled in the great parlour at the 'George'. Major and Mrs Gordon and pretty Flora and Mr Ludovic were all as bright and handsome and friendly as could be; but I could hardly attend to them for watching Mr Peter, and I saw that Miss Pole was equally busy. I had never seen Mrs Jamieson so roused and animated before; her face looked full of interest in what Mr Peter was saying. I drew near to listen. My relief was great when I caught that his words were not words of love, but that, for all his grave face, he was at his old tricks. He was telling her of his travels in India, and describing the wonderful height of the Himalaya mountains: one touch after another added to their size, and each exceeded the former in absurdity; but Mrs Jamieson really enjoyed all in perfect good faith. I suppose she required strong stimulants to excite her to come out of her apathy. Mr Peter wound up his account by saying that, of course, at that altitude there were none of the animals to be found that existed in the lower regions; the game, – everything was different. Firing one day at some flying creature, he was very much dismayed when it fell, to find that he had shot a cherubim! Mr Peter caught my eye at this moment, and gave me such a funny twinkle, that I felt sure he had no thoughts of Mrs Jamieson as a wife from that time. She looked uncomfortably amazed –

'But, Mr Peter, shooting a cherubim – don't you think – I am afraid that was sacrilege!'

Mr Peter composed his countenance in a moment, and appeared shocked at the idea, which, as he said truly enough, was now presented to him for the first time; but then Mrs Jamieson must remember that he had been living for a long time among savages – all of whom were heathens – some of them, he was afraid, were downright Dissenters. Then, seeing Miss Matty draw near, he hastily changed the conversation, and after a little while, turning to me, he said, 'Don't be shocked, prim little Mary, at all my wonderful stories. I consider Mrs Jamieson fair game, and besides I am bent on propitiating her, and the first step towards it is keeping her well awake. I bribed her here by asking her to let me have her name as patroness for my poor conjuror this evening; and I don't want to give her time enough to get up her rancour against the Hogginses, who are just coming in. I want everybody to be friends, for it harasses Matty so much to hear of these quarrels. I shall go at it again by-and-by, so you need not look shocked. I intend to enter the Assembly Room tonight with Mrs Jamieson on one side, and my lady, Mrs Hoggins, on the other. You see if I don't.'

Somehow or another he did; and fairly got them into conversation together. Major and Mrs Gordon helped at the good work with their perfect ignorance of any existing coolness between any of the inhabitants of Cranford.

Ever since that day there has been the old friendly sociability in Cranford society; which I am thankful for, because of my dear Miss Matty's love of peace and kindliness. We all love Miss Matty, and I somehow think we are all of us better when she is near us.